"That old, old question—what does it mean to be human?—is given a new configuration by DJ Daniels: what does it mean to be human *or otherwise?*

"And it's the *otherwise* that really counts, in a brilliant story that celebrates existence and survival on the newfound edges of life, and love. The fight back against disposability starts here!"

**Jeff Noon,
Arthur C. Clarke Award-winning
author of *Vurt* and the *Nyquist* series**

An Abaddon Books™ Publication
www.abaddonbooks.com
abaddon@rebellion.co.uk

Published in 2018 by Abaddon Books™,
Rebellion Publishing IP Limited,
Riverside House, Osney Mead, Oxford,
OX2 0ES, UK.

10 9 8 7 6 5 4 3 2 1

Creative Director and CEO: Jason Kingsley
Chief Technical Officer: Chris Kingsley
Head of Books and Comics Publishing: Ben Smith
Editors: David Thomas Moore,
Michael Rowley and Kate Coe
Marketing and PR: Remy Njambi
Design: Sam Gretton, Oz Osborne and Maz Smith
Cover Art: Pye Parr

ISBN: 978-1-78108-644-5

Printed in Denmark by Nørhaven.

GREEN JAY AND CROW

DJ DANIELS

ABADDON
BOOKS

WWW.ABADDONBOOKS.COM

CHAPTER ONE

Green Jay

I THINK OF it as a ripple, a ripple of favour and exchange. Of course, the effects spread wider than I can see—there is intersection and interference—but this is how it goes as far as I know it, how the ripples flow in the little world of Barlewin. Sometimes I imagine I'm a bird, that I can follow them along, but there's no need for that, not really, because I watch closely and I'm beginning to know this place well.

First of all, there's a package that enters Barlewin, up by the water tower usually. I'm still not sure why the couriers feel safe there, maybe it's the protection of something so large. The feeling you can hide. Perhaps because you're hidden from the gaze of the man *painted* on the water tower, the one with the huge head and the large eyes and the crazy hair and the comb. It's hard to tell if he's friendly or not.

I can tell who has a package because there's a certain kind of walk that lets me know something's going on. It's not a determined walk. I see plenty of that. Along with the shy, timid, don't-take-any-notice-of-me kind of stuff. This walk is sure, but relaxed. Deliberately relaxed. It says, I'm in control and there's nothing going on. Except there is.

More often than not the package changes hands close to the water tower. But the walk doesn't change, it's passed on to the next person in the relay. There's no favour, not yet, just a delivery. Drugs, it's probably drugs. And if it is, the parcel will most likely find its way to Guerra. Once it's there with him, it's all potential. All expectation. The package will be broken up, and later, at night, Guerra's people will take the smaller parcels back out into the world. Then there will be smaller, moonlit ripples.

Sometimes the package is something for the robots. I love the robots. They call themselves the Chemical Conjurers. Their package might contain chemicals for their routine, or it might contain other stuff people know better than to ask about. Though people usually don't think the robots would do any harm. And for those who know, the robots can be bribed to provide a distraction (a smoke, a smell, a spectacle) at the appointed time and place. They did it for me once, and I still owe them. But they don't often have deliveries from human couriers. They like to get their packages by delivery drone. It amuses them, I think. I've seen them set up mazes, see if the drones can find them, but they mean them no harm. Once, when one of Guerra's people tried to catch a drone, they sprayed him with something cloudy and dense so it could fly up and away.

Sometimes the courier walks in the other direction, goes north of the water tower. The farms are there, scratched-out places to grow tomatoes and spinach and beans and whatever else. Maybe the package is worms, or fertiliser. Most likely it's not. Most likely it makes its way to the shipping container at the side of the farm and hides between the spades and the secateurs and the rope. I don't like to think about the farms.

I can always tell if it's something for the Tenties by the look on the courier's face. She'll be walking fast, not even bothering to look relaxed. The package will be soft and squishy and the courier wants it out of her hands, she wants it gone, whatever it is the Tenties have asked for this time. Those deliveries make me laugh. The Tenties are crazy. I love the way they change. Every week there's something new and they never get it right. They know enough to realise I'm not real, but not enough to ignore me like the others would.

And sometimes the package makes its way past the big screen and the market shops and into the tenements. Up alleys and through doorways where there are special knocks to get in, or certain words to say to a man sitting to the side. Then there are stairs, there are always stairs, and a search for the right number. If a courier was looking for me, they'd need to climb up and up: I'm as high as Guerra. And in this room there's lots of glass to see out, down to the streets. That's how I know about the packages.

But there's never been one for me.

* * *

Crow

I'M STANDING IN front of the big screen for brain training. Morning Mentals. In theory you could defer it for later, do it at work, at home, log in on the train, whatever. But most everyone figures that if you're at least *seen* looking up at the big screen, then you're probably taking part. I mean, it's nice of the government to care so much for the state of our mental health. You don't have to tab your answers in. I never do. There's not much point. No chance of me reaching the 10,000s, of pulling off the prize. Mac could. Mac gets it right, gets it faster, gets it supersonic. Better than anyone I've ever met. But he never tabs in. There's some days he'll not even bother with his phone, just talk it, calling out the answers. Almost before they're asked. That's if it's something like arithmetic or word making. He's a genius. But he don't like to share. At best he mumbles something about patterns. But he won't talk about it. Just waves his thumb in the air. The creepy right thumb with the dark blue circular print on the base. Looks something like a blood blister, but it's not. He won't say what it is, where he got it. I'm not going to ask.

Brain training's early. Not that early, but early enough. Especially if you've been up the night before, looking after concerns. Rarely your own. Or perhaps always your own, as an underlying theme, in that you want to eat and sleep without too much worry. But for me that usually means errands for Guerra. Not many other choices. And there it is. No angelic life path. Not if you stay in Barlewin.

Guerra's business model encompasses a number of streams, some almost legal; but if you had to describe his empire in one word, it'd be drugs. If there's ever been any consistency in human nature over the course of time it would have to be devotion to a transformed state of mind. So that's our night, Mac's and mine, delivering, collecting. Mostly it's peaceful. You may not believe that, but mostly it is. Not everyone's a hate-filled, violent psychopath, though most of us delude ourselves to some extent. Mac carries this ridiculous knife in his wallet. The thing's folded up like a credit card. He took it out once and showed me. Yes, it works. Works good. Can't see anyone giving him the time to take it out of his wallet and unfold it, but you never know. It makes him feel better. Two ways: one, he's carrying a knife; two, he's not really carrying a knife. Mac's thought process is a thing unto itself.

But he's the brains. There's no cash exchanged in these transactions, understand. Mac keeps track of everything. He's the one who remembers the names, the numbers, the keywords, the passes, the locks. And I'm the something else. Suits me fine.

In any case, I'm standing here for Morning Mentals, poking randomly at my phone, no matter where the birds are or whatever it is you're meant to be looking for. 'Cause my peripheral vision's just fine, and right now it's more interested in what's happening under the water tower. It used to be guarded, but nobody seems so worried about that any more. Ol' Stick Man painted up there, he can't see what's happening down below. There's a courier under the tower, looks like he's not from around here, don't recognise him anyway, and he should've known better than to wear bright orange shoes like that. The ones with long toes and the weird soles. Most probably he can shimmy up the water tower if he needs to. Won't do him much good, but there it is. Some psychological crutch thing like Mac's credit card knife. But it's the other person under the water tower I'm really interested in. This one I know, Carine. The orange toe man won't be worried because she's a girl, but he should be. Carine is fast. And she's mean. But she's usually calm. There's some kind of an altercation taking place, which is not Carine's style and, despite the shoes, is probably not this man's either. He's still holding the package. She's not even making a grab for it.

Mac's mumbling numbers to himself. The training's moved on to maths bubbles and I hadn't even noticed. Don't want to disturb. I leave him there and walk up to the tower. Taking my time, watching close. Wouldn't hurt to have Carine owe me a favour, but wouldn't want to piss her off either.

Shit, there's a Tentie there. Didn't see it before. That's what all the fuss will be about. This one's got its tentacles pulled back like dreads. It's kept its beak but adapted the rest of its face to look more human. Standard Tentie look of the moment. Nothing's ever *clean* with the Tenties. Don't dislike them, but they give me the greeblies. And it's never simple. Don't let none of them hug me; never did, never will.

"Stay back, Brom," says Carine without even turning round.

"Someone's got to take it," says Orange Toes.

The Tentie starts forward. "Don't," says Carine. And probably she means the Tentie, but maybe she means me. In any case, there's no way I'm going to take the package. I can see it now. It's Time Locked.

A Time Locked package is a shit of a thing. Luckily, they're rare. Pretty damn expensive, I'm guessing. But the thing is, it's locked in all sorts of weird ways. First, it's locked to the courier. Don't seem so bad. But a Time Locked package has a habit of jumping back and forward in time, just like it says. Did it once; carried something in Time Lock. Makes you feel like shit. Like, fucking disgusting. You can barely function, you're just hanging on, waiting for it to shift back to normality. So, it's bad for the courier. Then you have to find someone to hand it over to. Which is almost impossible, almost nobody will take it, even the person it's meant for. You can unlock yourself and put it down, yes, but usually a Time Locked package doesn't contain something you can just leave on a desk and go.

And then there's the unpacking. The package will keep jumping around merrily in time as it sees fit, at random moments until someone decides to unlock it. And that person needs to know exactly how to do that. Codes and synching and shit. No idea really, but it's complex. Of course, that's the least of the problems for the courier, and most probably the courier don't know the answers to those questions, not if the security's worth anything.

But there it is. Expensive, wanky, weird shit. And Orange Toes wants to give it to one of us.

"You take it in, all the way," suggests Carine.

"Nup," says Orange Toes. "Water tower exchange, that's the deal."

The Tentie moves forward again. I'm not sure if the alien is just intrigued by the Time Lock or is attracted to whatever's in the package—which means something organic if that's it—or, for some unknown reason, the Tentie wants to get in good with Guerra. Or maybe Carine, though that seems unlikely.

"No," says Carine. And she looks like she's ready to walk away. The Tentie gets even closer.

"I'll take it," I say. Don't ask me why. Don't.

Carine stifles a groan; Orange Toes stifles a grin.

"Done this before?" he asks.

I nod, and he starts the transfer under Carine's watchful gaze. Which, considering, doesn't take that long. I already feel disgusting, so I'm pretty sure I'm in Time Lock. There's no Orange Toes, no Carine, no Tentie. But the water tower's still there and I can see the path up to the High Track. Away we go.

CHAPTER TWO

Green Jay

I WAS MEANT to come to Barlewin, but I was never meant to stay.

Even that's not really true. This body was meant to come to Barlewin, and it had jobs to do and people to see, all directed by the impulses of someone else. Mostly as a tourist, mostly here for fun, memories it could take back to its original before the body died. I try not to think about the original. Olwin Duilis. I'm not that person. But I rely on her knowledge. I have to. Otherwise I have no way of negotiating the world; otherwise I would never have been able to escape. I use her knowledge and build on it and bury what I don't need. I am becoming more and more myself.

I don't want to admit this, but I'm more of a plant than a person. Doubles don't need to eat. A bit of sun is all they need. So in my top floor glass house, I'm okay. And the Tenties look after me. We have our own exchange of favours and rewards.

I saw it happen once, a body being created. More than once, to be honest, but I don't like to watch anymore. First a protective skin emerges from the 3D printer. It looks like a bubble, it's translucent but very tough. Too many copies were destroyed without it. They're too vulnerable, the process is too slow. Then the body comes. Most of the time it's a blank. Maybe it would have been better if I'd been one of those. They're empty; it would have been easier to form myself inside one of those. But I'd never have survived. They don't last for long. I'm only here because I'm a double.

It's usually Tenties that load the printer, fill it with biostuff. Because they love it and they understand it and they can adapt materials if something is short. Everyone else is grossed out. Even me. Even though that's how I was made.

But it's the robots I love the most, because they're the ones that understood, they're the ones that allowed me to escape. I was drifting through the market shops, blending in with the people, trying to think of a way to disappear. They saw me there, told me about this place, created a cloud of grey smoke so that I could slip into an alley and then up to this room. I had some money to bribe the boy at the door then. How did they know who I was, what was needed? I like to think they recognised another new soul. If I am wrong, it means someone knew what I would do, and wanted to protect me. Or wanted to keep me close. I try not to think of that.

In my dreams, there's someone out there, the original, looking for her body back. Although she's older now and her body is falling apart. If she finds me, she will snatch me. She knows I must have come to Barlewin. But she will not think I stayed here. She will not think I survived.

Crow

THE THING TO do with a Time Locked package is to keep moving. That way, it jumps less often. Moving complicates things, I guess. Can't say I understand it. A Time Locked box is moving between one of several time bubbles. Little bubble realities that come and go, and are usually sufficiently like ours that everything stays on track. Some say alternate realities, and that all you've got to do is not change anything and then you can pop back. Which is probably bullshit meant to scare couriers, but what do I know.

The thing is, it's not really time travel. I mean, the jump's only a matter of a fraction of a second. 0.63 seconds at the most, I'm told. By Mac, who should know. Which is shit-all time to affect your past or your future, let me tell you. 0.63 seconds is pretty useless. But you can't really affect things because you can't interact; that's the whole point. Otherwise someone would just put their hand out, leave it there until the parcel moved into phase with that particular future. No, it's *never* in phase. It jumps around.

And that is the other point of the plastic box. Not just a torture device for the courier, but an interface so that it can sit on the desk, or what have you, and wait for you to come and open it. So that you can see that you've still got something to come and open. Freaky shit.

And apparently in all the alternate realities that we visit, the box and I, I'm taking it to Guerra. Guerra lives up on the High Track. Old freight railway tracks, coupla storeys high, believe it or not, fell into disrepair, remodelling by upstanding citizens—when such people existed—and, voilà. Something beautiful, something green and flowery, something to be proud of. You could visit and look down on the dump of a place you called home and almost feel good about it. Until a few years ago. When Guerra held a party up there one night, told the regular security to have the night off, brought in his own people, and never left. Well, that's the rumour. Truth is probably more complicated than that. It's nice up there. It's the same rain that falls on him—if anything, he's filtering it for us—the same polluted haze that drifts up and around, but somehow it seems cleaner up there.

The High Track isn't that far from the water tower. Actually, you can see Guerra's domain right beside and above you, but you do have to come up by the correct entrance. I'm already out from under the tower, moving up the path behind the big screen and then progressing, via a winding path, to Guerra's number 3 staircase. I presume the others are following; I've never followed someone who was Time Locked, so don't ask me what they see. But Carine's used to this shit and I can guarantee she's not going to lose me. At a guess, Carine is following at a distance and the Tentie is following close. It's the package that's attracting it, I'm sure of it, though the package don't feel squishy, and it don't smell. But then again, dummkopf, it's in a Time Locked box. I briefly wonder how the time jumps are affecting the substance inside, but then I decide that's an avenue of thought I probably don't want to stroll down. 'Cause if the Time Lock is affecting the substance, it's also affecting me.

I imagine Carine guiding me in as if she is remote docking a spacecraft. She'll be able to see the plastic box, if nothing else, although some people claim that the courier appears as a shimmer to people in normal time. I'm not going to look around to find out if I can see her. 'Don't look back' is often very sound advice. I just try to keep walking without puking.

There's no drama on the stairs. The guards see the box and wave me through. It seems this reality's not all that alternate. They're decent stairs. Metal, with a rail. There's a lot of them. And eventually I'm up, right in the middle of plants and gentility. Guerra's kept the High Track nice, I'll give him that. Kept it in its original state, perhaps even improved it, what with the new buildings he's put in. The supremely optimistic might say that when Guerra's empire falls, the High Track can be returned to the borough intact and unharmed. I'm not completely sure who actually lives up here. Just Guerra, or a retinue? But right now there's a stack of people. Or I should say there's a stack of people in my alternate reality bubble.

And I'm guessing there's a stack of people whatever the particular time circumstance. I know the drill. I find what I think of as 'admin' and walk in. There's a table to the left. Very empty, very obviously waiting for the box. I put the package down, start the process of disentangling myself. This, as you might have guessed, takes longer. I follow the instructions Orange Toes gave me to the letter. Nobody stops me, nobody interferes.

And I step back. A huge wave of nausea hits, I try not to double over, and fail spectacularly. Carine's there in the room, she gives me an encouraging nod. Or discouraging, depending on which way you want to look at it. And the Tentie's still close, I can't believe it's still here, that it's up on the High Track, right up in Guerra's sanctum. Of course, Guerra probably has an interest in the Tenties. The thought has probably occurred to him that they could synthesise whatever he wants. Actually, 'synthesise' isn't quite the right word, and neither is 'manufacture.' The Tenties could *create* whatever he wants. And there's the thing. Who'd want to put some Tentie-created concoction inside their own body? You'd have to keep their involvement quiet, keep it hushed.

But that's me done. Box delivered, favours earned. Pats on the back all around.

Only there's not. Instead there's Guerra. Himself, in person.

Guerra's somewhere in the middle-age, bits of grey, a few wrinkles, but looking good. No visible scars, no visible tattoos. Well-dressed, without being showy. UMC shit. And he's calm. The kind of calm that's really not.

Just like any remarks he makes are the kind of friendly that's really not.

"Wasn't expecting you today, Kern Bromley," is his opening line.

"He wouldn't come in," says Carine. "The courier. Wouldn't move past the water tower."

"And yet, that's what he was paid to do," says Guerra. "And what Kern was demonstrably not paid to do." Guerra taps the box. "Got any idea of what's inside here, Kern?"

I shrug, but it isn't enough. Guerra wants speculation, he's asking me to play the game and guess.

"Something expensive, something private," I say.

Guerra nods. "Bait," he says.

Bait for what is the question absolutely nobody is asking.

The thing is, Guerra's a little fish. Would never do to tell him that. But there you have it. The biggest fish in a little pond, I'll grant you. But you've got to know there's far worse out there. And Guerra's neat; he's tidy. I'd go so far as to say well-organised. And he definitely likes the pretence of being an up-and-coming businessman. Perhaps he is, so long as you skirt the concepts of 'legitimate' or 'legal.' The Tentie is hovering close, close enough for Guerra to bat it away. A small, orange cloud has formed above it, a sure sign it's getting overexcited. The two of them seemed ready for a private tête-à-tête.

"We'll be going, then," says Carine.

Guerra nods.

Carine pokes at me and we turn and make for the door.

I half-expect, half-hope that Guerra will call me back. Why, I couldn't tell you. Curiosity. But, of course, he doesn't call. And I'm better off out of there.

"Thanks," says Carine when we are halfway down staircase number 3.

"S'okay."

"You back to normal now?"

"Guess so," I say. And I am. Yes, I am.

CHAPTER THREE

Green Jay

IT'S STRANGE TO see the big screen in the square, stuck in with the cobbles and the old shops and the market stalls. But that's Barlewin, lots of old with bits of new pasted on top. The new never seems quite right.

The morning I first saw the big screen light up, the first morning I was here in my greenhouse, I ignored the brain training. I was scared the screen would alert someone and I'd be found just by thinking about it. But I've decided that won't happen as long as I don't tab the results in. I couldn't any way: I don't have a phone or anything like that. But I need to test my brain to see what it can do, to see if it can learn. My score is improving. My memory and vision are good. My maths is fine. I don't do so well at vocabulary, but I am getting better, trying to learn. I like finding the birds, I like unlocking the names. I pretended

I didn't know them to start with; that I had to work my way through all the letters. But now I know owl, heron, blue jay, seagull, pelican and many more. I know them; they're not Olwin Duilis' memories.

Of course, it does not test long-term memory or any type of analytical ability, but for now, it is good for me. I worry that one day I will find that I am deteriorating. But not yet. And if I do, I will ask the Tenties for extra help.

There is someone else who never tabs his results in. I noticed him first because he always stands in the same spot. Him and a friend. Though, in fact, most people stand in roughly the same place. People like to form patterns. They trace themselves slowly into the earth. I have done that too, here in my greenhouse. I don't think they want to be predictable. But there is something in them that wants the same path, that wants to form habits. The Tenties are not the same; and often there is great misunderstanding if a Tentie takes a spot that a human thinks of as his or hers. But the man that I watch is always in exactly the same place. And he is too fast. He answers the questions while they are still being asked. As if he is Time Locked a little ahead. Although that, of course, is impossible. I don't think he knows it. Some days, I forget my own training and just watch him. I call him Blue Jay, though I know that can't be his name.

I've taken off my clothes. I don't need them here and they're the only ones I have. This way I can sit naked, absorbing the sun, letting myself replenish. I sleep now, too. At first, I didn't want to—sleep probably meant death—but one day, in the sun, I slept without meaning to. I hope that means I am a little less plantlike, a little more human. Now I let myself sleep whenever I need to. Usually at night, though night can be the most interesting time in Barlewin. Sometimes in the day. I like to lie out under the sun. I imagine my cells growing and renewing. I imagine the true me forming. I refuse to let the thoughts of the original intrude, instead I instruct my dreams into new places, places only I could have thought of, and only I will ever be found in.

Crow

THE TENTIES HAVEN'T been with us that long. Five years, tops, though some people like to suggest they were hiding out for a long time before that. Hiding out where, exactly, is never specified. The Tenties are too weird to fit in. The first time I ever saw one, it was riding a bike down our street. No offence, but you couldn't tell if it was male or female. But even from a long way off, you knew it wasn't human: something about the way they sway from side to side. And they're large, you know, lumpy. Well, this was kind of early on. Anyway, this one was wearing a gigantic blue T-shirt and riding down our street singing in that whale song way they have. I guess 'cause it was drizzling; that always makes them happy. And it was kind of spooky, me standing on the front porch, watching this blue thing come closer and closer. As though I was mesmerised, but then I'd never seen one in real life and who could blame me. And I was younger then too. Younger and more impressionable.

"Mate," it called out in its bubbly way and then it lifted its feet off the pedals and let the bike glide in to stop in front of our gate. Its tentacles were gently waving around its face; that was kind of gross. I knew you were meant to be friendly, but it was just me and this... thing. But I walked down into the drizzle and up to the gate.

"Mate," I said in return and it wanted to wrap its sort-of arms around me. I didn't let it. I stepped back before it had a chance. It smelled good. I thought everyone had been exaggerating, or maybe even that they were being sarcastic, but it smelled so good and I was kind of sad when it got back on the bike and went off down the road. I stood there in the rain listening to it sing, watching until it was just a patch of blue in the distance.

And I was right not to have let it touch me. Never got any of the weird scaly shit on my arms and back, never got the feeling like you'd lost something—'cause you *had*. You know, all that DNA exchange stuff we found out about later.

But hell, I still think about it as a good experience. You know, first contact and all. I was never one for the red writing (which the Tenties couldn't read anyway) or the protest T-shirts. The Hooks went way too far. Not just the fish hooks in their hair and ears, but more their brand of unsolicited violence. That's not for me. Not that I ever owned a tentacle hat either, even when they were all the craze. Mac feels pretty much the same way. But I am surprised to see him sitting with a Tentie, down on the seats by the big screen. Brain Training was over, long over, of course. I figured Mac would wait for me. Didn't figure on him finding a friend.

This Tentie's a hell of a lot calmer than the one up with Guerra, but Mac has that effect. It's wearing a green T-shirt with the words *Love and Understanding* printed in the same font as the *Fuck Off* T-shirts. Which just goes to show that the Tenties are a lot more aware of what's going on than most give them credit for.

I don't know why Barlewin got stuck with a truckload of Tenties, but then probably most every place thinks that. It's true we're mostly over the biggest misunderstandings now: the scales, the transformations, etc., etc. I mean, all things considered, we've taken this alien thing in our stride, almost gone overboard in our welcoming ways. This one, like most, I couldn't tell if it was boy or girl. They did their best before they turned up to look as much like us as possible. And God knows they did their best after they got here, to complete the transformation. But apparently, the specificities of gender is one thing they don't want to change. Thought they were all male at first. Stupid us.

Anyway, the Tentie in the green T-shirt is sitting there with Mac and they're having a nice, low-key, but fairly intense chat. Which is par for the course for both Mac and Tenties.

"Hey," says Mac. I want to tell him I've just popped through a couple of alternate realities on my way here, but somehow the news seems inappropriate.

"T-Lily, Brom, Brom, T-Lily."

I nod and the Tentie releases a cloud of something bluey-green. I try very hard not to look amused, askance—

anything, really—at the Tentie's name, which, after all is reasonably sane for a Tentie. And, I guess it means the Tentie is a she.

"T-Lily wants to show us something."

"Lead the way," I reply. It's nice, just for the moment, to have my feet on reliable earth.

We walk up to the west, away from the big screen, up past the Chemical Conjurers, skirting the market shops and into the narrow streets and the apartments. For a while it feels as if the Tentie is leading me home, which gives me the slight greeblies, but then it turns into a particularly narrow alley, offers something quick and sly to a young one by a doorway, and then we are in and climbing up what seems like a thousand stairs.

You'd think I'd be fit, running round, doing good deeds for Guerra. I'm not. If you are truly dedicated, you can get up early, do a round of exercises they show on the screen before Morning Mentals. Not for me. Mac I suspect of surreptitious exercise, and my belief is borne out when neither he nor T-Lily are at all troubled by the endless stairs.

We come to the top at last, up to what looks like a door to the roof. Well, not like a proper door, to a proper apartment. I try not to breathe too loudly. Mac gives me a funny look, which I can't quite interpret. T-Lily knocks at the door, twice, then three times. Locks are drawn back and the door scraped open. There is a girl, wearing clothes that have seen better days. That probably could be said of us all, but these ones have actual tears and the bottom fringe of her skirt is extremely tattered. The girl is beautiful, but there's something wrong, something vulnerable, something that will make her too much trouble. The Tentie hugs her and, unbelievably, this girl hugs T-Lily back.

It is only then I notice the room. We aren't on the roof at all, but in a space that looks like nothing more than an old, abandoned greenhouse. A greenhouse without plants, mind you. A greenhouse without furniture of any kind. If this girl lives here, she's living a pretty austere life.

T-Lily withdraws from the hug and attempts to introduce us. "Kern Bromley, Mac Limburg." There is no mention of the girl's name.

The stranger attempts a smile. Mac steps forward, gently, cautiously, and extends a hand. She takes it, shakes it in a very businesslike manner and then withdraws as if her actions surprised her. There's a hole in her shirt under the arm. Mac draws off his T-shirt with one quick movement and presents it to her with a bow.

"For you," he says. "Way too big, but no holes."

The girl takes it and pulls it on over her rags. And then we stand around, silently, admiring the dark blue tracings on Mac's shoulders and back. Same colour as the thing on his thumb, and something I've never known he had. And I've known him for a while.

"Blue Jay," says the girl. This time she smiles as if she has let us in on a private joke.

To my surprise, Mac grins too. "Do you have a name?" he asks.

The girl shakes her head.

"She is from the printer," says T-Lily.

"A copy," I say. Without thought, because really that's quite rude, but then I've never seen a copy this good. Even doubles are fairly obvious.

"A double," says T-Lily. "But leftover, now."

The girl is watching us closely, waiting to see if she needs to run, what she might need to do.

"Perhaps not leftover anymore," says Mac.

The girl smiles at him, again, then looks away.

"How long?" I ask.

"Four weeks," says T-Lily.

"Shit," says Mac. I believe I share his sentiments.

"How is that even possible?" I ask.

Mac turns to T-Lily. "You helped her," he says. And it is nothing of a question.

T-Lily nods. "But..."

"You need something from us?" Mac holds out an arm, ready for T-Lily to put her hands on him, to take whatever substance the girl needs and the Tentie can't make.

T-Lily shakes her head, tentacles flailing just a little too much for my liking. "It will help, but she needs something more."

"Something Guerra has?" I ask. Because I just like to lay my stupidity out on the line.

"Yes," says T-Lily. And, for the first time, I fully realise what an unbelievably dumb thing I'd done this morning.

CHAPTER FOUR

Green Jay

BLUE JAY AND I are lying on the floor of my room, soaking up the sun. He said to call him Mac, but I still think of him as Blue Jay. It makes me laugh, inside. He brought me new clothes, but we are lying here naked, soaking up the sun like beautiful lizards. I watch the way the sun lights up the tracings on Blue Jay's body. They are all over him. Growing, I think, although I have not seen him enough to be sure. He has not said what they are. I can guess, if I allow my old memories in. But I have enough of my own mysteries. The person I used to be knows a little about this body of mine. But not enough. I know I can eat, but that it is not necessary and not especially helpful. It comes out the usual way. I have few of the internal organs that Blue Jay does. But I have a skeleton and muscle. Skin and hair. Teeth, lips, tongue. From the outside I am just like him. I touch his skin and I touch mine. It is not different. Perhaps his is hairier. Of course, that cannot be true. Our skins cannot be the same: it is my skin that is keeping me alive. I am lucky that my skin is dark brown; if it wasn't, you would see the green, and even in this light, the bright light of my greenhouse, the green tinge is clearly visible. Blue Jay doesn't seem to care.

"You need a name," he says. "A name of your own."

I have an old name. Olwin Duilis. Deep inside, it won't go away. But I keep it down, I don't let it surface. At first, when that name bubbled up, I would turn, I would jump as if I'd heard it called. But now, I can keep it down. It is not me.

"I can't choose," I say. And it's true. I cannot think of a name that encompasses all of me. I am so misty still.

"It will grow," he says. "The name will become you." He turns to look at me. "We could choose a bird. You like birds."

Green Jay, I think, but I am too shy to say so. I shake my head. "Eva," I say, because that is how I want to think of myself. As someone new.

"Eva," says Mac, and he grins. Blue Jay and Green Jay, I think. I stretch out my fingers and touch his hand. We lie here in the sun.

Crow

IT'S A SHIT of a hot day. It's not that early and already I can feel the sweat gathering and the light pouring in, trying to poke at ungrateful eyes. You'd think we'd be getting used to the heat waves, but no, not really. There's enough of them, there's truly enough, but not enough for the average person to be prepared. The weather can still lull you into an unsuspecting apathy. But the worst part is that you really don't know what to expect when. I've lived in Barlewin all my life. You'd think I'd know what's what. But there are no seasons any more. There are areas of damage, broad times of possible danger. A homeless person could freeze and then burn. But shit, we're all that much closer to being homeless now.

Mac is waiting for me in our usual spot for Morning Mentals. About the only time I see him lately. He's besotted with the double. And I know there's something he wants from me, something to do with the package and Guerra, but he's not asking yet. And I have no intention of offering. We're stuck in a holding pattern.

We do the brain training, Mac tapping away at his usual light speed, me spotting some peripheral birds and completing some arithmetic at my discretion. Then comes the half-arsed memory test set in a cafe with relentless customers who want you to not only remember their absurd orders but their names as well. The whole gathering groans. For a start, it's a ridiculous set-up. Nobody, but nobody who has ever served me has felt the need to remember my name. Not even when they'd asked for it with the dubious pretext that they would yell it out when my order was ready.

"My name's Beryl and I would like some eCrunchies and half a drop," says Mac. It's our usual joke.

"A bottle of tequila," I add.

"With some Ace."

"An ambulance."

"And a stomach pump."

At last, the endless array of pretend customers finally leaves the screen, dissatisfied, for the most part, with their orders and our collective lack of interest in their names. People start to drift away; the market starts to encroach onto the road. Mac suggests coffee before it gets too hot. It is already too hot, but I say yes, because I figure today is probably the day. The day of the favour. We get our drinks from the place we always do. They probably know our names, but they never see the point of using them.

"You ever have any flashbacks?" he asks while we wait. "I mean from that time-walk you did."

Not the question I am expecting. In fact, I am faintly surprised that Mac even knows about that. "Nup," I say. "But then it was only about fifteen, twenty minutes."

"Anybody open the box yet?"

"Not my concern," I say.

"But you'd know if it was opened."

"I'm not still linked to it."

"You sure?"

"Totally sure, Mac. And Guerra won't be telling me if and when he opens the box, either. Strangely enough."

Our coffees present themselves and Mac pays for mine as a peace offering.

"He say anything about it?" Mac asks. This is deeply out of character. You could almost see the man forcing the words to come out of his mouth. But for all I'm sympathetic, I know what this is all about: the double Mac is besotted with and her need for whatever it is Guerra has.

"He called it bait, Mac. Bait. You need to stay away from it."

Mac shakes his head. We are wandering, but I know where we're going. Away from the shops, through some alleys, down into the apartments. Mac tosses a doughnut to the kid by the door. "You don't have to be part of it, Brom," he says.

I grunt something noncommittal, but I follow him into the building and up the stairs. Mac gives the knock the Tentie gave. Two raps, then three.

The door swings open and there she is. The double, dressed in some of Mac's old clothes. Looking... much darker, much greener, still beautiful, still completely wrong. A cloud of black curls partially hides her face. But the smell... The greenhouse is already hot and the stink of the double has filled it up. A composty smell that reminds me of the farms out behind the water tower. Not completely bad, but there is something underneath, some decay. She looks deeply disappointed to see me.

"Eva, you remember Brom?" says Mac. As if we're at a party.

"Eva," I say. Not highly original as names go, but then what does it really matter?

We all sit on the floor in the sun. I would have preferred some shade, but there isn't a lot of that available in the greenhouse. Eva and Mac link fingers, they can't help themselves. I feel somewhat redundant.

"We're going up to the High Track," says Mac after a while. "We have to; Eva needs to get the box."

"It's a trap," I say.

"We have no choice," says Mac.

You do, I think. You have another choice, not very pleasant, but then again, this is a double, not a real person.

"You could open the box." Eva is talking to me, and her tone isn't quite so cutesy as it was before.

"No, I couldn't," I reply. "I linked with it once, yes. Don't mean I can link with it again. There's a whole... procedure. Not to mention it's up at Guerra's. Not to mention it's a really stupid thing to do."

"But you can," persists Eva. "I have memories. Knowledge, from... You *can* link with it again. Quite easily. I know how."

"It's okay, Brom. It doesn't make sense for you to get involved," says Mac.

"She can't go," I say. "It'd be suicide for her. It's exactly what Guerra wants."

"All you need do is touch it again," says Eva.

"Just walk up to it, and touch it," I say. "That's all you want. Just walk into a place I hardly ever go, certainly not without invitation, somewhere I'm not especially welcome and just touch a box which is probably quite heavily guarded or at the very least securely stored. Under guard. With surveillance measures. So just touch that box."

Mac closes his eyes. "Brom," is all he manages. It's a kind of groan.

"I know how to open the box," says Eva again, "but I need someone who's been Time Locked to it."

"Then get the original courier, old Orange Toes."

"Yeah, Brom," says Mac. "That's feasible."

"More feasible for him to show up than me."

"He's touched too many boxes," says Eva. Looking at me as if I am the chosen one, which I most definitely am not.

"Tell me," I say. "Tell me what I have to do."

Eva shakes her head. "We must all go."

"Well, that's unlikely," I say.

"You don't have to go with us," she says. "Just let us know when you're there."

"Who the hell are you?" I ask. Because it seems pretty obvious to me that however much this double imagines herself a unique individual, that there are memories belonging to a real person in there that would be much more relevant to the situation in hand.

"That person is not me," says Eva.

"That person can help us now." Actually that person, that real person, is probably out to destroy her renegade double, and likely sent the box in the first place, but there is no point muddying the waters with speculation.

Eva looks away.

"You'll come with us?" asks Mac.

"All for one," I say.

"And one for all," says Mac happily.

Apparently Eva's memories don't include *Three Musketeers* references.

CHAPTER FIVE

CHAPTER FIVE

Green Jay

KERN BROMLEY IS a crow. I won't even give him a colour. The kind of bird that drifts around picking up scraps with no direction of its own, no beauty. I don't like him, I don't trust him; but we need him, Blue Jay and me. We need him because he is the one who can open the box.

I try and sneak up on Olwin Duilis' memories, to see what she wants with me, what she plans with the package. I am sure that she sent it. But she won't let me know, there is nothing there to find. I don't know how she did this, and it scares me a little to find a gap where there should be information. Perhaps it should comfort me, perhaps it means that she is fading away and that I am truly taking over. But I don't think so. I have the information of how to open the box. I have the surety that the package will contain something to help me. These things keep popping into my mind. They are not my thoughts, they are the thoughts of Olwin Duilis, but they are very real.

When Kern Bromley the crow visited, he looked at me the whole time with his beady eyes, with his questions that he didn't speak but that we both knew were there. Who are you? he wants to know. What is inside you? How human are you? Why do you think you should be alive? How do you know what you know? He doesn't look at Blue Jay that way, and that is the only reason I have hope. I watch the Crow through the glass when I can. He is making no attempt to go to the package; he is never anywhere near the High Track. I watch the ripples that he makes and they are so few that it is almost as if he is gliding. He is trying not to be seen. But that is impossible, especially if Guerra is watching. A crow is a loud, noisy bird. Smart, but not small. Always in the way. Always noticeable.

I watch a body copy as it makes its way through the market. This one is the androgynous model, with jeans and a T-shirt and short red hair. It has a job to do. It's moving so deliberately that it creates its own ripple, like a swimmer in a calm lake. People give it a little more space than they would give to another person. If I watch carefully I can see the moment they recognise it as a copy, step back just a little. Nobody wants to acknowledge that they can be built so easily. And the copies have such short lives, like butterflies. It is disconcerting, I think, for people to see something so much like themselves born and then die. To learn that the stuff that they are made of is not so special.

* * *

Crow

IT ISN'T ENTIRELY true I haven't had any time flashbacks. But I am choosing to ignore them, treat them as dreams. Worse side effects than the first time I did it, but so far, so good, they don't seem to be affecting my day to day life. But they do mean that when I see Carine I am sitting down, watching the Chemical Conjurers, letting myself acclimatise to what I hope is my regular world. They crack me up, the Chemical Conjurers. Ol' Felix and Oscar. They have names, long names they'll recite given half a chance, complete with numbers and addendums, but I call them Felix and Oscar. There's no particular correlation in appearance or personality with the old TV show characters: in fact, as far as I can tell the Chemical Conjurers are pretty much identical twins.

Every day there's something new. You'd expect repetition, but no, they seem to get bored quick, though some routines are definite favourites. They're always getting deliveries. Usually with those drones. Which also cracks me up, especially as what they seem to be delivering is insignificant shit.

I mean, what does a robot want? An endless array of meaningless junk, if you're thinking with a human brain. Not drugs, not sex, but yes to the rock and roll. They love music, the robots do, although their taste, as they say, is questionable. Now some might say I'm unfairly extrapolating the preferences of the two robots

I know best onto all of robot kind. Forgive me, for I have sinned. The Chemical Conjurers love them some beats. But also, it must be said, also the chemicals. Their favourite at the moment is concentrated sulphuric acid added to p-nitroaniline. They told me this one day when I had nothing better to do but take the information in. In any case those two chemicals mixed together produce an angry punch of weird arse black stuff. That seems to be incorporated into the show most days. It's a bit aggro, I tell them. But they pump up the bass, put the music on loud, spin a few lights and then, hey presto. It's fun stuff, the way they do it. Quite why they decided to settle in Barlewin, nobody knows. But everyone loves them.

They're up for a bit of helping hand too. A bit of cover. I've used them myself. For me, they used an old rubbish bin, put some liquid nitrogen in and added ping pong balls. Man, those balls went everywhere. And to add to the chaos, that moment also turned out to be one of the rare times a car chose to use the road as an actual road. The market shops—which, naturally, had drifted out onto the bitumen—had to quickly drift back in again. I had some major restitution to do with the shopkeepers, but I managed. Spent a lot of time picking up squashed ping pong balls, for a start.

So when Carine comes and sits down beside me, we watch the Chemical Conjurers in silence for a while. Today's routine involves hydrogen peroxide mixed with potassium iodide. If you're imaginative, it looks like there's another robot, a third conjurer, with all the body movements of a balloon man swaying with the wind. Which is pretty much how I feel, and Carine, for once, seems to appreciate that. This is my chance, I know it, to get up to see Guerra. Just can't quite seem to form the words to come up with something plausible.

"How you feeling, Brom?" she asks after a while.

"Fine," I say. Which we both know isn't completely true.

"Got time to come up to the High Track for a bit?" Which, despite the syntax, can't strictly be viewed as a question.

"Sure," I say. Yes, too good to be true, gift horse, etcetera, etcetera. But also beggars can't be choosers. I text Mac, being a cryptic as I can, and then Carine and I walk up to staircase number 3, taking a path vaguely reminiscent of my Time Locked walk. The nauseous quotient is about equal, I have to say.

"Don't dick around with him," Carine offers once we're past the guards at the bottom of the stairs. It takes me a while to formulate a suitable comeback: so long, in fact, that we are standing inside admin and I still haven't said a thing. The same table off to the side, this time with various papers on it and, surprise, surprise, no Time Locked box. There's a Tentie hanging around, same one as the other day, I'm fairly sure. It's dithering, but essentially it's hovering close to a cupboard in the back right-hand corner. No prizes for guessing what's in there. We wait, not for long, but long enough. Eventually Guerra arrives. Carine disappears, and so, after a long, hard look from Guerra, does the Tentie.

"Remember that box you brought up for me the other day?" begins Guerra. No hellos, none really necessary.

I nod.

"Remember what I said it was?"

"Bait," I reply. As nonchalantly as I'm able.

"Bait that hasn't worked," he remarks.

"Hasn't been that long," I say.

"Long enough," says Guerra. There's a pause in which neither of us appear to have anything to say. "You do a lot of work for me, Kern," he says. "A lot of deliveries. And you've earned my trust."

I nod, I smile, I realise he means almost the exact opposite.

"But, in the beginning, as a sensible precaution, I took the liberty of having you tracked. I can see where you go and when, Kern. That way, if there are complaints of non-delivery, I have evidence to back me up, I can accurately point the finger at the guilty party. So far, that hasn't been you."

This is no revelation; I'd already figured as much. Not sure if it's my own person, my phone—the most likely culprit—or even traces from the parcels I carry, but it amounts to the same thing. But I also know the tracking isn't a hundred per cent reliable, that a lot of suspicious types, which for some reason includes many of Guerra's customers, put up blocks around their home or business. I am reasonably sure that Mac's true love is hiding out in a place that can't be tracked. First sign was the kid at the entrance, second sign was the hardware clearly on display in the staircase. Of course, I can't be sure. And, probably more to the point, my tracks would take me quite close to the door of that apartment building before they were blocked. Guerra could figure the rest out for himself.

I convey all of this in a shrug.

"So, Kern, seeing as how you and I both know where you go and, for the most part, what you do, I want to ask if you've come across anyone interesting of late. Anyone who possibly shouldn't be here. Anyone with something to hide."

"You already know all the secrets," I tell Guerra. "The citizens of Barlewin, they're not that interesting."

Guerra walks over to the cupboard and opens the door. There is the Time Locked box. Not the only thing in the cupboard, but the thing I am trying hard not to notice. "It's not the citizens I'm talking about." He taps the plastic of the box. "Strange feeling," he remarks. "There and not there. You want to move it for me, Kern?"

"I'm still feeling a little"—*fucked up* is what I want to say, but Guerra don't take to that kind of language—"strange from the last time."

"But you know what to do?" asks Guerra.

"Sure."

I don't advance any closer.

"The thing about alternate realities is they usually turn out to be immensely dissatisfying," remarks Guerra.

Alternate Reality One: I refuse to move the box for Guerra. Black mark in Guerra's eyes, black mark in Mac's eyes. But probably redeemable. Well, possibly. But at least I haven't linked with that bloody box.

Alternate Reality Two: I move the box. Gold star in

Mac's eyes. Not quite sure what in Guerra's eyes. Why the fuck does he want me to move the box, anyway?

Alternate Reality Three: I run away. Not feasible. Not even close.

Alternate Reality Four: I move the box, switch to some other time bubble and get the fuck out of here. Three flaws: the box will still be visible, I'll probably be stuck to it and last, but not least, there's no way to do that.

Why am I even debating?

"Know what to do?" asks Guerra. Which is more of a prod than a question. He looks again at a small screen he's carrying, but then looks at me expectantly.

"I know what I did last time," I say. Which is about all I do know. You would think Guerra would be better informed, or at least have a set of instructions, but he seems to be winging it. Pretty much just as I am. But then, that is supposing that his purpose in having me here is to have the box moved.

I walk up to the cupboard and fiddle with the top of the box, all the time aware of Guerra's watchful eye. On top of the box are two pads that unhook and attach to your hands. The hands slot in to panels at the side so that they're pretty much encased in plastic. So you're physically holding the box and also connected to the box by the pads that are still attached to the box by some sort of cords. That's the limit of my technical knowledge. Unhooking yourself is more complex, and someone has always told me how to do it. God knows what will happen at the end of this particular trip.

"All ready?" asks Guerra.

"Yep," I say. With the confident tone of someone who has no idea at all.

I slide my hands into the panels, pick up the box, experience the familiar failure of my body to cope with the mangling of the correct order of things, and think, *shit, Mac, this better be worth it.*

CHAPTER SIX

Green Jay

IT IS STRANGE to walk outside after all this time in the greenhouse. Blue Jay and T-Lily have found me clothes so that I don't stand out. I worry that my skin is too green, that everyone will know, but the day is cloudy and nobody seems to be looking. That's good, I think. A good thing. Brom is up there already, we need to hurry, but we're taking the long way around. It's safer, Blue Jay says. Staircase number 2 is not so heavily guarded, and it's in a place where the old railway line curves around, so that it will be harder to see us climb. Someone has painted a large hand on top of the posts the High Track rests on. As if a giant was holding it up. I trust that giant, somehow.

I like the feel of the air around me, but I miss the sun of the greenhouse. Outside it is murkier, there are shadows and clouds. We manage the staircase; the guard is sitting down, having a smoke, his back to the stairs. We sneak up behind him and he doesn't even notice. I feel exposed on the way up, but there are vines halfway that offer some protection.

The High Track is beautiful. It's a shame that someone like Guerra owns it, that it isn't for everybody. There are seats and paths and plantings in patterns and you can see out over Barlewin and a little beyond. From where we are standing, I can see apartments, the tip of the big screen and some of the water tower. The markets are too low to see from here. And so are the warehouses which hide in the middle. In the other direction, there is more city; mostly small houses. It's the edge of Barlewin, and the beginning of somewhere else. Somewhere nicer. I let those memories drift up for a moment, but then I press them down. We need to get to the package.

It took Brom so long, it is almost too late, but Blue Jay is right, it is a miracle he has done it at all.

A few steps on and Blue Jay stops. He points to the right. There, very visibly, is my greenhouse. It seemed so hidden, to walk to it requires so many turns and alleys and corners. But here, on the High Track, it is close, very close. It makes my heart doubt, but we cannot go back now. We are close to the main administration, a building that Guerra has obviously added to the High Track. He has tried to make it fit, but everything else is so delicate, so natural, that this large building stands out painfully. There are more people around, and Blue Jay nods to them and they nod back. No-one's stopped us so far. But we need to get right inside. I reach for the two plastic interfaces Blue Jay found for me. They are nestled in my pocket, waiting to connect me.

There is the door. There's no sign of anyone here, no security, not even a Tentie. It's too easy; surely there is something wrong. Blue Jay and I both stop. I place my hand on his chest, to feel his heart beating. I have no choice but to walk into the building, but he could hide, he could leave now. I love that he doesn't.

The first thing I see is the plastic box, mid-air with a shimmer around it. It means that Brom has the box, that it is jumping through time again. It means I have a chance. I step towards it, but Blue Jay holds me back; Guerra is there standing in the shadows to the right. He looks up. "I've been expecting you," he says, and he shows us the screen he is holding. There are our faces, or in my case, a face that is not really me, but that Guerra thinks is mine. A face that is close enough to mine to trap me.

"I see you've brought me Olwin Duilis' renegade double, Mac," he says.

"Her name is Eva," says Blue Jay. He is brave and true, but there is no point. I don't wish to speak with Guerra. I concentrate instead on the box.

"She's not real," says Guerra.

"Then how has she survived this long?"

I take a step towards the box.

"You'd not be here, except that she won't survive for much longer," says Guerra. "Let her stay; I'll care for her, make sure she has everything she needs."

Another step. He doesn't look at me. Neither of them do.

"Why?" asks Blue Jay. But we both know the answer to that. Because Olwin Duilis has asked him to, has paid him to. Another step, another. Too greedy. Guerra reaches out, grabs me.

"Because," says Guerra. "That's all you need to know."

"Don't hurt her," says Blue Jay. And then he runs, he flies, because there is nothing else he can do. I understand.

Crow

SO FAR, ALL I've been experiencing is various views of Guerra's admin. If I didn't feel like throwing up, I'd go as far as to say I was bored. I've walked the box back and forward around the room. I've put it down; I've tried to unlink myself. Quite a few times. Tried and failed. Monumentally failed. So all I can do is wait. I'm still holding on to the box, because I don't really know what else to do and I figure that Guerra is not so stupid that he don't have a plan at all. I mean he actually does need what's inside this box, so surely he's not going to let me fart around with it for too long. There's a moment, not a long one, but it's happened more than once, where I'm not inside a building at all. There's grass under my feet and leaves tickling at my hair. It's only a moment, but it's there. Which just goes to show that Guerra isn't everywhere.

I've been bouncing around like this for a while now, and, apart from the nauseous feeling that pervades the whole experience, I'm getting restless. There has to be a way to get offa this train. Surely someone will unlock the box. If Mac and Eva have made it there, they'll try. That was the whole point. Even if they're been discovered and Eva's well and truly under Guerra's thumb, which, almost inevitably, she must be.

There's something like a stripy cane flitting in and out of my vision. You know me, poor impulse control, next time it comes around, I grab it. Got nothing better to do. Can't hurt. Can't make things worse. One hand's holding the box, still slotted into place, the other hand's holding onto the stripy cane. And if I thought I felt bad before, now I feel worse. But there's no letting go. And then, ladies and gentlemen, I pass out.

The first thing I'm aware of after that is something itching at my nose. Something fluffy that I can flick away, but which comes back to taunt me. I open one eye, am dismayed by the amount of bright light, see that it's a piece of grass that's got overexcited and produced something like a flower. I think about sitting up, decide against it and wriggle to the side so that the grass is no longer touching me. I close my eye and, in the peaceful darkness, I think about what may or may not have happened.

That don't take long; I have no idea. I do know one thing, I'm no longer doing a Time Dance. Actually, I know two things, I'm no longer holding the box. It takes a while, but eventually curiosity overcomes me and I open both eyes. Can't see much. A bit of sky, a bit of leaf. Moving my head hurts, but the view to the right provides pretty much more of the same. The view to the left may contain a plastic box. I sit up slowly, orienting myself to the left.

I groan. It's a whole new battered feeling. Different from being Time Locked, but not better. Well, perhaps better. In that I'm hoping this feeling is residual; that the only way, as they say, is up. Possibly that's overly optimistic.

Yes, the plastic box is sitting there. Fully in view. Looking, perhaps, not quite as pristine as it used to. I do not want to touch it. I can see the marks on my hands where the pads were attached. They're not pretty; it's a combination of graze and burn that's just beginning to heal over with that silvery grey shit. The left hand's worse because it's the one that was still holding onto the box. So yes, my hands are hurting, but I hadn't really singled them out from the rest of my bodily aches. I have now.

I find a stick, poke at the box. It sits there, as it always does, impervious. But the thing is, I can poke it, so it's stopped jumping around and it's here with me in the wherever this is. Well that's my reasoning and I'm probably wrong, but if the box is still jumping around, at least it's doing it on its own time.

This place, all things considered, looks pretty much like the High Track. I'll go for a walk in a minute, have a proper look. But as far as I can tell, from my admittedly not vast experience, that thing about alternate realities being full of interesting shit is a crock. There's no monsters, or castles, or magic, or what have you. Disappointing, perhaps, but on the plus side, in this particular time bubble there's probably no Guerra either.

I stand, I groan, I stretch, I persuade my feet it's okay to walk. I leave the box where it is. Frankly, someone else is welcome to it. The High Track looks, to me, just like it always does. I'm not an expert, unfortunately, but the path winds around much as I remember it, there are the tall fluffy grasses I first became acquainted with, some bizarre hedges, places to stop and see the world, mosaics, mazes, all the artistic shit you'd expect. And seats. Fantastic bloody seats and I take advantage of one and sit down. I'm looking across at buildings. If I stood and looked over the edge I'd probably see the market shops. But I can't be bothered. The apartments look right. I can see the greenhouse the double is living in. That surprises me, but it makes sense. Guerra has probably been keeping an eye on her all this time. The whole thing smacks of a set-up. You'd think Mac would be smart enough to see it.

This seat is painted with red stripes, something that I'd not immediately associate with the High Track. And it makes me think of that candy striped stick I grabbed onto. And only now, for the first time in my slow, slow brain, I think about who might have been holding the other end of that stick. On the corner of the armrest, someone has painted a pair of lips in the middle of a red circle. Only the circle has been chopped in half, so that one side is lower than the other. Which pretty much symbolises how I feel at the moment. The circle that is, not the lips. Don't know what the fuck the lips mean. And this symbol, I'm reasonably sure, does not belong on the High Track I know. Definitely not pre-Guerra. That aesthetic was arty, but not this kind of arty: more leaves and twigs and woven things. Nature arty. This is... Alice in Wonderland.

Right now, I don't care. My brain hurts too much to

think for long. There's no-one here that I can see. No OCD rabbits or addicted caterpillars or cats with nothing better to do than to smile. No-one at all. I close my eyes and lean back. There's a nice breeze up here on this High Track. My hands still hurt, but the rest of me is recovering. I sit here for a while, but it doesn't take long before I'm bored. I move from the seat, which suddenly feels like foolishness, and walk the six or so steps towards the railing. Another place to lean. It feels as if I could almost touch the buildings across the way. I look down. And yes, sure enough, there's the market. Is it any different? Can't say I've ever observed it from this angle. But I see people; that's a comfort, I suppose. I look for the familiar brown awning of the coffee hut, and yes, I think I see it.

I begin to feel slightly ill from dangling over the edge. My body has been *fucked up*. I straighten up, and then I see it: Eva, looking straight at me. It's a painting, of course. An idealised Eva with her head in her hands, surrounded by all sorts of green and with her hair floating up and around artistically. The look on her face is… questioning. Not that she's in a position to be asking the questions. It's me, that has that right, to my way of thinking. But the disturbing thing is, looking at that picture, it's almost as if I'm inside her head. I don't like it.

CHAPTER SEVEN

Green Jay

GUERRA LETS ME go, with a push towards the box. It's what I wanted anyway, what I was trying to do, but he is the type of person that likes to show he is in control.

I take the two interfaces out of my pocket. Guerra watches me. He's like a hawk, ready to pounce, but so far he is letting me do my job. I peel the plastic off the back, place one on my left hand and then, with more difficulty, one on my right. I feel a flicker of triumph. This body is right-handed, though I am only a plant. *I* am right-handed. I do not care what handedness Olwin Duilis possessed. I am right-handed. But that doesn't matter now.

I close my eyes for a moment, still my mind, I need to let the memories come up. I have kept them there, just below the surface, almost ready. I step into the space that

Brom is in. I think he is on the other side of the box, but it doesn't matter. Not at this point.

The box has flickered out of sight, but that happens, especially when someone inexperienced like Brom is holding it. I'm not too worried. He's tried to free himself of the box, I'm sure of it, and that makes things harder, but not impossible. It should be easier for me, far easier than for Brom. The box is meant for me.

I put my hands where I think the box is, I imagine I can feel it. I let the interfaces do their work, guiding me, finding a moment—it needs only a moment—when they can sense the box. And it's there, I can feel it. I can touch it. And then... no, it is gone. This is strange, but not entirely unexpected. I try again. But now, there is nothing. No pull, no hint. The box is gone.

Brom has taken it. He has stolen it. The Crow. Prince Crow. I must give him his due. Thief Crow is perhaps a better title.

I turn, face Guerra. He is still watching closely, but his face has changed.

"It's gone," I tell him.

"Gone?"

"There is nothing there. Kern Bromley has stolen it."

Guerra laughs. "How is that possible?"

I begin to carefully peel the interfaces from my hands, return them to their casing. I only have this one pair and it seems likely I will need them again. "I don't know how it is possible, I just know that is what he's done."

"It's not possible," repeats Guerra.

"Possible, impossible. That is what he's done."

Guerra takes a moment. He is annoyed, but he is poised. "You need to stay with me," he says.

"No, I need to go."

"You'll not survive."

I shrug.

"And if the box comes back?"

"I will not wait here."

"Yes," says Guerra. "I think you will."

People appear at the doorway, people who were not here before. One of them is a Tentie and she comes towards me and touches my arm. An act of sympathy, I suppose at first, but then I feel dizzy, tired and I feel myself drop into her.

Crow

LOOKING AT THE markets has made me hungry. Not famished, about-to-die hungry, but my curiosity is piqued. I have money in my pockets. And my phone, though God knows who I'd call right here. I decide to test out the shops, see if the coinage I have will buy me anything at all. I think about walking all the way down to staircase number 2, but, seriously, I can't be bothered. I know how to blend in, even if I am making an entrance down from the High Track.

I wander back through the grasses and the mosaics and what have you and casually descend staircase number 3. The food smells are getting stronger. There's breakfasty stuff: eggs, rolls, coffee. Shit, I want coffee. But—and this is where I didn't think things through—there's no big screen. Nothing to hide behind. Not that anyone seems to be noticing. The markets here have covered the whole of the space where the big screen usually stands. There's no indication that any cars ever use the road at all. It's all bustle and shops and people and food. It all looks vaguely familiar, but there's nothing I definitely recognise. I wander past a few stalls, as if I'm just looking, gauging my options. But really I'm trying to scope out the nature of the currency. It looks right. No way to really tell without picking some up, but it's right enough to maybe pretend that I made a mistake if I hand the vendor the stuff that I've got. And the prices don't seem so out of whack. I could always try some liberation discount, but I like to make a good impression on my first visit to a reality.

I decide on pancakes. Not health food, but then, perhaps it's the best thing for a body that's just jumped out of its normal space and time. Who could say? I get three with maple syrup and ice cream and even some berries. The exchange of money goes without a hitch, and I have a moment or two of happiness, stuffing food into my mouth. I wander, just looking, blending in. I think I'm pretty successful. Disappointing to see there's no Chemical Conjurers. On the other hand, no Tenties. Well, none out at the markets anyway.

There's more shops here, more room for them without the big screen, and plenty of people bustling around. I'm almost up at the water tower when I feel my happiness drain away. There, where Ol' Stick Man should be, with his crazy hair and his optimistic comb, is another picture of Eva. A large head-and-shoulders thing, again with her head in her hands. Big eyes staring at me. Less questioning, more demanding, but perhaps that's my paranoia. I'm beginning to think she planned this whole thing.

My mood is definitely damaged. I lick the remains of syrupy pancake off my fingers and find a bin for the plate. Yes, there's no harm in being tidy even in alternate worlds apparently constructed at the whim of a manipulative plant woman. I decide to return to the High Track. It's as good a place as any to collect my thoughts. Halfway up the number 3 staircase, it occurs to me that the picture could just as well be of the original, and that this makes a lot more sense. Not, 'oh, yes, anyone could run out and do that' sense, but more sense than Eva being in charge. This makes me feel a little better. Which, I realise, is not a logical reaction. Just that Eva gives me the irrits.

I reach the top of the stairs, check on the box—it's still there, happily sitting under some fluffy grass—and find me a comfortable place to sit. There are long wooden seats up here, where you can stretch out your legs, almost like deckchairs. I lie back, hands behind my head, and devote myself to the contemplation of my predicament.

The thing about me is that I've never wanted to travel. Born in Barlewin, lived out my not-yet-all-that-long life in Barlewin, saw the Tenties come and the big screen go up and... shit, it's my home. And if I'm being completely honest, that's why I work for Guerra.

Should probably make that 'worked.'

It's easier. It means not having to commute, to convince

someone else of my worth and status. It means I can stay in Barlewin. Not even the other side of the High Track counts, in my mind, the side that thinks it's becoming gentrified, part of Wilton. Nobody's tried to have a crack at the area under the High Track. Can't say that I blame them. That's where Guerra stores his stuff. And that's where his saddest customers live. Every now and then the two populations—up and coming and down and desperate—meet and it never ends well. So Barlewin's not for everyone. Even my parents have moved on, but not me. I guess I'm a homebody. Though that isn't turning out so well just now.

I must have momentarily drifted off, because the next thing I know, there's something poking me. I open my eyes to see a man with another of those red striped candy cane sticks. The angle of the sun makes it hard to see what he looks like, but he don't seem menacing so much as curious. I sit up a bit and offer my hand.

"Hi," I say.

The man uses the stick to poke at my feet. I draw them up and sit cross-legged as he perches on the end of my seat. His clothes are more like robes, coloured in green and black. Clean, I think. Well, he don't smell, anyway; with those colours it'd be hard to know if there were stains or not. His hair is longish and pretty wild. He has one of those beards that make you think Old Testament or serious hippy. And all this time he hasn't said a thing.

"My name's Kern Bromley," I offer. "Most people call me Brom." And then, because it just occurs to me, "Have I taken your seat? I'm sorry, I was just a bit—"

"Lost," says the man. And yes, he's right.

"As it happens."

"Lost, lingering, leftover."

I smile, because quite frankly there's no reply to that. He has a deep voice, and somehow reminds me of someone. That kind of tickle at your brain where you know you recognise the face, but you don't know why.

"Korbin," he says. And he sticks out his hand. It's a strong grip, and for a moment I wonder if he's ever going to let go, but he does at last. I resist the urge to wipe my hand on the seat rest. Not that Korbin's in any way grubby. Just odd, very odd.

There's a faint sound of singing drifting up and over. Korbin stands and turns to face the sound. He takes a few steps, realises I'm not moving and impatiently gestures for me to follow. I mentally shrug. Why not? It's not like I've got anything else to do.

We walk in the direction of where Guerra's admin would be. Korbin gives the box a tap with his red striped cane, but gives it no further attention and we walk on. The singing is getting louder. We're heading close to the water tower and up where the farms are, or should be. I've never been on this part of the High Track. But I do know there's another staircase further up, and I decide that I'll attempt an exit stage right.

Before I get the chance, a flock of women come into view. They're wearing the same robes as Korbin, though the greens are brighter. They have bits of green in their hair too. And flowers, much in the way of the Eva graffiti. The thought makes me shudder, but really, there's no need. It's just a bunch of women singing. And, to be fair, doing a fine job.

"Prophets," says Korbin. He steps to the side as they approach. I expect them to stop, talk to him, he was so determined to find them, but they keep going, their song drifting away as they continue back up the path of the High Track.

"Green. A good day."

I see the stairs to the right. I want, very much, to walk down them and away, but Korbin has his eye on me. I saunter along. There's nothing doing, no aggro, no tension. Until Korbin pushes me down the stairs and I find myself being bumped and thumped and generally mangled on the way down.

It's a long way.

CHAPTER EIGHT

Green Jay

THERE IS A Tentie hovering over me and I feel as if I cannot breathe. I'm not sure if I have lungs to breathe with, or if my skin does my breathing for me, but the feeling is still there, of suffocating, of being overwhelmed. I try to push it away, but I am weak. The Tentie understands, though, and moves back to give me space.

"How long?" I ask.

"Three days," says the Tentie.

I try and sit and it makes me dizzy. The Tentie watches me closely and I make myself sit straight. I won't let myself lie down while it is still here.

"What is your name?" I ask.

"Rose-Q." She offers me her hand and I take it, because I have no need to fear them as real humans do, and because she has already injected me with substances of herself. There is something in me that wasn't there before. Something new. I'm not sure if it's harm or help.

Rose-Q seems kind enough, though I know I should be cautious. I should not be surprised that some Tenties associate with Guerra, but I am. I thought of them as angels; strange, ugly angels. The way they cared for me. T-Lily especially. But this is a different Tentie. And it was foolish of me to imagine they were all the same.

Not that she is cruel. She seems to be making sure that I am as well as I can be. Rose-Q is not the same one that I fell into three days ago. At least I don't think so. Her head is barely tentacled, and the small hole that releases their coloured clouds is visible on the top of her head. Her face is very beaky and her eyes are small. She hovers, ready to bring me what I ask for, and I ask her to take me out into the sun. She pauses, not sure if it is a trick, but she agrees, because she knows my body needs it, and because she sees that I am too weak to run away. She doesn't know about Blue Jay, though he is safer away from here.

I have dreamed of him. I think, perhaps, he may have visited me. Although that may not be true, it may just be wishes. In the sun I will be better.

Rose-Q helps me stand and we walk, slowly, so slowly, out into the sun. There is a long bench outside, almost a bed, and Rose-Q helps me onto it. Already I feel better. I let the warmth fall into me. I bask. I wonder if I am more of a lizard than a plant and the thought makes me want to giggle. I close my eyes and there is still some brightness left. I am almost happy.

* * *

Crow

I CAN'T DECIDE if coming through to this fucked-up world felt worse than my trip down the stairs. Of course the stairs feel worse right at this moment, being the most recent and all, but perhaps they're only in second place. A very close second place, mind you.

Who *does* that?

The more I think about it, lying here on the cold, hard metal of the landing, the more Korbin reminds me of Guerra. Not that Guerra would have got his hands dirty. It would have been someone else who did the pushing back in my world. Carine, maybe. Definitely not Guerra. But then Korbin seems to be a lone operator. I decide that at some future point in time, I'll climb back up the stairs and reinstate my rights as a citizen on the High Track. But for now, I think the most prudent way forward would be down, so to speak.

I sit, I stretch. All body parts seem functional, with the possible exception of my head. No pools of blood, which I suppose can only be a good thing. My jeans are ripped and one of my knees is scraped and bloody. It hurts to buggery when I stand, and walking down the rest of the stairs becomes a foolish exercise in throwing my body around in the least painful way possible. On the bright side, I still have a body to throw around, and it seems amenable to the directions I'm putting to it.

I make it down the stairs and all the way to the other

side of the water tower, away from the gaze of the graffiti girl. If all things were in their rightful place, I'd be at the farms now. And from the look of things, this actually seems to be the case. Can't say I've visited the farms a lot, so I couldn't tell you if the particular placement of trees and whatnot are exact. But it seems right to me. The shipping container's clearly visible. I go looking in search of some sane human company.

The farming area is much bigger than I remember it. I mean, it's not exactly large-scale agriculture here, just a few people deciding that there's better things to do with the space than fill it with weeds and rubbish and dog shit. And it's the one place, believe it or not, that Guerra hasn't made his influence felt. I mean, you'd figure it'd be a prime target for the growing of certain herbs, but no. Rumour is they refused, way back in the day, and Guerra's left them alone ever since. I guess it's too small-scale for him to bother, and that probably suits them just fine. I mean, it's not much more than a community garden.

All this reminiscing has made me a little homesick. It's only been a few hours, but even this morning's pancakes seem a long time ago. There's a person up ahead: a woman, I think, but I'm not sure. She's wearing a huge hat. She turns, sees me. Hesitates, and then starts running towards me. It's probably a good thing. I keep walking, which means throwing my hurt leg out without bending the knee too much, and trying not to put too much weight on it when the other leg moves. I smile, try and look normal. Hope there's not too much blood about my person, and especially not on my face. It might have been good to check before I came visiting, but still. And then I'm leaning on her and then there's another person, a man this time, and I'm half being carried over to the house. And it seems to me I've reached a kind of haven.

When, eventually—after introductions, food, tea, bandages and sympathy—I tell them what happened, they're all understanding. As if this throwing-down-the-stairs thing is a semi regular occurrence.

"Did you hear the prophets sing?" the woman asks. Turns out her name is Judith, which, in my humble opinion, is a nice, regular, comforting name. She has cut her hair short, but it gives the impression that, at any minute, grey and black curls might spring out.

The man, or Ed as he likes to be known, humphs a little. He isn't going to be a talker, I don't think.

"The women in robes?" I ask.

Nods all around.

"Yes, I heard them. They were very good." It was a strange, beautiful moment up there on the High Track with Korbin. But I don't want to get too carried away.

"And the colours?" asks Judith.

"Green," I say. "With a little black. But mostly green."

Judith smiles and even Ed manages to look happy. "A good day," she says.

"That's what Korbin said."

"That's what he called himself?" asked Ed.

"We call him the Barleycorn King," says Judith.

"It suits him," I say. And it did, in a mad-king kind of a way. Which, after all, was pretty much the vibe I got. I wait, to see if there is more. I don't want to ask directly if he really is mad or why the fact that the prophets were wearing green was good. I don't want to seem too strange or unknowledgeable.

We sit and contemplate the peculiarities of the Barleycorn King for a while. The silence becomes awkward and I realise it's about time to go. "Thank you," I say. And I straighten up as gracefully as I am able.

"You can't leave!" says Judith, horrified.

"It's not that bad," I say. "Mostly cosmetic." And, while I'd like to stay for longer, it would just seem weird if I did.

"I could stand some help around here, this afternoon," offers Ed. "Nothing too demanding. If you've got time, that is."

"He can't," protests Judith. "Look at him. He can barely move."

"I'm fine," I say. "And," in an admission that amazes me, "I'd be happy to help."

I realise that it's mostly pity that's got me this far. That, and something about my encounter with Korbin. And possibly because Ed, in particular, wants to keep an eye on me. But right now, more than anything else, I can't quite seem to think of my next move.

Gardening, as you may guess, is not my natural milieu. Soil and worms and bugs and shit. Ed's got me sitting down, putting small seeds into small containers of dirt. It's quite soothing in its own way, and probably not something I can stuff up. I'm wearing a huge hat like the one Ed has on, except more battered, and that's saying something. It creates a small, shaded world. The chair is uncomfortable, else I'd be asleep, and I have to put my left leg out to the side 'cause it don't really want to bend. The scabs on my hands are still gross and probably won't respond well to added dirt, but they've calmed down to the point where they blend in with all my other bodily aches and pains.

Ed's pottering around doing his thing. Judith, for the time being, is somewhere inside. They're not so much old as contented. I mean, older than me, yes; older than, say, Guerra; but I like the way they're doing their own thing. Though any minute now, I'm going to be asked where I live and whether there's someone who'll come get me. Questions I just don't have answers for. I'll go in a bit. When I can work up a plan.

Ed's bending over some complicated bit of tubing and swearing softly to himself.

"Could you get me a hammer from the shed, Brom?" he asks. And obliging as I am, I hobble over to the old shipping container that I seriously doubt has ever had any connection with the ocean. In any case, it seems fairly bonded with the earth now; there's vines growing up and over and all manner of junk has found a home resting against the side. I pull back the door and, contrary to appearance, it slides open easily.

It's even darker inside, cool and musty. But it's well-organised and it's easy to see where the tools are kept: over to the left above a shelf. I head in that general direction, still moving like Frankenstein's monster. And then I see it. A Time Locked Box. Looking, frankly, as battered as the one I'd been carrying.

'Course, this could be meaningless, harmless, entirely coincidental. But it's not gonna be, is it? Not the way things have been turning out lately.

CHAPTER NINE

Green Jay

I'VE SEEN BLUE Jay a few times now. I'm not sure how many, because I'm fuzzy and tired. Sitting in the sun helps, but the Tenties always bring me back inside. I'm sure that they're drugging me, that Guerra has asked them to drug me. Something that keeps me hazy and only half-conscious. I have dreams of plants and lizards. At times, I've thought I was dying. But when I didn't fall back any further, I realised that Guerra has also asked the Tenties to keep me alive.

And I am still myself. I am still Eva; I am still Green Jay. Olwin Duilis knows nothing of this existence, I have moved far enough away from her to be free. That is a lie, and I know it, but it's something I want to cling to. I try and minimise my contact with the Tenties, try to keep the drugs levels to a minimum, but it's almost impossible. I need them to keep me alive.

Blue Jay is hiding up here on the High Track, I think. We only see each other for moments and we cannot talk loudly. I tell him about the package, tell him how Brom has disappeared with it. I tell him he must find it, though I don't know how. I cannot help him. I don't understand what Brom would want with it, except that he's a crow.

Except to torment me.

Blue Jay sits beside me, holds my hand. There are only moments. There is no time to lie in the sun as we used to. He has to get the box. He has to.

Guerra visits me from time to time too. He thinks that I am sleeping, that I can't hear him. He talks—not to me, as I thought at first, but to someone who can't be seen. Someone I think is actually his phone. I peer out from between my eyelids, try to see, but I cannot tell. The voice I hear is normal, not electronic, not scattered. He is a lonely man. I suppose he has to be. Who can he trust, who can he confide in? When he visits me he paces, talking to his phone. But sometimes, he stops and listens to the voice.

Today, for the first time, he sat with me while I was outside. I was sad, at first; it meant Blue Jay could not visit. But then the annoyance turned to interest. I was stretched out on one of the wooden lounges and instead of taking another seat, he sat at the end of my lounge, by my toes. He talked to his phone and she talked back and then, almost as if by accident, he put his hand on my leg. I was startled, but I managed not to jump, not to withdraw my leg. I would have if he had done anything else, or if his hand had moved. It didn't.

It almost made me laugh, having this strange hand on

my leg, but nobody really there attached to it because Guerra was all caught up talking to his phone. Maybe it was a type of intimidation. That is Guerra's way. But I wonder if he was pretending I was the girl he talks to. After all, if I could be another Olwin Duilis, perhaps I could also be the girl he dreams of.

He is wrong.

Crow

I TAKE THE hammer out to Ed. I mean, what else am I going to do? He takes it, grunting, then asks me to hold this, hold that, while he wrestles the tubing back into shape. I figure it's something to do with the watering system. And while I stand here helping out like a five-year-old, I take a look at the water tower. There's no picture of Eva here, thank God, but someone's painted a picture of a giant bird feeding a worm to three small baby birds in a nest. The nest kind of melds with a scraggly bit of vegetation at the bottom of the water tower. It's a strange combination of domestically cute and macabre. I think about birds for a while and then I remember I'm not really that much into plants and gardening. That there's no need to solve the mystery of the box in the shed, that it's probably time to be moving on.

"Thanks," Ed says at last. There's no visible difference in the tubing, but he seems to have stopped messing around. "How's the planting going?"

"Pretty much done," I say. "I probably should get going now."

Ed pushes his hat back with both his hands and takes a long look at me. "And where will you go, Brom?"

"Home," I say.

"Really?" asks Ed.

I splutter a bit, because, well, I do. But I gather myself together. "I mean, you've looked after me, and I'm thankful, and I've enjoyed our time in the garden, but I feel a lot better now and—"

"There's no point, Brom," says Ed.

"We know you don't belong here," says Judith, who's snuck up on us, bearing more drinks and looking completely motherly, but somehow now she's acquired a sinister edge. "You'll need somewhere to stay, and we'd be happy to help."

"No," I say. "No, it's alright, I've somewhere to go. But thank you, thank you." I would run, if I could, but the best I'm going to manage is a fast hobble.

Still, I start moving, try to give the general impression that I'm a man about his business and not to be stopped.

Ed puts a hand on my arm.

"We don't want to alarm you, Brom, you're free to go, of course you are." His arm notwithstanding. "You're not the first, you realise."

"The first what?" I ask, because actually I want to know, and why not be as stupid as I can be?

"The first person to be caught from elsewhere," says Judith. "Why else would the Barleycorn King throw you down the stairs? We figured you must be a friend of our Olwin. That's why you came here."

That name is familiar. Something tells me I should know

who Olwin is, but it's not information that's making itself accessible just at the moment. I shake my head. "No, I'm sorry. I don't know her. I was just—"

"Hurt and lost and barely alive." I'd not go that far, myself, but I figure Judith's sympathy is not something to throw away. "He's a dreadful man," she continues.

Ed comes to a decision. "Whether you know Olwin or not, an enemy of an enemy is a friend." He puts out a hand and I shake it. I'm not sure that I'd class Korbin as an enemy, even taking the stairs incident into account, but on the other hand, I'm quite partial to having someone on my side.

"Stay," says Judith. "Just for tonight. Tomorrow you can go your own way, if you want to. We've a bed, a room, it's somewhere..." She looks hopeful, almost pleading.

And, not completely unexpectedly, I agree. It's very seductive, this: the bringing of food, the offering of shelter and even friendship. Not something that I'm used to. Not something I'm sure I should want, but there you have it. It's nice to be fussed over.

I help Ed tidy up in the garden. It's late afternoon by the time we're finished. I make several trips to the shed, assiduously avoid looking at the box, don't yield to the temptation to examine it to see if it's still Time Locked.

Then it's more food and drink. Fresh from the farm type meal. There's lots of salad. But also bread and cheese. No meat. The talk starts off polite enough at first. I mean, on my part, I doubt if Judith and Ed have ever *not* been polite. But after a while, I can't help but probe a little.

Ask a few questions, seek a few answers. And they're completely forthcoming.

"What happened to the big screen?" I ask

"Brain Training? Oh, they got rid of that years ago," replies Judith. "It was silly, really."

Possibly more forthcoming that I would've liked. "Oh," is about all I can think of to say.

"Don't worry, Brom," says Ed. "Everyone's the same. It looks like the place you know, but it's not. It's different. Different place, different history."

Everyone? Different time? I want to ask, but don't. Instead I forge ahead with compare-and-contrast. "And the Tenties?"

Ed shakes his head. "Oh," says Judith. "That's a sad story. And, you know Brom, that's not a very nice way of speaking about them. Nobody says Tenties. Not anymore. They're called the Trocarn."

I'm as conflicted about the Tenties as the next person, but if anything, their nickname is a term of affection. I've heard a lot worse.

"What happened?" I ask.

Ed shakes his head again. "They went too far," he says. I'm not sure if he means the Tenties or some other group: the Hooks, possibly. The Hooks have maintained their fixation with the Tenties, even in the face of everyone else's apathy. It don't usually come to much, not anymore, but their hatred has a tendency to arc up in unexpected and dangerous ways.

Judith is looking away, fiddling with her food. This is obviously a topic beyond the bounds. I don't press.

And I don't have the heart to ask about the Chemical Conjurers. "Then tell me about the Barleycorn King," I say. And they're off.

"The Barleycorn King," says Judith, "And you're right, Brom, his real name is Korbin, though nobody's called him that in a long time. He was a normal person, once. Not a particularly nice one."

"Criminal," adds Ed.

"But powerful," says Judith. "He took over the High Track. It used to be for everybody, once." She pauses for a moment. "But that wasn't the thing. He somehow got caught up in something bigger than him. A technology that pulled people here from other places, other times. And…"

"It drove him mad," says Ed.

"I think he was the one that pulled me here," I say.

The both look at me closely.

"Well, perhaps not intentionally," I admit. "But there was a stripy cane I grabbed on to. The cane Korbin uses to walk around. At first I thought maybe he was trying to rescue me."

"Rescue you from what, Brom?" asks Ed.

"I was holding a box," I say. "A Time Locked box. And I couldn't get free."

And here, I think, is where the forthcoming might end.

"A Time Locked box, you say?" remarks Ed.

I nod. I look, to the best of my ability, inscrutable and yet trustworthy. And then I notice Judith has begun to cry.

"The same as the one in the shed?" asks Ed. But it's barely a question.

"I left the one I was carrying up on the High Track," I say. And because the looks are all expectant, and the pressure to say something is mounting, I blurt out, "I could go back and get it, I guess." They seem keen on the idea, though what good that box is going to do them, I have no idea. But I'm going to have to follow through, because Judith cries some more.

CHAPTER TEN

Green Jay

I LIE HERE in the sun, watching a package come in on a
drone. It must be for the robots, they're the only ones
who really do this. I miss them, suddenly. I miss my
greenhouse, looking down on the streets and watching.
I have all the sun I need, now that they've let me outside,
but all that I can see is sky. Clouds. Birds, sometimes.
I can't even see the big screen. They won't let me walk
to the edges. Perhaps they think I'll jump, or attract
attention. Perhaps they're worried it would tire me out.
I am getting weaker, despite the Tenties' care, despite the
sun. My skin is beautiful, glowing, but it holds together
a disintegrating sack. That is how I think in my worst
moments. I almost welcome the drugs now. They give me
an excuse, a reason to explain my lack of energy, my lack
of clear thought. I am scared that without them, I would

not be alive at all, that somehow they are providing me with a malicious scaffolding. I hope I am wrong. This is just fear. And helplessness.

Blue Jay has not been to see me a while now. I don't think Guerra has him. He would taunt me with the knowledge, if he did. I am all alone, and I am fading. I need to find a way to come back to myself, become stronger. Sometimes I feel the memories of Olwin Duilis springing up, unwanted. She is trying to tell me something, something I do not want to listen to. Something, she suggests, that will keep me alive. Keep who alive? Me, Eva, Green Jay, or you, Olwin Duilis? I know the answer to that question, so I push her down again.

I'm beginning to grow fond of Rose-Q. I know that it's a mistake. It's mostly her that looks after me, and she is so kind. Sometimes, it is true, she fusses too much and at first I found that annoying, overwhelming. But now I welcome it. It reminds me that I am still here, that I am a person worth fussing over.

I am too lonely. I have become like Guerra, with only a machine to talk to. He talks to her more and more while he is with me; he seems to have forgotten that I am alive. Her name—I want to be generous and say 'her,' because if I am allowed to live, then surely so must she—is Eila. It is too much like Eva, too close. Perhaps that is how he got the idea? I shudder with the thought that he wants, somehow, to make me her. Or make her me. He forgets that my memories are organic, that hers are electronic. Something different. A different way of thinking. And that my memories are entirely my own, memories I have chosen and forced myself to think. Hers are only Guerra's. A cruel person would say that he is in love with himself. And, of course, he is vain and self-obsessed. But I think that he is truly in love with another. Perhaps that other is a creature of his imagination, but it is still love.

The drone disappeared for a while, but it is back now, hovering close to my chair. Sometimes the robots like to make it difficult for the package to land. They like to test the drone. Perhaps they too are looking for signs of life in unlikely places. But then the package drops close to my chair. Rose-Q is nearby, but she hasn't noticed. I make myself sit up, force myself to stretch towards the package. I don't want to stand; that would attract Rose-Q's attention. I stretch so that my stomach hurts and my arms ache, but I manage to pull the package slowly towards me. And then, quickly, quietly, I slide it under the chair. It must wait until I am truly alone.

Crow

JUDITH RUNS ME a bath. She justified it to Ed by listing my (actually quite minor) injuries, but I think it's probably a reward of some sort. Something to do with the Time Locked box in the shed and my promise to retrieve the one I brought with me. It's a big, big old-fashioned bath, that seems to belong to another country altogether. Which is an odd thought, seeing as this is a whole other reality, but, you know, it's still Barlewin to me. The bathtub has its own feet and everything. I'm ridiculously excited; I haven't had a bath in a long, long time. Not since I was a baby, in fact. I mean, who has the water? I suspect Ed and Judith make use of the water tower, although I don't know if it's still actually a water tower. I don't really care—I'm in a bath. There's bubbles and everything. I try not to think that I'm actually sitting in a soup of my own blood and scabs and dirt. There's too many bubbles for that.

I let myself relax for a bit, but my mind can't stop whirring. The thought occurs that there should be a lot more than two people living here. I'm reasonably sure that in my rare, brief farm excursions, there were something like ten folks pottering around. Who exactly *are* Ed and Judith? It'd help, maybe, if I knew their surname. Something more about them. But I figure I've asked enough questions, what with Judith crying and all.

There's something about the name Olwin that niggles at me. A friend of our Olwin, they said. And then, as the bubbles collapse a bit, a conversation I had with Mac slowly presents itself and it all slots into place: Olwin Duilis. Eva's original. The probable sender of the Time Locked box. The bath no longer feels so comfortable. These people are most likely Olwin Duilis' parents. Unless, and this thought comes to me out of an unwelcome corner of my mind, life is really fucked up and they're Mac and Eva, masquerading as contented farmers Ed and Judith. Unlikely. Judith could be a plumper version of Eva, I suppose: her cleavage is comforting rather than compelling, but it's a possibility. On the other hand, I would've recognised Mac, surely. Age or no age. He would've recognised me. There's no blue mark on Ed's thumb, I'm almost sure of it. I need to calm down. Get a grip. I'm becoming totally paranoid. I sink into the bath a little more and ponder my allegiances.

The thing I need is a plan. To get back home, hopefully. To get away from here, at least. I promised to go back up to the High Track, get the box I came in with. I'll do that. It might be a way of getting back, you never know. It's not like Ed and Judith hold the secrets to alternate reality travel. Not that I'd've thought Guerra-aka-the-Barleycorn-King does either and, if I'm getting Judith's story right, that's what they're claiming. Different histories or no, it's clear the Barleycorn King is key to this. I like that name, I'm sticking to it.

The High Track, at least the High Track I know, is a loop. If you want, you can walk around the whole thing and come back to the place you started. I got the feeling that's what those singing prophets were doing. 'Course, I could be wrong, the High Track here could be totally different. But there's no point thinking like that. That way lies madness.

So, the beginnings of a plan are beginning to bubble through my brain. That is, when it can be bothered functioning at all, given that the body it's attached to is very much enjoying this bath, although intermittently reminding the brain that's it's been through a lot today and enough might just be enough. I'll go up to the High Track, but this time, I'll be a little more wary. For a start, I won't let the Barleycorn King get anywhere near me, especially in the vicinity of stairs or railings.

I lie back, put a washcloth over my face. Even my brain, possibly the most active but the least functional part of me, is protesting now.

MORNING COMES ALL too soon. There is, of course, food to be consumed, wounds to be fussed over, plans to be discussed. Although there's less of that than you'd might expect. Apparently, they're leaving most of it up to me. I learn the times that the prophets do their rounds, I learn where the Barleycorn King is likely to be found and when. Although he's an uncertain bugger, by all accounts. Ed, unexpectedly, offers me a gun. I refuse, much to his surprise. I've never liked guns; they have a way of pointing in the wrong direction, in my experience. Judith looks approving at this decision, and Ed somewhat proud. Not that I'm about to invite the Barleycorn King to engage in hand-to-hand combat. No, running away and hiding are my main strategies.

But there's one piece of equipment that I have accepted. Ed has devised a pair of gloves which, he claims, will allow me to carry the Time Locked box without problem. They look, I have to say, much like heavy gardening gloves. I am sceptical, but it's the lining of the gloves that gives me cause for hope. Inside, instead of cloth, is a plastic substance which reminds me a little of the box itself. It's weird to put on, so I keep the gloves in a back pocket—they're not the kind of thing you want to be seen wandering around wearing.

I have to admit they'll be useful. My original plan

involved a certain amount of wishful thinking that the box wouldn't be jumping around in time anymore and, possibly, the vague idea of pushing it over the side of the High Track before it really caught hold of me. Possibly not the best plan I've ever had. Worse comes to worst, I could walk the box back to the farm Time Locked and wait for Ed to figure out how to unlock me. No, actually, there's no way I'm going to do that. I take a moment to internally vow that things are not going to be allowed to get that bad.

Then I'm off and out and away from the farm.

Once I'm out on the other side of the water tower, in among the market-goers, I feel like I'm almost home again. Everything seems alarmingly normal. It's only when I'm up near staircase number 2—the closest to the box, if it's stayed where I left it—that I see the eyes of Olwin Duilis staring at me, watching my progress.

"Who the hell are you?" I ask.

She don't see fit to reply.

"I'm not doing this for you," I tell her. "I want to get home."

She remains silent.

"What were you thinking when you made that double?" I ask. "Did you know she'd go off, try and stay alive? Is that what you want?"

Olwin Duilis stays as uncommunicative as ever. I fart around, trying to find the bottom of the staircase, and discover it hidden behind a vine artistically arranged over a wire sculpture that could almost be mistaken for a Tentie. Well, this is something new, something that isn't here back home. I wonder if Guerra got rid of it, or it's part of the whole mystery of the disappearing Tenties Judith couldn't quite bring herself to talk about. I decide I don't care.

The stairs are noisy. They're metal and it's almost impossible not to clang as you make your way up. So much for the discreet entrance. The ascent also reminds me that my left knee could be in better shape, and, to be honest, that I'm not as fit as someone my age possibly should be. There seem to be more stairs here than on the other staircases, but I'm probably kidding myself. Nevertheless I make it to the top, take a moment to catch my breath, look around and am greeted by an empty High Track. It's almost disappointing.

I wander for a bit, realise that my notions of where I left the box may not be entirely pinpoint accurate, but I manage to convince myself that I've narrowed the area down. I look for that fluffy grass, which now seems to be growing everywhere, but after a while of what to the untrained observer might look like mindless wandering, I find my original point of entry.

And there, sitting happily on the grass as if nothing much has been going on, is the Time Locked box. My Time Locked box. And I don't know if I love it or hate it.

CHAPTER ELEVEN

Green Jay

THE PACKAGE WAS from T-Lily and not from Blue Jay as I had hoped. But it is almost as good. She has sent me some of the cloths that she uses. They are very light, like gauze, but infused with things I need. I am feeling lighter, less drugged; I think Blue Jay has asked her to help with that as well. He is clever, and so is she; but I must be careful not to let it show too much. I wonder if Rose-Q can tell. I'm not sure how sensitive she is, whether she must deliberately test for information or whether she can tell, at a touch, my biological state. If she can, she hasn't said anything, and so we keep a secret, although it is one I must be careful not to expose.

The box is hidden in a cupboard in my room. Or, I should say, the room that I am staying in. I would destroy the box if I could. But the tissue paper T-Lily wrapped the cloths in is more dangerous, and I've hidden it as far under the mattress as I am able. T-Lily had embossed a small lily on the corner of the paper. That is how I knew it was from her, that the cloths were safe. It is beautiful, too beautiful to destroy, but it would be immediately obvious who had been in contact with me if anyone found it. I wonder if I could safely eat it. And yet I do not.

Rose-Q has been telling me a little about her people. They are strange, wonderful beings, and I would have liked to have met them before they came here, before they started copying humans. She told me that their form was different before they came, but when I asked her why they changed, she just smiled and shook her head. It is disconcerting, the shake, the way her head tentacles wave around, even for Rose-Q who has fewer tentacles than most. I think: this is something humans have taught them too, this body language, this shaking of the head. It makes me sad to think that they are so unlike their original selves, but then, I am hoping for the same thing, hoping to become more human. I cannot blame her for her desires.

But I have one question, one I hope is not too invasive, too rude. I ask Rose-Q why her people did not go to the oceans, meet creatures of their kind. The whales and the dolphins, the squid. All as smart as people.

"No," says Rose-Q. "There is no technology there."

And so I learn what has drawn them. The human capacity for gadgets and things. No wonder they love the 3D printers. Though nobody has ever truly discovered how the Trocarn came here. That is their true name, at least true enough for this place. Better than 'Tenties.' There must have been some technology to get them here. Something far more wonderful than anything we have ever made.

But Rose-Q sees my question, sits down and tells me a story. It is so strange that it is almost unbelievable. Perhaps it is a myth, the story of her people that holds a truth without being true. I listen as best I can and try to understand.

Crow

I SIT DOWN beside the box and feel for Ed's gloves. They're still in my back pocket, but I'm reluctant to put them on. The thought that I might be able to reconnect to the box and get the fuck back home keeps bobbing up. I mean, so far I haven't done anything wrong, at least nothing that I can't convince Guerra wasn't really my fault. There's no doubt that he'll be wanting the box back. And yes, it means I'll get involved in all that Mac/Eva shit again, but after all, that's what friends are for. And, look at it this way, I've held up my end of the bargain, and the rest, whatever it may be, is up to them.

But I don't connect to the box. Instead I stretch out in the sun. My leg is shaking a little, if you must know. I pluck a tuft of grass fluff and stick it in my pocket as a memento. I hear singing in the distance, and it must be those prophets, but it's a fair way away, and, in any case, they're not the ones that pushed me down the stairs.

Then my phone buzzes, which scares the shit out of me. I almost forgot I had it. My normal life is an endless sequence of buzzes, beeps and other salutations from the phone, but apparently I haven't missed it. There, on the screen, is something that looks like one of those video stamp things people stick on parcels. QR code. At least, I think that's what it is. It's crap quality, grainy and strangely focussed. Whatever it is, my phone don't recognise it. The message isn't playing, the image is just sitting there on the phone without unspooling as it's meant to do.

I send a question mark as a reply. Just in case there's more to it. And just in case, and this is probably my strongest motivation, it's something from Mac. This whole reality shit is probably too much for even Mac to figure out, but if anyone can, it's him. But then I put the phone back in my pocket and turn my attention to my current dilemma.

Shit, I'll just do it. I pull on the gloves, stand up, reach down for the box and pick it up. Probably I should've tested them in some way before going all in, but now that I'm committed, everything seems okay. I'm certainly not doing that dimensional shift thing I did last time. The box isn't that heavy, but it's going to be a bugger getting the thing down the stairs. I'll deal with that when I come to it.

I retrace my steps, heading in the direction of staircase number 2—and, I think, away from the singing. I'm walking as fast as I can, without running or seeming hurried; the old casual speed has kicked in. I see the top of the stairs, I'm feeling good, I'm focussed on getting out and away, and maybe because of that I fail to see the man sitting on the bench. The Barleycorn King himself.

Naturally.

He gestures at me with his stick. I suppose he wants me to come closer. There's no way that's going to happen. I keep walking.

"Kern Brom," he calls. Which is more annoying than anything else.

"Brom," I say, "Just Brom." I keep walking, all the while reminding myself that I shouldn't have engaged with him.

"You stealing that box from me, Brom?"

"Box is mine," I say. The stairs are so close. Only a few more steps. As long as I can get onto the stairs, I think I'll be okay. Why I think that, I'm not sure. The combination of stairs and Barleycorn King hasn't proved reassuring in the past. But then, he's still sitting on the seat, though his red-striped cane is bobbing up and down impatiently.

"You sure about that?"

I'd shrug if I could. The truth is way more complicated than I need to go into.

My foot is on the top of the stairs, the metal landing. Drifting up from below is the sound of the prophets, accompanied—without much sympathy for the underlying rhythmic structure of the song—by the clanging of steps. I see the top of a prophet's head. Dark blonde hair wound up and threaded through with flowers. She lifts her face and smiles as she ascends the top few stairs. It's a wondrous sight, but tempered by the fact she obviously expects me to stand aside. And really, what other choice do I have? I take a few steps, just a few to the right, but it's a mistake, The Barleycorn King is right beside me, his breath on my neck. I can just about see his cane off to the side. I am not going to look at him. This is exactly the position I had vowed not to be in.

"A touch of yellow today," says the Barleycorn King. And, if I'm not mistaken, his voice is sad.

The head chorister bows her head, but she don't give him anything other than that. She keeps on moving, up the High Track, back in the direction I'd just come from. Her acolytes follow her. A few of them look at me and the Barleycorn King, but most just keep on with their singing, as if they were in a trance, in another world. Although one, I swear, winks at me; and I'd be lying if I didn't admit to some admiration of the way her robe swings against her body. But this is not the time or place, not to mention that there is a distinctly off-limits vibe about the whole prophet choir thing.

"I'd hoped the green would continue for a little longer," the Barleycorn King continues.

I sneak a glance at him, mostly to gauge the depth of his madness. He is standing straight and tall, as if watching the passing of a parade. A salute would not be out of place, although his hands are at his side. His robes are the same as yesterday, a mixture of muted greens and browns. They are held in place by a wide rope belt. The striped cane is still there, close to me.

"The idea first came from the Trocarn, although the technology, of course, is completely different. It's the inks in the robes, you know, that react to the air quality.

The green you saw yesterday inspired that remarkable singing. Today's song has touches of melancholy."

This is all very well and good, but that's not why he's here and we both know it.

The last prophet comes up the stairs. I move to take her place, merging myself into the tail of the choir.

"Not so fast," he says. It's the tap of the cane that stops me, rather than the words, but stop I do, although I don't turn around.

"It won't help, you know," he remarks. "She's tried before. She always fails."

"I promised," I say.

The Barleycorn King taps his cane again and this time I turn to look at him. For some reason I fixate on his features, try to determine if this is in fact an older, madder version of Guerra. The man's hair is grey and unkempt. He has dignity, but he's less sure of himself than Guerra is. His face is so lined that it's impossible to know. It could be Guerra. It could be someone else altogether. It could be that this place is fucking with my mind.

The Barleycorn King takes a step towards me. "You don't strike me as someone who always keeps his promises," he says.

I decide—if an impulse to flee counts as a decision— that this line of conversation is getting me nowhere. I clang down the stairs as fast as I am able, holding the goddam box. I almost trip and fall and my knee protests most of the way down, but I make it. I slow myself to a casual walk once I'm past the Tentie vine sculpture, and I pointedly ignore Olwin Duilis as I pass her. I get away from the area under the High Track; it seems safer out in the open, although, logically that's probably not true. I see people, fellow Barlewin citizens, albeit not of my time or reality. If they see anything unusual about me, or about my parcel, there's no indication. And if the air quality is less pure than yesterday, nobody seems to mind or care. We're all going about our business, free as birds.

I have a sudden longing for the Chemical Conjurers. They'd be up for a bit of much-needed distraction, but even without their assistance I manage to make my way through the market shops without noticeable pursuit. I look Olwin Duilis in the eye as I approach the water tower, but not for long. I walk underneath its cool shade and out the other side. My right hand feels a little weird and I'm slightly queasy, but I ignore that and I press on. Almost home. I hear something and, despite my better judgement, I half-turn; and then it happens.

I glitch out of here and into the Time Dance.

CHAPTER TWELVE

Green Jay

ACCORDING TO ROSE-Q, thousands, maybe millions of Trocarn formed themselves into a living spaceship. Some hardened to become the outer hull, some were softer, part of the internal. They all fused together. They all died, really. They had to, they couldn't keep their own thoughts, their own lives. They let their minds grow together, become one. One creature, which could manoeuvre through space. How strange, how lonely. But inside the creature were eggs, kept fertilised, but in stasis, ready for a time they could be born. New, fresh beings in a new place. Parts of the ship broke away, parachuted down in protective sacs containing the eggs, ready for the planet, ready for life. And then the ship sailed on. Is it still travelling, orbiting some other earth, or has it disintegrated in space? Rose-Q could not say. And why did we never know this, here? How could we have not noticed thousands of beings floating down to earth?

Why would they do it? There was no catastrophe that Rose-Q spoke of. I imagine them a long, long time ago, before Rose-Q or any of the Trocarn we know were born, living in another place. Somewhere, if I understand it properly, that cannot be reached by normal means. No space ship that we design will ever be able to fly there. Or perhaps I have misunderstood that part altogether. Everything Rose-Q says is hazy, but I think she has told me that Trocarn society was based around manipulation of life, sometimes at the most basic level, sometimes as an adjunct to their own forms. Their art was the art of cells and flesh, their laws were the laws of poisons and infiltration, their relationships were based on the level of biological sharing. They morphed and changed as they grew, deliberately. But then, perhaps inevitably, there came forms that were more highly prized. And of course there were some that grew tired of the limits of the life they knew. There are always adventurers.

But this is all my imaginings, mixed in with something of what Rose-Q told me. I know I will have it wrong, misunderstand in some important, fundamental way. But there is something there, something true. I am envious of her story. I don't know why. It is almost ridiculous, after all. I would have liked to have floated down to earth, separating from some giant creature, created just for me and my brothers and sisters. I know Rose-Q's tale is just a story, a way of telling others about the Trocarn.

I would like a creation myth too, but I know exactly

how I was made. And there is nothing romantic about it. But if I manage to separate myself from Olwin Duilis, that will be a story of courage, a story someone could tell. It will sound ridiculous, I know, but that does not mean it will not be true.

Crow

MY FIRST INSTINCT is to drop the box, but that seems difficult to do. I close my eyes, try some slow, deep breaths, more to distract myself from the nausea than anything else. I've stopped walking, and I know I'm hunched over a bit, because shit, I feel sick. But the deep breaths are doing nothing and having my eyes closed just makes me feel trapped in the nausea. I open them, knowing whatever I see won't be helpful.

To a point, I'm right. It's just a flickering of water tower images. The only difference is the graffiti on the tower. There's one of a girl stuck inside a jar of berries that, I have to say, is very much in tune with my current state. Some of the berries are whole and some are mushed and the same could be said of the girl. It's an interesting artistic depiction, but not one that lingers. I'm moving on and through. There are other images and in one reality, sadly lacking in imagination, nothing at all except the grey wall of the water tower. I try and remember what this side of the water tower looks like back home—my real home—but I'm buggered if I know.

The next best thing is to look for that large bird in Ed

and Judith's reality and hope that this particular artist's imagination hasn't been replicated in too many places. I remember Mac telling me that each time jump is less than a second. That seems wrong, these jumps seem longer, but in any case, there's not much time if I'm going to make a move. I wiggle my fingers as much out of the gloves as I can. I wait for the bird, wait and wait, and then as soon as it appears, I force myself to drop the box, fling it down on the ground and then whip off the gloves. My right hand is red and looks more than a little burnt, but yes, I'm in the land of the bird water tower and I hope to hell there are some friendly farmers close by.

I see figures that I hope are Ed and Judith running towards me. I'm not sure if they're just very slow runners or if my brain is having its own quiet meltdown, because they seem to be taking a while. I decide that my previous decision to stay standing until they get here was an unnecessary one. I fall forward, luckily in the same slow motion and luckily in a different direction to the box. The grass here is not as fluffy as up on the High Track. There are spiky plants and yellow flowers that live close to the ground. Yellow isn't as good as green, I think. I wonder why the hell not.

SOMETIME LATER AND everything's sorted. Ed managed to lever the box up onto a trolley and wheel it back to the farm. We had a long discussion about the gloves during which he imparted a lot of technical information which went over my head and which was punctuated by Judith remonstrating with him for letting me burn my hand. Ed appears exceedingly proud that the left hand glove remained totally functional throughout. It's the reason I managed to come back to this reality, in his opinion. I, for one, am grateful that the left hand glove was generous enough to let my entire body follow along with the wayward right hand glove and not insist on keeping part of me for itself. But more than that, I'm happy to be back. I've not been so fussed over in some time and I'm not sure that it's going to get old. Mind you, I could do without the reasons for the fuss.

Ed and Judith don't open the box. At least not as far as I'm aware. Not in front of me, anyway; and right now, it's sitting in the shed. It can stay there unopened, for all I care. I feel I've done my bit for Ed, Judith, Olwin Duilis, Eva, Guerra. Even for Mac.

And so I sleep. For how long, I'm not sure. But then I discover Judith sitting on the end of my bed, holding a cup of tea and looking wistful. There's some kind of insect burring against the window and I wish she'd just up and let it out, but instead she sits there looking at me.

"I brought your phone," she said. "You dropped it by the tower." She hands it over and I wonder if she's snuck a look. The messages I can see are half-hearted and blurred and all from the same number as before. Nothing much else seems to have survived the journey. I know the feeling.

"They make no sense," I tell her.

"How do you feel? Do you need anything?" asks Judith.

I shake my head, but that movement alone contradicts

my valour and so she slips me something she had in her pocket. The time for caring what the something is, or whether or not it'll do me harm or good, is well past. She hops up, pours a glass of water from a jug by the bed and hands it to me. She watches the insect buzzing away, trying to find its way back out to the world, not understanding the glass.

"There's a story about those dragonflies," she says. "Waiting for an old woman and then turning her into sprites, half mechanical, half organic."

"Maybe we should let it out," I say.

"It's about to die," says Judith. But she opens the window anyway and persuades the poor creature out into the air. She pulls at the window some more, trying to coax it down, but it's old and stuck. Instead, she props a piece of wood underneath to stop it paying sudden homage to gravity.

"How do you know her?" she asks.

I sit up some more, put the glass back down on the table. "I don't." It's possible I've never felt more crummy.

Judith examines her tea.

"I know someone a lot like her," I offer.

The tea is still remarkably interesting.

"A double," I say. And I know I've probably made things a lot worse.

But Judith brightens. Or at least she looks up, looks straight at me. "And she's survived?"

I nod.

"How long?"

"Eight weeks." Adding quickly: "I think."

"Oh, she's just beginning."

"There's been more than one?"

Judith nods and she turns to stare out the window. "You know we even had her stung with bees. It was meant to help. She was so young." She turns back to me and we both ignore the tears. She puts her tea down on the windowsill and scrapes at something on her left inside wrist. It takes a moment, but eventually she peels away a thin, floppy membrane. She flicks it and it becomes rigid, but it's still a translucent nothing. "This might help," she says. She must see utter incomprehension, because she adds, "It's not fancy and there are newer ones out, but it might have less glitches than yours." She hands me the card. It reminds me a little of Mac's fold up knife, it's about that size, the size of an overly ambitious credit card.

"Thanks," I say as I take it. Judith presses something on the bottom and the thing springs to life and then, immediately, I know it's a phone. It's probably a lot of other things as well, but here, for the first time, I'm seeing some weird future shit I really have no idea about.

The cynic in me wants to ask if it's helped before, how many other people have been pulled through to this strange place and tortured by the Barleycorn King, but I hold that cynic down and stomp on his head.

She looks at me for a moment, then quickly darts in and kisses me on top of my head. And then she's off, disappearing out of the room, back to her life. She's a woman of many secrets, is Judith, but I can't help but like her.

The phone is empty. There's no evidence it's been used before at all. It's easy to navigate, no strange future symbols or capacities that I can see. I send its details through to the number that keeps desperately appearing on my own battered phone. Shit, I hope the sender's Mac.

The message whirs quickly away, but there's no reply. I fiddle with the phone for a while, but there's not much doing, really. I think about attaching it to my wrist, future style, but instead I slip it my pocket, along with my olde worlde heap of junk. Unfair, really. I was in love with it only days ago.

Judith's pill, whatever it was, has taken effect. I lever myself out of bed, take a piss, splash my face with water and run my fingers through my hair. Which is just as well, because it turns out I have a visitor.

CHAPTER THIRTEEN

Green Jay

I'VE BEGUN TO read the books in the room I'm staying in. I need something to do now that I'm more alive. Because if I don't occupy myself, I think I might run to the edge and throw myself over, hoping perhaps that the Chemical Conjurers might catch me, or that the Trocarn will fix me after my fall. I dare not imagine that Blue Jay would catch me. He seems to have left me here, and without him there is no hope.

But I will not let myself think about him. Instead, I tell myself that books are of benefit, that once again I can develop my own brain, lay down memories that are completely mine. Rose-Q must know that I am better, but she's given no indication of it. Or perhaps she's just stopped drugging me. Maybe Guerra thinks I am compliant now, maybe Rose-Q trusts me; but I must continue to be careful. If I run, they will catch me and I am not strong enough for that.

I want to ask Rose-Q if there are books of Trocarn stories. But I haven't found courage for that yet. Perhaps their stories are part of themselves, biological threads rather than words. I content myself with the books in this room. I wonder who they once belonged to. I doubt that Guerra has ever read them.

The saddest story I've found so far is about a lonely woman, a woman who I think could turn out to be me, if I manage to live so long. And I feel I understand her, because Blue Jay has not shown and there is no sign of the Crow and the box, and I seem forgotten, up here in Guerra's castle.

The woman had lived a long time, a very long time, but now she was alone except for a dragonfly. Not a real dragonfly, but a toy, a childhood gift that had turned into something more. A companion, a friend, a repository.

She'd been all alone for at least ten years and, in the end, she didn't mind. She'd imagined a life, once, surrounded by people, but she hadn't managed to find it—or no-one simpatico, anyway—and the wear of souls who failed to understand proved too much. Sometimes in the book, you weren't sure if the woman was telling the truth, but the dragonfly knew what was true because it had been there for almost all of it.

She loved the dragonfly. It and her house by the sea had been enough.

"Let me die," she said, more than once, knowing that

the dragonfly could keep her alive as a type of memory ghost. And so, when the time came, the dragonfly did.

But not long after her last breath had drifted from her mouth, the dragonfly got to work. It extracted cells and other matter, it manufactured strands of its own substance. It was only a small being with gossamer wings and a tiny body, but it could spin and make. It used whatever it could find, and in this fine empty house by the sea there was plenty of material.

The old lady's body was desiccated and still by the time the dragonfly had finished. It had not wanted the body to jelly and decay, and so it had injected the remains with something to keep it mummified, just in case. There would be no skeleton lying on the bed. But it did not matter; the dragonfly's plan had worked.

A cloud of sprites—half human, half machine—flowed through the dining room, up the stairs and into the library. They found nests between the books. All they needed was a few centimetres of space. They built homes and shelters. They lived their own individual lives, but they remembered the old lady and the dragonfly too. Because all too soon it was the dragonfly's turn to die. It had lived far longer than it was meant to, and its final act of creation had depleted it. The sprites took over the house by the sea and lived there until its stones crumbled and fell into the waves. Which, as the story says, may not yet have happened.

It's an odd kind of fairy tale, what with artificial dragonflies who live longer than humans. It can't be something old, can it? It must be something new. Or have people always dreamt of machines and of ways to stay alive? Probably they have. I do.

Crow

I DON'T RECOGNISE her at first, seeing as she's not dressed in robes, but it turns out one of the prophets has come to call. A minor prophet, I dare say. But Judith, as usual, has plied her with food. You'd think Ed and Judith would be larger with all the eating that's done here, but maybe it's the fresh farm air or what-have-you that keeps them trim.

So I find myself sitting at the kitchen table, eating some kind of orange cake and drinking coffee—yes, coffee— and admiring the dragonfly tattoo on the inside wrist of the prophet, whose name as it turns out is a relatively unmystical Catelin. She's got rid of the robes and is wearing jeans and a T-shirt. She's not, as everyone feared, an emissary from the Barleycorn King; or, she claims, a messenger of any type. Instead she's come of her own accord, to buy some fresh veg, she says, because she missed the best stuff at the markets. Or, more truthfully, she's quite possibly come to see me, as Judith obviously suspects. But that seems to be okay with everyone. Including me.

Ed talks with her a little about the yellow robe days. Sure it's a sign of contaminants in the air, but nothing too dreadful, nothing he can't cope with. Catelin reassures him on that front, and for a while they reminisce about the orange robe days, how those times seem to be gone. I sit back and enjoy my coffee and whatever other pleasures are on hand. I have no interest in pollutants, yellow, orange, or any other colour.

"He's sorry, you know, that he pushed you down the stairs," says Catelin. Apropos, as far as I'm aware, of nothing.

Still hurt, I think but don't say. I let my many and varied wounds speak for themselves, though most of them, admittedly, are not on display.

"Brom was lucky it wasn't worse," says Judith loyally. "I'll never forget him staggering towards us that first day. I thought he would collapse before we reached him."

Ed says nothing. They're both obviously not moving on their anti-Barleycorn King stance, but entertaining minor prophets seems to be permissible.

"He'd like to talk to you," says Catelin.

"Not up on the High Track," I say.

And that shocks everyone. Apparently the Barleycorn King never, but *ever* leaves the High Track. If he is Guerra, then he's gone spectacularly mad. Makes you wonder what set him off.

"Who is he?" I ask. "I mean, has he always been there? Was he always the Barleycorn King? Ever the Barleycorn Prince? A baby in waiting? Heir apparent?" I'm raving; the look on the three faces around me is not encouraging.

"Different histories," says Ed after a moment.

We all begin to talk at once and, because I'm a fool, I'm the one that keeps going. "Back where I come from, if you're asked to come and talk with the man who owns the High Track, it usually don't mean anything good." I don't mention that I work for him. Or I used to.

"Oh, no," says Catelin, scandalised. "He just wants to apologise. Perhaps he can help."

"That's unlikely," says Ed. Judith shakes her head. But at the same time, she offers Catelin more cake, an offer which Catelin gently refuses. I take another piece, because why the fuck not.

The conversation winds down back to banalities, until Catelin finds a way to extricate herself. I catch her looking at my wrist at one point. Perhaps she is scoping for a phone, and as much as I'd like to be able to contact her, I find I'm grateful I didn't attach Judith's gift to my skin. Judith and Ed take her out to the garden to load her up with the vegetables she may or may not want. And I'm left alone, none the wiser.

I take the future phone from my pocket. It's showing a type of screensaver. That, or I activated something without meaning to. The image is a head-and-shoulders portrait of Olwin Duilis superimposed over what appears to be an old map. Very arty, sepia tones. I can look at it because Olwin's eyes are closed. She's not examining me for failings. Her hair is back in a bun. It's very peaceful, almost deathlike, but not in a creepy way. She is truly beautiful, this person. I can admit that.

On the map are tiny, tiny words, so small they could be mistaken for mountain ranges or some such, contour lines on a map. I move my fingers over one of them, mostly to see if they'll enlarge. The writing gets big enough to read. *Jump through*, it says. Which makes no sense. Or, perhaps

I kind of sense I don't want to think about. I don't want to touch the screen again, in case it takes my probing as assent and moves me somewhere else. What I'd really like is a message from Mac. Clear and unequivocal.

Judith comes back to the room. The phone's reverted to the original picture and I show her. "Is that yours?" I ask. Wondering if I've stepped too far into her personal space, but needing to know if this is a genuine message or just something I opened by mistake.

"I know the picture," says Judith, "but not like that." She turns her right wrist over, taps it a few times and there, hanging in front of us, is the same portrait of Olwin. Brighter colours. No map. I don't know what to say. We admire it for a while in silence.

"I think Catelin probably wanted to talk to you alone, Brom. I'm sorry if we got in the way."

"She's probably a spy." I don't want it to be true, but there it is.

"Probably," says Judith. But she smiles to reassure me. Perhaps a spy is okay, she seems to suggest.

"Maybe I should talk to him?" I say.

Judith releases the picture back to her phone. "Olwin will help you."

I don't want to say that much as Olwin, or for that matter Eva, would be interested in getting hold of the box, neither of them probably cares much where *I* end up.

"Has anything else come through?" she asks.

I don't tell her about the map message, but I do show her my future phone, because quite frankly I don't think I'm around all its thin, bendy intricacies.

She fiddles with it for a while, shakes her head and then shows me how to attach it to my wrist. "If you want to?"

I agree. And there it is, attached to me, barely discernible. Unless, of course, you think about it, and then it's a weird sort of itch.

Judith shows me how to activate connections: if you shake someone's hand, or even just tap them lightly on the hand with a finger, their details will come through to you, and yours to them. I think wistfully of the prophet and her dragonfly tattoo for a while. In the meantime, Judith tells me of ways to set up various privacy screens and precautions, but there's not much to me in this reality: no credit details to skim, no identity to steal.

"It collects biodata too, if you want it to?"

No, that's not for me. Because, seriously, what am I going to do with that knowledge?

There's a pause, which is nothing to do with technology and then, finally she's out with it. "Stay," says Judith. "Just for a while. It can't hurt."

I smile and she seems to take that as a yes. It's not like I have the means to go anywhere else. Not really. Not unless you count a cryptic message hidden in a map. Well, *jump through* isn't that cryptic, but I'm choosing to treat it as such. As much as I'd like to be back home in known surrounds with known enemies, I'm not up for whatever jumping as that may entail just yet.

Who puts an option like that on a phone anyway?

CHAPTER FOURTEEN

Green Jay

I HAVE GUERRA'S phone. I can't keep it for long, but while I have it, I search. I scroll through messages. There's too much here to search properly, quickly. I skim over the messages from Olwin Duilis. I should read them, but I can't. I can't face them. But I see messages from Kern Bromley and I click them open.

It's strange, this stuff. Pictures, almost codes, and many of them don't seem to have been sent properly. And then a final message, a new number. I memorise it. I need to tell Blue Jay. I need to see Blue Jay. But I find that new number and see only one message sent. A portrait. Of me. Or, more likely, of Olwin Duilis. Without meaning to I remember the photograph, the day it was taken. The place. I think of my mother and father and the farm and then force myself to remember that they are not mine.

That is not my past. They are not my parents. I'm angry at myself for letting her in. I see my hand is shaking and I focus on that, try and make it stop.

"You seem upset," says a voice. The phone, of course. Eila. I ignore her.

I force myself to look at the photo. Why would Guerra want to send this to the Crow? A warning?

"I am trying to get him back," Eila says.

"Get who back?" I ask. I know it mightn't work. My voice is not Guerra's voice, but she must already know that I am not him.

"Kern Bromley," she says. "He has the box. I hope you don't mind. I thought you would want the box back too."

Does she know who I am? Who she is talking to? "How will this photograph help?"

"It's a short cut for Time Lock. A way to shift between realities."

"But that's…" Impossible, I think, but I stop because there are footsteps close to the door.

I stuff the phone under me, because there is not enough time to put it anywhere else. Guerra will be searching. He will know he left it here. He visited earlier today, and caught me reading. If he thought anything of it, he didn't say. He wandered the room. Sat down beside me as usual. He must know he left the phone.

I close my eyes as the door opens. The pretence will do me no good if Eila speaks. I can feel the phone in the hollow of my back. It buzzes, but there is no voice. They're trying to find it by ringing. I hope that my body is enough to dampen the sound. I open my eyes just a fraction, enough to see who has come in. Not Guerra, but one of his people. Carine, I think. It does not matter. No-one can find me with the phone. I keep track of where they go, where they look. I need to find a place to put the phone, a place where nobody has searched.

When Carine leaves I get up, put the phone on the floor by the chair and kick it to the back of the room. I want to look at it more. I don't let myself. Instead, I leave my room and go in search of Rose-Q. She will ask how I am, she will fuss. She will be my barrier.

Crow

IT'S NIGHT AND Judith and Ed are fast asleep. Me, I'm as restless as hell, so I decide to go for a walk. It's not as dark as I thought it might be. The farm itself isn't lit up, but there are lights up on the High Track that shine down and light the way. Somebody has seen fit to light up the water tower. Not that I'm going to risk walking underneath it. It's usually a bit of a magnet for assignations, dubious and otherwise, at night. So I skirt around, make my way to the marketplace. The shops have pretty much shut down, except for the kebab place. I'm not sure if it's the same guy, but it's the same idea. Late nights require a certain sort of quickly available grease- and salt-enriched food. Back home I'd go have a chat to the Chemical Conjurers. The thought occurs that I could go visit myself, but seriously, why'd I do that? Especially as I'd be older. The thought also occurs that the person to visit might be Mac.

Would he still be in Barlewin? Doubt it. But I do want to explore a bit. I want to drift. There's secrets to be learned, and usually this is the best way to find them.

Kebab in hand, I wander through the tenements, past the picture of Olwin Duilis and vaguely in the direction of Eva's apartment. Maybe it's because it's night time, but things appear startlingly unchanged. Not that I recognise anyone. It's just the vibe; the ambience, if you will. The usual suspects are out and, of course, they don't know me, so they're out to test my intentions and capacities as well. It's been a while since I experienced this. In fact, it's been never, because Barlewin's own have always known who I am. But there was, understandably, a time when I was more of an underdog. Or, tell the truth, not Guerra's man. So I walk tall, make it seem as if I belong. Which, weirdly, I do. Try not to look around too much.

There's only one difference that I see—make that two. Up on the walls, there's some kind of glowing stuff. Looks like fungus. Makes the alleyways slightly less dark, though the colour it gives off is hardly conducive to thoughts of upright citizenship. And the second difference, the one I don't like. It's a light too, but it flickers in and out. And I have no idea where it's coming from. It's as if someone has designed their own idiosyncratic lighthouse. Interestingly, the light's not coming from the High Track, which is the habitat of the only mad man I know.

I receive a few silent enquiries in the sign language of the alleys. A certain tilt to the head, a certain stance, a certain positioning of the feet and arms. I don't think the passage of time—or, indeed, realities—will have changed the interpretation that much. In much the same way I endeavour to show them who I am, but they have the advantage of home turf. It troubles me that this should be so. So close to home, and so far.

And then, because it's close to inevitable, I realise there's someone behind me. Close but not too close. I can feel it in the stones under my feet, because they're my stones too, and, damn it, I was here first. I don't like this bit, what's coming next. It's necessary, there's no way around it, but still. You'd think I'd be out of practice, but there's always someone desperate enough, wired enough to decide the only way out is through.

I've reached a spot where I hope things can play out in a reasonably quick way. I move back and to the left, quickly, without indication, just enough to draw level with my follower. I swing a leg, catch him in the back of the knee, watch him fall. He stays down. I like that. A sense of the inevitable, of the necessary, of the required. All sensible. There are others, of course there are others, but they seem to have paused in their intentions. I decide the time is not yet right to pull out my knife, and I try not to contemplate the shitty way my leg feels. The Barleycorn King's wounds have not yet healed.

"Where you going?" asks the man on the ground.

This does surprise. His voice is thin, and higher than it should be. On the other hand, he's lying on the ground. No sense in replying. I keep walking.

"She's not there," he says.

Enough to make me pause. "Wasn't visiting," I say.

"Sure, you were," says the man.

Some people just don't know when enough is enough. I'm close enough to Eva's apartment block for it not to matter, so I keep walking. But then there's some scrabbling and a rush and then there's a figure standing at the top of the steps by the front door. Not blocking it, exactly, but enough to be in the way. There's no-one else there, there's no door guard the way there used to be, but then by the look of the building, even in this fungal light, there's nothing much to guard.

"You really want to do this again?" I ask. I take the first two steps, just to show the direction I intend to move.

The man's shaking but he's standing his ground. He's pulled his hoodie halfway down his face—apparently some things never change. He's a small thing, really, and I feel slightly guilty for knocking him to the ground. Only slightly, mind you. The night lights up with the mad lighthouse search again, and I watch him stand completely still. He'd melt into the wall, if he could. There's a pause in the light, it rests on the bottom step. I press myself up onto the third step, close to the door, subtly, without seeming to move, the way I did when I was kid. I used to practise rolling over under the sheets. I figured if I did it slowly enough, the monsters wouldn't see. Sometimes it even works.

The light's on the second step now. I push a little harder against the door, hoping it'll give. It don't.

Third step. This thing's playing with us. I look over at my hoodie friend. He reaches over, does something funny with the handle. The door falls back, and he rushes in. I'm not that far behind. The light is in the building now, just behind us, and we're running up the stairs, all pretence of cool gone.

We're running for real. Right up to Eva's greenhouse. I half expect the man to give the two-three knock at the door. That's not what happens. But the door is opened, gently, reverently, and the man steps inside as if into a temple. He waits for me to come in, closes the door softly behind him and we both admire the view. There's a ton of bioluminescent fungus up here, and it's less of the murky green of the alleyway and more blue. It's beautiful, in its own strange way. The faint light from the High Track light helps, I suppose. And apart from the fungus, the room is clean. Cleaner than I've ever seen it. On the walls are pictures, and there's a double bookshelf to one side. It's almost feels like a library. I can't say I've been inside a lot of libraries, but this is without a doubt the weirdest one I've ever stepped into.

The man's been quiet for a while, and I look at him, because it don't usually pay to forget the whereabouts of the person who recently followed you in an alley. He's standing close to a window, looking up at the High Track, and his hoodie's fallen back.

There's something about his hair I don't like. I step over, push the hoodie back all the way. There's no tentacles, only dreads, but the man is clearly not a man. The green tinge I'd figured was a function of fungus lighting is still there. And the features are more delicate than I'd first realised. This is a woman. But not a human one.

"You're not humant," she says.

"I think you'll find I am. Cut me and I bleed. Though that's not an offer."

"Hum*ant*," says the woman. I could swear there's a touch of exasperation in her voice. "Plant/human hybrid. You know."

I don't, but I'm not going to tell her that. "What made you think I was?"

She shrugged. "Who else would come here? It's a pilgrimage."

"Yeah, well. Not for me."

"Were the time nets after you?"

I figure she means those creepy lights that had us running up the stairs. "You didn't look too pleased to see them yourself."

"No-one wants to get caught in the nets."

I think, suddenly, of the Hooks and the Tenties, but now is not the time to ask.

"It's cleaned up nice," I offer. And she looks at me at first as if I'm mad and then as if she'd been right about me all along.

"You're a friend," she says.

Now, *that's* a question I'd like to know the answer to.

CHAPTER FIFTEEN

Green Jay

IT WAS A mistake to see Rose-Q. She has sent me under again, given me enough drugs to have me swimming through a heavy ocean. I suppose it was Guerra. I have used several of T-Lily's cloths to try and fight it. They have helped, but not enough, and there are too few left for me to dare use any more. But I have learned my lesson; I will be more careful.

I lie out in the sun, hoping it will help me. Rose-Q sits close by. She has walked me to a different chair today. From here I can see the water tower. I don't want to see it, even though the stick man is out of sight. It brings back memories that I don't want. The drugs make it harder for me to resist Olwin Duilis. I keep thinking of her picture. It rests behind my eyes, even when they're closed. I try to pretend that it's a picture of me. A picture that Blue Jay has drawn. I make up a story that he is sitting here in a chair close by and has drawn this picture. But I cannot keep up the fantasy. There is no chance that he could visit, even if he chose to. Not with Rose-Q close by. And I know the picture is not of me but of Olwin Duilis.

I think, instead, of what Eila said about the photograph, how it could be used to shift reality. This is knowledge Olwin has blocked from me, if she ever had it. She probably does. Olwin Duilis, it seems to me, is too clever for her own good. She places herself where she is not wanted. She tries to change things to suit herself. I must try and forget her. I must.

I wonder if the Crow is smart enough to use the map. Probably he is. But that is not how he will be thinking. He may want to get home, but he will not think to bring the box. Perhaps it's better where he is. I wonder if I would choose to come back if I could escape. But I am not Kern Bromley. He belongs here, and he knows that he does.

There is a dragonfly flying close. It buzzes loud, or louder than I expected; I have never seen a dragonfly before. I let it rest on my arm. I am still, perfectly still, watching its iridescent wings and its searching eyes. Its tiny feet prickle my skin, but I do not move. It feels like an important visit, a message of some sort, but I am not able to decipher its intent. It reminds me about the story of the old woman, but that was just a story and this is just an ordinary dragonfly. The dragonfly leaves after a while. I stretch, I try not to cry. Crying used to make me feel human—no plant cries, after all. But now it seems a measure of the drugs I have floating in my system. I am too close to tears, too close to frailty.

There are people up on the water tower, painting. It's a strange design; I can't make any sense of it. Patterns rather than a picture. It reminds me of a rock pool, or of the kind of stone that has layers and ripples. I force myself to watch even though I can feel my eyes wanting to close.

Crow

I DISCOVER THE woman's name is Fay, that she lives here in Barlewin, "for now," and that she likes to keep an eye on the greenhouse. "There are still haters," is her only explanation for that. She seems to think I can offer her something, but she don't say what. And other than give her a few much-needed lessons in self-defence, I don't quite know what she's after. I'm getting used to the look of her. She's different from Eva, more substantial. Perhaps it's just that she's whole and healthy and not in need of constant care and attention from Tenties and the like. I cast my mind back, see if I can recall seeing other green-hued beings in the past couple of days, but no-one comes to mind. Not that I was exactly looking. Not that I didn't have other things on my mind.

Fay fusses about the greenhouse. She's happy working in the blue half-gloom and that's fine with me; I'm still a little freaked out about the lights and I don't really want to draw attention to my lack of calm. I look out the windows. The High Track is harder to see than I expected. I mean it's right there, but something about the angle of the windows and the curve of the High Track means that you don't really get to see *in*. What you do see is a vista of Barlewin: the marketplace, the water tower, even the High Track's number 3 staircase. And there's someone on those stairs—in fact, a couple of someones—climbing up. The lights of the High Track make them clearly visible, but I can't tell much about them.

Once at the top, they turn in my direction. I stifle the urge to duck down, but they don't seem to be looking at the greenhouse. They seem to be heading to what I can't help think of as admin, which is just a bit further up and out of sight. I expect I'm going to lose them, but they stop, almost directly in front of me. Another figure joins them. The Barleycorn King? Doubt it. Not tall enough, too sprightly, no crazy hair. Most importantly, no *cane*. Although I'm beginning to think that's more an instrument of torture than a walking aid.

All three of them walk to the very edge of the High Track. They've pushed their way past plants and to the railing lining the whole thing. It's not much of a railing, it'd not stop anyone jumping off, but it's there in a non-functional, symbolic way. They seem to be attaching something to it, something small, possibly metallic, because the light glints off it every now and then.

I can't help myself. "What the hell are they doing?" I ask Fay.

She comes closer, too close. She reminds me of Tenties that way. "Oh, that's nothing. Just a protest."

"A protest against what?"

"They're putting on locks. To protest what happened to the Trocarn. It's only symbolic. They're not real Time Locks, just old-fashioned metal locks. But they do piss him off."

"The Barleycorn King?"

"Yep," says Fay. She's already wandering away, back to her fussing.

"But the Barleycorn King couldn't be responsible for the Time Locks."

"No! Of course not."

The depth of my ignorance is beginning to wear at me and that's unusual. I'm not usually someone who needs to know. Although I am happy to rejoice in anything that pisses off the Barleycorn King.

"I'm finished now," says Fay. Which is obviously an invitation to leave. I grab a book from the shelves while Fay's not looking, a spur-of-the-moment acquisition. We're both cautious as we walk down the stairs, but there's no searching light and the alley is just an alley. Fay says goodbye and turns away into the night before I think to offer to walk with her. There's a path up here that will take me back to the marketplace, or there should be. It's smaller than an alley, almost a mistake, as if they forgot to make the houses bigger, or forgot to include room for a garden. You have to know the spot—there's some not very clever graffiti, a scraggly tree—and then you duck under a bit of fence and there you are.

I look for my landmarks. I should be able to find the place without thinking. I've walked this way so many times, but I second-guess myself and it takes longer than it should to find the fence. Mostly because the tree has gone. But then I'm under the rail and up the path and I almost feel as if I'm home. It's the kind of place kids find, that's how I found it anyway, and I've never seen anyone else there. And tonight appears to be no exception.

I stand at the end of the path, looking out at the marketplace. There's no-one around. In the Barlewin I know, there's always some activity if you know where to look. I guess I just don't know what direction to head as yet. There's a buzz of something up to the left in the buildings that have their backsides facing the High Track. I head that way, mentally counting the coins I have left. Enough for something. I definitely need a drink.

The bar is artier than I remember it. There's a handcrafted sign above the front door which would not have lasted in the Barlewin I know and love. And there's no scaries. Strange music playing. Something scattered and hard to hold on to. I'm underdressed, but I really don't give a shit. I acquire a drink without too much of a fuss—a rum, Black Kraken, and it's just as good as it should be. There's a table by the window and I take it because I don't especially want to converse. My view holds no Eva/Olwin graffiti, thank God; or none that I can make out. But I can see the water tower, which is all wrong, the big screen should be in the way.

Sometimes I convince myself I'm at home, and then something small like the absence of the big screen really hits me. I wonder if it'd be possible to settle in here. Assuming I can stay, which is a big and probably unfounded assumption. Maybe the laws of physics will bounce me back home after a while. Which is an odd thought, and possibly one I should pre-empt by returning myself before it turns out to be true. But as much as I'd like to get myself home—and that's the plan and all— can't say I'm in a rush to Time Lock in a hurry.

There are lights strobing the water tower and I remember my headlong rush up the stairs. If I'd been with Mac, we'd've been almost laughing as we ran. But Mac isn't here. And then an image flickers up. It's that bloody map, of course. Thankfully without Olwin Duilis' face, but the map nonetheless. I half expect the writing to expand and a message appear saying *Kern Bromley what the hell have you done with my box?* But, luckily, nothing like that. Not even a *jump through*. I take another few sips of my drink and enjoy—if that's the right word—the view.

The water tower goes back to being its ordinary self and the strobing lights appear to have gone for now. I decide it's time for home. Ed and Judith's, I mean. It's safe, it's known, and I can keep an eye on the Barleycorn King.

The walk is uneventful. It's safer, this future Barlewin, at least down here on street level. I don't know if I like it.

I'm back by the gardens, close to sleep and bed, when an insect starts buzzing around me. It's a noisy little thing, and I wonder what it's doing here. Surely it should be valiantly attacking the water tower lights or buzzing up to the High Track. I guess the farm is an attractant. But why me? I make a few casual sweeps of the arm in front of me, but the insect don't take a hint and accompanies me all the way home. I think I've lost it inside the house, but up in my room it's back, coming in through the window Judith left open. I flop down on the bed, take a look at the book I nicked from the greenhouse. The insect lands on the top of the spine. It's another dragonfly. It sits there buzzing happily.

"I don't know what you want from me," I say, "but I'm not really from around here."

The dragonfly pays no mind. After a while of me pretending to read, it flies down to the pocket of my jeans. An invasion of privacy; I try to bat it away. It becomes insistent, and I shift away from it, but still it pesters. I take my old phone out of my pocket, because at this angle it's digging into me, and the dragonfly settles on that.

"You can have it," I say. But as I move the phone to the bedside table, it creeps along it, back towards me. This is one persistent insect. And then the phone lights up and it's Mac's voice talking to me, and I'm so freaked out I drop the whole thing on the floor.

CHAPTER SIXTEEN

Green Jay

SOMEONE IS SHAKING me, waking me up. I recognise the voice; I want to move towards it. I don't think they're trying to hurt me—it's not that kind of shaking—but I don't like it. I want to stay asleep. But I also want to move towards the voice. I know the voice. I—

"Eva," says someone who I think might be Blue Jay.

I force my eyes to open. He is there, misty and out of focus. Perhaps this is a dream.

"I've found him."

Found who, I wonder. Who did he want to find?

"Please hold on. It won't be too much longer."

I want to tell Blue Jay that I am not as sick as I seem, it's just the drugs, it's just that Guerra caught me, that I can hold on, of course I can hold on, but the words won't come out.

Blue Jay sits down beside me. He takes my hand and I feel his body against mine. I try harder to properly wake up and I manage to open my eyes. I see him looking down at me. I should tell him to go, that Rose-Q is close by, that this is not safe.

"You can always make another one," says a voice.

Blue Jay turns, but I don't, because I know who it is: Guerra. Blue Jay should run, he should leave. I can feel the twitching in his body, but he stays close beside me and I'm glad of it.

"She's not the first," says Guerra, and I feel Blue Jay stiffen. "But you know that, don't you?"

I want to ask Blue Jay what he means, but I don't dare. Not in front of Guerra. I think I could speak now, but I'm not sure I trust my voice to come out right.

"Olwin will be here soon," says Guerra. "And we'll have Kern back. The nets will find him."

"What do you know about the time nets?" asks Blue Jay.

"Not as much as you, obviously," says Guerra. "But all I really need to know is that they're there, at my disposal."

"It's torture," says Blue Jay.

Guerra shrugs. "Can I help it that Kern has run away with my property?"

"It's not yours."

"And neither is she yours."

Guerra is close now, close enough to touch, but I still haven't turned to him. I can see Rose-Q, she's come closer, she's shaking her head, trying to tell me something, and there's a murky yellow cloud above her head. She's upset, of course she is. If only she was one of the Chemical Conjurers she'd use that cloud to hide Blue Jay, let him run away, but she's still, waiting.

Blue Jay stands. "Let me get him back," he says. And then he turns and runs.

"You have today," calls Guerra, but I don't know if Blue Jay has heard him because he's far, far away.

Guerra sits down beside me, mimicking Blue Jay's position, but on the other side. He puts a hand on my jaw and turns my face towards him. "Any questions?" he asks.

"No," I say, although I have many.

Guerra lets go of my face, but he remains sitting beside me. I want to shift my body away from his, but I don't dare. Rose-Q is very close now, standing where Blue Jay was a moment ago. Guerra takes out his phone and taps at it. He shows me a picture. It's a picture I've already seen, the one Eila sent to the number I have memorised. I test my brain, quickly; yes, it is still there.

"This is the real one," says Guerra.

"I know that's not me," I say. And I shouldn't, I know I shouldn't, but I can't let him speak me out of existence.

"No," says Guerra. He becomes absorbed by his phone. We sit there, the three of us, and I try not to shake because I know if I do, Rose-Q will bend over and fill me with something. She is wiping my face and I recognise one of T-Lily's wipes. She shakes her head, so gently that her tentacles remain in place. And we sit together, the three of us, waiting, listening to the sound of Eila's whispers.

* * *

Crow

I HAVE TO tell Mac to shut the fuck up, because my brain needs time, plus he's been babbling on while the phone's been down there on the floor and as far as I'm concerned it's just been a whole lot of squeaking. But I've pulled myself together and I'm holding my phone. I can't see him; I doubt that he can see me. Instead I see one of those QR coded messages that scan to video, exactly the type that had been sent to my phone before but didn't unlock. I can feel the future phone on my wrist vibrating a little. It's obviously trying to make contact with this old time tech. I have no idea if it's successful or not, and even if I did, I don't know how to stop it.

The dragonfly's sitting on top of the old phone. I can see now it's not real, though it's a pretty good copy, very close. I would definitely not have noticed unless it had drawn itself to my attention. Which, of course, it did. For a second I think about Judith chasing the dragonfly out the other day, but I push that thought to the back of my brain, take a deep breath and say, "Okay."

The QR code floats away and I have Mac back. Well, his voice anyway. "You need to come back, Brom." His voice is not as calm as usual. He sounds tired, a little desperate, very un-Mac.

"I'm quite enjoying the alternate future," I say.

"Guerra'll drag you back."

"With that freaky light shit?"

"Time nets, Brom. They hurt like hell."

"Since when do you know anything about time nets?"

"And the box?"

"Don't have the box," I say. Which isn't strictly true, but it isn't strictly a lie, either.

"We need it," says Mac.

"We?"

"Eva. Eva needs it."

"So she's still alive?"

"Brom. I can get you back, if you'll let me."

"Okay," I say, because—well, I don't know why, but it seems wrong not to. And then, because this is Mac after all, and I don't want him to have to ask, I tell him I know where the box is, and that most probably I can get it.

There's a pause, during which I understand that Mac would very much like it if I went and got the box right this instant, but he doesn't want to harass me.

"Okay," I say to break the silence, "tell me what to do."

Mac's plan involves a whole lot of stuff I don't even try and follow. I do, however, focus on the safety features, because if I have to do this shit, I'd rather do it with the least possible damage to my person. I put my old phone back in my pocket. I think about peeling the new one off, decide to keep it, feel supremely guilty about Judith and Ed, decide to keep the future phone anyway. I packed light on my first trip, so there's not much to gather. I leave the book I liberated from the greenhouse. I haven't had a chance to really look at it yet, and, who knows, maybe it's a good read, but I'm not going to find out. It's a goodbye and a thank you and an explanation, I hope. Or maybe it's just another old book that Judith and Ed already knew about. It's the best I can do.

I stand by the door for a minute and listen to the house. It's an old house, full of its own creaks and groans, but I don't think any of the creaking and groaning is Judith or Ed awake. The dragonfly's still with me. I wish it had a mute button. It follows me down the stairs and to the front door. The door creaks when I open it, of course it does, but I manage to slip out unheard and head through the gardens to the shed. I can see the mad lighthouse lights again. They're not searching this way, and I don't want to give them the chance to. I have my doubts about the existence of 'time nets,' but if such a thing does exist, I don't want to be caught in one. I also doubt if a shed can stop them finding me, but there you have it, there's nothing like hiding if you can.

Inside the shed, it's dark, super dark, and I regret volunteering to bring the box back. Ed could do with some of that luminescent fungus stuff in here. But the dragonfly proves itself mildly useful, producing a thin stream of light and then buzzing over the boxes. I get the message. There's no point going home without it. I see Ed's left his unreliable gloves on the bench beside the box. I shove them in my pocket for later use and decide that the box I want, my box, must be the one that's closest. There's no real way of knowing. I decide not to dwell on the possibility that it's actually the same box having arrived by different pathways. That kind of shit freaks me out.

The dragonfly buzzes a little louder. Mac seriously could have made it less annoying. It's an OCD creation if ever there was one. I put on Ed's gloves, pick up the box and begin what I hope is my last journey in this reality. It's not an especially exciting journey, just out of the shed and up to the water tower, because I don't really want to materialise in the farm back home. The gloves are holding, for now. I say a mental farewell to the Barleycorn King, who I won't miss, and to the prophets, some of whom I will. I reach the water tower without incident. The time net lights are in the marketplace, so I can't delay. The box probably has them out, all excited, sniffing like bloodhounds.

I put down the box, take off Ed's gloves, shove them in my back pocket. My old phone protests, but Mac's synced things to the new one which, of course, he is deeply impressed by. Even from afar. It's all lit up now. Maps and shit. No Olwin Duilis, thank God. I enlarge the screen, find the bit I'm meant to use, and now here's the fiddly bit, because I have to attach myself to the box without activating the jump. Somehow, Mac's got it set up so that the box won't jump around on me until I ask it to. I'm attached, I'm all ready to go, it's only the anticipation of nausea that's holding me back.

I hear a cough and I turn, which is a mistake, because I see Ed standing in among the tomatoes. He's just standing there, not running towards me, not even beckoning. Just watching my foolishness as if he'd seen it all before.

I nod, and as a goodbye it's crappy but it'll have to do. I move my left wrist in towards the box, hope that I've tapped the right bloody part of the map and then we're away. No, it don't feel any better, but it's short and sweet.

I feel someone grab me. I've got my eyes closed and though I'm not particularly inclined to open them just yet, I do. It's Mac. As expected. He's intent on separating me from the box and it's fiddly, as usual, but then it's done and I'm sitting on the grass by the water tower and laughing my head off.

CHAPTER SEVENTEEN

Green Jay

"Go," says Rose-Q. She is leaning over me, very close, too close, but not touching. I cannot believe I have heard her correctly. Guerra has disappeared, but only just, only long enough for me to stretch a little, breathe deeper. But now here is Rose-Q trying to persuade me of something without speaking. There is a blue-green cloud around her, that is the best colour, the colour of love, acceptance and calm. Not excitement. Not joy. I don't think the Tenties can fake the colour, it's a true indication of their state. But perhaps I am wrong, perhaps anyone can fake anything.

Rose-Q leans so close that I feel I am breathing her breath. She smells of salt and something sharp. "Go," she breathes into me and then she jerks up and away and back to her seat.

I sit up, I place my feet on the ground, I stand. Watching

her all the while, to see if she will stop me. The blue cloud grows thicker, almost a smoke screen. And then I run, away from Guerra, towards the staircase near the water tower. My legs are trembling underneath me, they don't want to do this job, but they know that they must. I reach the staircase and I make myself slow as I go down, because I know I could fall. My feet are untrustworthy, but they find each metal stair and they move me down and down and around. My hands grip the railings, too hard. I miss a step. I pull myself up and then I'm careening down the stairs. They clang as I go and I can't stop it. I have to be out.

I don't know where I will go when I am out of here, but at the bottom of the stairs, I see that it doesn't matter. Blue Jay is waiting for me at the water tower. He is sitting still; he doesn't move or come to help me. I almost fall as my feet touch the ground.

I wave at him, but he is looking away, looking towards the man he is sitting with, towards something on the ground. My eyes are blurry, I am not even sure anymore that it is him. But I run anyway. I see the farm, there are people out with the plants and they are staring at me, their hats make them look like scarecrows, and I am running still.

He is too far, I will never reach him.

Crow

MAC LOOKS CRAPPY, I have to say, but then I've looked better myself. We sit in silence for a while, because there's no real need to talk. The box is on the grass in front of us and the dragonfly is annoying it for a change. Actually, I think the dragonfly might be trying to open it. I'm happy just to let it all be. Mac is taking a look at Ed's gloves and he seems mightily impressed. I should tell him that they weren't one-hundred-percent effective, but I'm not in the mood for talking just yet. There are people up on the water tower, painting, I think. But they're up there, and I'm down here and doing just fine.

Of course, it can't last. There's a woman running towards us. Well, that's generous, staggering towards us. I see the farm workers staring at her, but nobody's coming out to help. It's a bit of déjà vu with regard to my untimely exit down the stairs via the Barleycorn King, but surely I looked better than this. She's heading right towards us.

"Mac," I say, as a general warning. He looks up and I see his expression change from deep involvement to something like fear. But then he's up and running towards the woman. And I recognise her now, it's Eva, though she's obviously seen better days.

Mac lies her down on the grass beside me. He props her head up on his jacket, fishes a few things out of his pocket, tears open a squishy packet that looks like wasabi and puts the contents into her mouth. Then he takes out a cloth from a packet and wipes over her skin, her face, her arms, her legs. She's wearing shorts and a tunic. He runs the cloth across her stomach. He seems very coy in the treatment of somebody I presume he's seen completely naked, though there's me sitting here watching and all. She's stopped shaking, but that's about as positive a prognosis as I can make for all Mac's ministrations. Mac's over at the box now. He's got Ed's gloves on and he's ripping it open, though the dragonfly had already made pretty good inroads.

Inside, there's another container, something like a cooler, and he lifts this out gently and places it on the grass. The dragonfly's still at the casing of the Time Locked box, but Mac's delving into the cooler. He lifts out a very small sealed tube, puts the lid back on the cooler and the tube on the lid, then sits back on his heels. There's a hesitation which I can make no sense of. We both look over at Eva. Her eyes are open now and she smiles at Mac. If I was paranoid I'd say she was trying hard not to look at me.

"It's okay," she says to Mac. She moves her arm up so that her hand is above her head.

Mac's all business. He puts a cloth down close to her arm, opens another package and puts on surgical gloves. He swabs the double's arm with something, presumably antiseptic because this is looking more and more like an operation. Lo and behold he injects something into her arm. Eva looks away, and I don't blame her, because the next thing you know Mac gets hold of her arm, makes an incision and then forces the tube into her arm. Why this had to be done right here, right now, I've no idea. There's still mopping up to be done, but I decide to take an interest in the how the dragonfly's progressing.

The Time Locked box is in pieces. I prod at it with a stick, but it seems to have lost its here-but-not-here properties. I take a quick look inside the cooler. The vials seem to contain something I can only describe as gloop. Minute quantities; it must be some magical high-powered shit.

"She'll need a minute," says Mac. "Then we can go."

"Go where?" I ask. Because I haven't forgotten Guerra's ability to track my whereabouts, or the likelihood of him chasing after Eva come what may.

"I found a place," says Mac. He grins at me and I figure that if he could work out a way to bring me back from the world of the Barleycorn King, he can find a way to keep us hidden. I don't like it, all this hiding out, not when I'm back home. But I don't much like the prospect of Guerra's attentions either.

The unmistakeable clang of staircase number 4 drifts through the air. Commotion is definitely coming our way. "Time to go," I say. I gather up the leftover remnants of the Time Locked box and the cooler containing Eva's gloop. Mac's tidied up from the not-so-elective surgery. He helps Eva stand and she manages it, though she's leaning on him heavily. I follow them, but we're moving far too slowly. We've only got as far as underneath the water tower before we stop. There's a metal ladder attached to one of the legs of the tower, and Mac puts his hand on it. If this is far as we can go, we're stuffed.

"The only way is up," he says. He grins, and so do I, because I realise where he's been hiding all this time. Inside the bloody water tower.

I'm up the rungs before he has to prompt me a second time. I push back the covering, heave all the crap inside and then pull myself up, then lean down and give Mac a hand with Eva. She's over his shoulder. Not very dignified, but better than waiting for her to make the climb herself. The cover's back in place and I take a moment to look around Mac's hidey hole.

It's not as dark as I thought, light's getting in somewhere. There's a kind of mezzanine level. And more mod cons than you'd have a right to expect.

"You built all this?" I ask.

"Nup," says Mac. "Found it. Made some improvements, but the most important thing is the tower's shielding."

He's pretty damn proud of it, just the same. I help him manoeuvre Eva up to the mezzanine and onto the bed, of which there is only one. She appears to be unconscious. Mac spends some time fussing with her. If it was anyone else but Mac, I'd ask him about his newfound surgical skills and how you measure the vital signs of a double. But I don't. It may be wise, it may be foolish, but it's the way it's always been.

"Not a lot of water for a water tower," I comment.

Mac smiles, but then he's all serious. "Look, Brom—" he begins.

I shake my head.

"You've a right to know," he continues anyway.

Yes, there's a shitload of questions I'd like to ask. Why, for example, Mac seems intent on growing himself a girlfriend. How long he's been in situ here, and whether he was ever living in the place I thought he lived. But I don't imagine the answers to those questions will be either satisfactory or comforting. So I peel off the alternate-reality future phone and distract Mac with that instead.

He pokes at it for a while and he's fascinated, he's enthralled, but the peace and quiet don't last as long as I'd hoped.

"There's messages here," he says.

"Yeah, from you."

"They're not from me, Brom. Not these early ones, anyway."

"It's not like anyone knows that number." But then I remember sending it through, very early on, to someone I thought was Mac.

"Did you try and send messages to my phone?" I ask.

"No. I should have. I didn't think that'd work, to be honest; I was working on the dragonfly."

And distracted by Eva, I think, but don't say.

There's a clang which makes us both pause for a moment, but then nothing else.

"You made it?" I ask, because it belatedly occurs to me that the dragonfly represents some fairly impressive technology which you probably can't knock up at home.

"Just modified it," says Mac. He's vague enough for me to think that he's not going to be all that forthcoming. "But we need to know where these messages came from."

"They look a lot like yours," I say, partly to excuse myself.

Mac don't reply. He's fiddling with the phone.

"Guerra?" I suggest, because after all, I'm not that wildly popular that my friends and associates would seek to contact me in alternate realities.

"Not Guerra, but maybe Guerra's phone."

"Guerra's phone." I know I'm not adding to the conversation. It just seems a little hard to believe.

"He has a natural language interface."

"So basically that's just Guerra, then."

Mack shakes his head. "A natural language interface is AI. Some of them are pretty advanced. This one seems to be…"

"Rogue, power hungry, a little too proactive?"

"Independent," says Mac.

"That's hard to believe."

"Well somebody sent you those messages. Somebody was trying to get you home, pretty much the same way I was."

"Somebody who knows about Eva." And I realise I've taken the first step towards knowing more than I really want to.

"Yes," says Mac. "And about Olwin Duilis."

"Well that don't have to be Guerra, then," I say. "Or Guerra's phone, just to clarify things."

"I suppose not," says Mac. I can see there's more to say, but he doesn't elaborate.

"They're her parents, right?" I ask. "Judith and Ed, the ones on the farm?" Thinking all the while, *say yes, don't say it's really a future you.*

"Yes," says Mac. "I think so."

"So if we go to the farm, we'd find them there. Their younger selves."

"Probably," says Mac.

"And we're hiding out right beside them. Is that wise?"

"I don't think they know much, right now, Olwin's—"

But then Eva stirs and calls out, and Mac hurries to her. I watch him fuss over her for a bit. But then I ferret around in the cooler, think about the advisability of taking a vial and slipping it into my pocket. There's plenty left, one less is not going to hurt.

CHAPTER EIGHTEEN

Green Jay

I FEEL SO strange. As if part of me is dying and part of me is coming alive. My arm hurts, of course, but that's normal, that's to be expected. I can never be truly human, but somehow I believe it's possible. I am a strange, plant-like Pinocchio. This is one of Olwin Duilis' memories, that is true, but I am adapting it for myself. I am stealing it from her and making it my own. That way she cannot touch me.

Blue Jay is here. He helps me sit up, move around, and I walk with him to make him happy. I would prefer to stay on the bed; when I move I feel dizzy and not myself. It will take time, he says, but how long neither of us know. It is all a strange experiment.

The Crow sits downstairs, lurking. He has not been up to visit me and I have not been down to talk to him. I suppose I should be grateful. He brought the box back, Blue Jay keeps reminding me. The Crow has a strange story to tell about being pulled away to a different world. It is less than believable, but something happened to him. He walks too stiffly and he has lost his calm. There is something on the inside of his left wrist which he looks at all the time. He takes it off, puts it on, plays with it. I cannot tell what it is, and, I think, neither can the Crow. Not really. There are scabs on his hands and legs and he spends a lot of the day picking at them when he thinks no-one is looking. Blue Jay wants him to tell me about the girl that he met in my greenhouse. The hints he has given almost makes me think I am in one of the fairy tales from Guerra's bookshelf, but the Crow is untrustworthy.

Blue Jay is working with the casing of the Time Locked box, trying to fashion something that looks to me like armour. He has gloves too, gloves which the Crow brought back from his fairy tale land. They look just like dirty old garden gloves to me. There is something about them that makes me happy, but that is probably only because Blue Jay is working on them.

The water tower is protecting us, like a castle. One day we will have to burst out and fly away, but not yet. For now, it is comforting to hide.

But not for the Crow. He wants to get out now. It is only Blue Jay that is keeping him here. That, and he has nowhere to go.

* * *

Crow

IT'S COOL HIDING out in the water tower and all. That is, it was cool for an hour or so. But it's been three days and now I'm bored. Mac's playing with Ed's gloves and the stuff the Time Locked box was made out of; between his scientific investigations and his doctoring, he's got something to do. Eva's time is pretty much all caught up with languishing. I suppose I could go talk to her. I don't really want to.

The thing about the inside of a water tower is that it echoes. I suppose if whoever had started the renovations had got around to finishing them, it would all be different. But right now, sound travels in weird and disconcerting ways. And there's just the three of us. Or really there's the two of them and the one of me. There's a set of stairs that takes you right the way up to the top of the tower. And I've found me a room a couple of flights up. That's good. But it's not enough.

My phone, my new phone, gets another message from time to time. It's a bit creepy, but Mac says not to worry. Stay in the water tower, says Mac, and you can't be traced. But seriously? Staying in the water tower is a joy that is far past its use by date.

So I've started replying, and probably that's ill-advised, but then what else is there to do?

Who is this? I ask my mysterious correspondent. That is to say I text them, I don't phone them directly; even I'm not that stupid. The texting thing took a while to figure out, but it's easy if you peel off the phone and shake it into its stiff card form. Whole thing becomes a touch screen. Pretty cool. I tried to show Mac, but he's more interested in the leftover pieces of the Time Locked box. God knows what he thinks he can do. Move himself holus-bolus into an alternate reality, most likely, without the aid of dragonflies, or phones, or being attached to a box with its own agenda. He's got the dragonfly buzzing around helping him, but sometimes it buzzes over to me, just for a hello, and I'm so bored I'm kind of glad when it does.

In any case, it turns out the name of my messenger is Eila. Which tells me precisely nothing, but it's nice to have a name.

Eila and I have embarked upon an intermittent and at times incomprehensible correspondence. She won't tell me why she contacted me back in the Judith-and-Ed days, only that she knew I needed help. Does she know Olwin Duilis? No, apparently not. But then why is she sending me her picture, albeit superimposed over a map? It was just a picture that she'd seen. Which, I have to say, is most probably a lie. She seems to know that I'm not in trouble any more. That I'm back in—wherever, whenever you want to call this. But she don't ask.

And so it goes, back and forth, tall tales and true. But the curious thing is that she bothers to engage me at all. I know what's in it for me, but what's in it for her? Until she wants to show me something. Something that means stepping out of the water tower. I say yes and I immediately feel guilty. Not that I'm a prisoner, not that Mac wouldn't let me go if I asked him.

But I'm not going to ask.

It's night. The tower's quiet except for the hum of Mac and Eva's conversation. I climb the flights of stairs to the very top and make my way out onto the roof. I more than half expected to have to scrape back a heavy, noisy door, which would have alerted Mac and stopped me making a fool of myself. But no, the exit to the roof is quiet.

This isn't where Eila's asked me to be, incidentally. This is me being cautious and wise and scoping out the lay of the land before I make my move. This is me hedging my bets. Also, I'm bringing along one of the gloop vials as insurance, a kind of bargaining chip if the situation gets all desperate.

It's good to breathe proper, non-tower air. I mean there's vents and shit inside the tower, but not enough, not when you're stuck there day and night. I spread out my arms and suppress the urge to whoop. Actually, I don't suppress it entirely, but it's a quiet whoop just for me and the night air. I look down at the farm and it's all quiet. There are lights on in the main house, the one I stayed in, but the rest is dark. There's music drifting faintly from an open window. Some kind of folk shit, adding to the hippy vibe.

And then I look over at the High Track. It looks pretty dark apart from the lights along the railings. But then I guess my eyes adjust, and I see that there's a kind of coloured fog in the area just to my left. Tenties, it has to be Tenties, and if you can tell anything by the colour— and with Tenties you always can—they're not happy campers. Is this what Eila wants me to see? It's not like she was all that forthcoming with details. On the other hand, she wanted me over at the marketplace, and I doubt that you can see this part of the High Track from there, not with the big screen and all. So this is another mystery altogether. One which I'm sure Eva and Mac would be mightily interested in, one which I hope I can leave alone.

If I remember things right, there's a long metal ladder that leads up from the ground right to the top of the tower. I find it, it don't look particularly safe, but it's a way out. I have a moment of doubt as I fling my feet over the side. Why the first rung can't be closer to the top I don't know. But then I'm climbing down, I'm away, and I find myself on the cool ground at the bottom of the tower with a grin on my face.

It's easy enough to sneak into the marketplace from here. I've done it before, hundreds of times. And before you know it, I'm truly back home, back into my Barlewin. I get a kebab, just to cement the feeling. This, I acknowledge, is probably a mistake, and it's the last of my meagre supply of ready cash, but such is my mood that I don't care. I've taken some time with my clothes and I don't think anyone's going to look twice at me. I've left my old phone at home, and the new one's inside my shirt pocket. Probably I should have left that back in the tower too, but it's turned off and detached from my wrist. That's as much caution as I'm willing to take.

I take a look up at the High Track. From here, everything looks peaceful and right, or as peaceful and right as it can be with Guerra in charge. I see the Chemical Conjurers and I toy with the idea of saying hello, but as much as I trust them, the thing with robots is that it's relatively easy to get inside their brain. Not that I think Guerra's tried that yet, but I wouldn't put it past him. People seem to be gathering in from of the big screen, and so I position myself at the back of the crowd. I'm off to the side and a few people in, so I'm not conspicuously at the back, but I'm still close enough to the water tower that a quick getaway's not out of the question. That or into the tenements, but that's a last resort option I'm hoping I don't have to take. The idea of tonight is to scratch the itch of curiosity before it becomes too annoying. That's all.

There's no sound, just images, and at first they make no sense to me. It's almost as if the Tenties made the footage—it has the same kind of bio-obsessiveness that reminds me of them—but then I see it's showing the internal workings of a 3D printer. It's showing the layering of biostuff. It's all sped up so it don't get boring, although people are beginning to get restless, because it's not like we haven't seen this kind of thing before. And then out of the printer comes the complete copy. Only it's not a copy, it's a double, it's Eva. At this stage she's not really green at all. And I can tell that, because she's completely naked, and while she waits for the clothes to be printed out, she stretches, tries out the body. This results in some appreciative comments from sections of the audience, though not too loudly because it's a fine line that nobody wants to advertise crossing, and then Eva's up and away.

You see her moving through the marketplace, and then out to the farm. It's not continuous footage, it's obviously been put together from security video and the like, but there she is, walking into the farm, talking with some gardeners, going into the shed. And then she's out, running, and you see her with the Chemical Conjurers and you see, very obviously, that after a bit of a chat, they're providing some smoke screen distraction, but not before there's a flash of tentacles, and a Tentie—probably T-Lily, but who can say—grabs her and drags her away.

CHAPTER NINETEEN

Green Jay

I CURL UP with Blue Jay the way we did in the early days. We are on the floor in the very middle of the tower. There is only moonlight, and even that's probably my imagination. A while ago we heard the Crow climbing the stairs. "Let him be," said Blue Jay, "he's restless and bored." We heard him climb higher and higher and I am sure that he is out on the roof.

I envy him that. I have tried to persuade Blue Jay to let me bask on top of the tower, but he won't agree. He says it is too dangerous, too clearly visible from the High Track. I am sure that no-one will be looking, though when I think of the High Track, I think mostly of Rose-Q. I hope that Guerra has not blamed her, although of course he must. I hope she thought to run, too. I hope she was able to escape.

But mostly, I am glad the Crow is not here. I mentally push him off the roof of the tower, urge him to jump, to fly away, although of course that would mean we would no longer be safe. Blue Jay curls his fingers through mine, and for a moment I allow myself to be happy. It is only now, now that that I have pulled his life into this strange shape, that I wonder if this is enough. I know that Blue Jay is devoted to me—I do not doubt him—but I am always reminded that I am not human, even though I was fashioned from one. So much has been done to me that I hardly know how to describe my body. What to hope for. How to be.

Sometimes I wonder if Blue Jay is not just trying to keep me alive, but also trying to make me more acceptable. I could hardly blame him, if that is so. But if I am honest, I don't really care if I am human or not. I just want to be me, truly me. Green Jay.

Silence streams down through the tower. It has been a long time since we have heard the Crow move and it worries me. What is he doing? I shouldn't care, I should lie here with Blue Jay, relaxing. But that strange man troubles me, and I still do not trust him. A minute ago, I wanted him gone; now I want to know where he is.

"What is he up to?" I ask.

"Hush," says Blue Jay.

It would be so easy for the Crow to betray us. Get back in with Guerra, by showing him where we are. I don't think he'd do that to Blue Jay. I know he'd do it to me. "What if he is caught?"

"Brom won't get caught."

"Are you sure?"

"Mmm," says Blue Jay and it is half a snore.

Crow

WELL THAT WAS a curious piece of propaganda from, presumably, Guerra. Designed to flush out Eva. He has an interest in her that's bordering on obsession. Perhaps she represents a very well-paid commission. What's really interesting is the way the crowd reacts. Seems to me that in their minds they've either been shown the wanton capture of an innocent double by some Tenties and the Chemical Conjurers, or they've been shown a renegade double escaping with the aid of some Tenties and the Chemical Conjurers. Either way it don't look so good for my robot friends, but it's the Tenties people seem to have decided to blame. There's a few of them in the crowd, though I don't recognise any of them. But they seem surrounded by people with, let's say, pressing questions. They're filling the air with a murky yellow cloud, and there's enough of them that the air's become foggy.

But not foggy enough.

Time to slip away.

"Kern Bromley," says a voice I know well. "Good to see you back."

It's one of the Chemical Conjurers. This one is Felix; I recognise the stars he's had engraved on his face. The fact he was able to sneak up on me is disconcerting, but it don't pay to show that.

"Hey, Felix."

"How is Eva?"

I owe the Chemical Conjurers a lot. And they're friends. Weird kind of friends, but friends. But I don't trust the fortress of their brains. Not if Guerra is the one trying to storm the castle.

"Felix," I say and I spread my hands.

"We can help. Mac's been working with us."

"I'll let him know," I say. And then it's a little awkward, which may sound a weird thing to say with a robot, but there you have it.

"We made the dragonfly," he says.

Well, that explains a lot. "Cool, very cool," I offer along with a high five which does some measurable damage to my hand. "Though next time, maybe work on a softer buzz."

"Will do," says Felix. He raises his hands up in a gesture I recognise but don't fully understand. It's something like amused resignation, but there's a robot meaning to it as well.

"That footage," I say, "that's not going to get you in trouble, is it?"

"Half-truths," says Felix. "Quarter-truths, but it's not trouble for us."

It's hard to see what's going on with the Tenties. Oscar has possibly gone over to investigate. Which means that Felix knows and, I'm guessing, thinks the situation is under control.

But really it's past time for me to go. I raise my hand to say goodbye. "She's okay," I say and then I'm off, slipping into the crowd, through the Tenties' mist and away from watching eyes, and back to the water tower.

I catch my breath when I'm under the dark cool of the tower. I can't see much of what's going on because of the big screen, but it sounds like it's devolved into a free-for-all. I'm not sure that's what Guerra had in mind; he's usually one for calm. Terrified calm, obedient calm, yes, but he don't go in much for terror. He hates any kind of a fuss, he's been known to sneer at my escapades with the Chemical Conjurers. What he doesn't understand is that they're fun, but I get it. They've a way of drawing attention, and that is probably unwanted. Also, and I'm out on a limb here, I think it's an age thing. Older you get, the more you value calm. Could be totally wrong, of course. It's my fervent hope to be able to find out personally.

Which is why I fully intend to climb back inside the water tower. Any minute now. My phone's been buzzing me for a while, and I have no intention of responding to its call just yet. Especially as I thought I'd turned it off. If that footage was what Eila wanted me to see—and what else could it be—then she knows more about me than I'd like. Is that a surprise? Probably not. But the one person I trust is sitting up in the water tower with his strange green love, fiddling with the universe in disturbing ways, and quite frankly, he needs my help. At the very least, not to give him away, not before he implements his escape plan. I have my own theories on what that might be.

The bottom door scrapes open and Mac climbs down the ladder. "You may as well come in the easy way," he says.

Both of us stand there a moment in the night. It's seductive, this water tower. When you're standing underneath it, you feel safe, almost invulnerable. No wonder Mac chose it as a fortress.

"Is she worth it?" I ask. I never meant to ask, but Guerra's footage must have been working on my brain as well.

"We'll be gone soon, Brom."

"Stay as long as you like," I say. Because that's not the answer to a question I'd like to ask. What's in this for Mac? Because, at the end of all this, wouldn't Mac prefer a human, a woman with all the bits, internal and external? Without the green skin and the languishing and the ongoing need for rescue and resuscitation? I've seen Mac with girls, it's not that this isn't a possibility, but I've never seen this level of unreasonable devotion.

"I know it makes no sense," he says. And he looks at me as if to say, *well, if I want to fall in love with a double, who are you to stop me?* And, indeed, he's right. Who am I to judge? My own track record is hardly stellar. I think of the minor prophet and wonder if she'd be worth a visit, but that connection is uncertain to say the least.

There's a rustle somewhere in the direction of the farm. We're back up the ladder as quick and as quiet as possible, which, after all, is one of our specialties. Mac's inside first, so it's just me that Carine discovers, both feet still on the ladder.

"You may as well come down, Brom," she says. She may be right, but I've no intention of obeying. I turn, so as I can jump down and run if I have to, or at the very least use my legs to take a swipe at her. "Guerra'd like a word," she continues.

"Nothing much to say," I tell her.

"Nevertheless…" And I recognise the strategy, because it's one I've used myself. Leave the subject to put two and two together and come quietly of their own accord. And who knows the two and the two better than me?

"The thing about that box is that it didn't survive the trip," I say. "And my apologies to Guerra, but that's a well-documented downside of Time Locked jumps. Or so I've heard."

"Don't give me that shit, Brom." Carine's getting impatient now, which don't usually play well.

"But I saved what I could." I pull the vial from my pocket and throw it down to Carine. She catches it and I jump and I'm running towards the farm and I hear her swearing and I figure I've got enough of a start, and plus, now I know the farm better than ever, and sure it's pretty obvious Eva and Mac are up in the tower, but if they just pull the opening shut it should give them time to get out and away. Or just stay put. I mean it's pretty much impregnable. But then I hear exactly the sounds that I don't want to hear and that's Mac's voice all calm and reasonable and somebody climbing down the ladder. I stop. I can hear them talking and it's a great big circle because Mac knows what Carine wants and Carine knows that he has it and it's only the fact they used to work together that stops Carine just pushing Mac out of the way and getting Eva herself.

There's a rustle beside me. A very slight rustle, but I

realise that Mac's only stalling, that he wants to give Eva enough time to climb up and out and away. Didn't think she was strong enough for that, but the evidence looks to be against me. That's assuming this is Eva and not another Guerra associate. But I don't think so.

I stay as absolutely still as I can. Eva's obviously heading for the farm. That pretty much wrecks my plan. On the other hand, I'm the least attractive quarry at this point.

Someone grabs my arm, and of course it's Eva. "Give me the phone," she says. Her voice is quiet, but her breathing's not. That climb's a bitch and don't I know it.

But I say, "No." Because, what the hell, not everything's about her.

"The phone can get me away."

"And what about Mac?"

"Blue Jay is protecting me."

I can feel her fingers on my wrist, searching for the phone and, naturally, failing to find it. It's creeping me out. I pull my wrist away and although there's more strength to her than I'd anticipated, it's not that hard to get out of her grip. I grab her arms and pin them to her side. We're standing so close that I can smell the double smell of her. It's different from before, but she still don't smell human. Not completely.

"You want all Mac's efforts to go to waste?" she asks.

"Not at all." I hope she understands that her idea of a waste probably does not converge with mine. She wriggles for a while but then she's still, planning her next move. I've no interest in what this may be so I say, "I'll let you go and then you run, okay. No phone, just go."

She nods and I release her arms, but she reaches up with one hand and hits my chin and reaches into my pocket with the other and grabs the phone. I try and grab it back and that's a mistake because she's already activated something and that familiar nauseated feel comes over me. I don't know how the hell she did it, but I'm back out of step with the true and proper world, only this time I'm stuck with Eva.

CHAPTER TWENTY

Green Jay

"How do you stop it?" I ask the Crow. He's closed his eyes and he looks pale and far away. I have the phone, but he's caught hold of my wrist and doesn't have the sense to let go. "What did you do last time?"

"I thought you knew all about this."

He is being mean, but he is right. I don't know enough. Blue Jay was beginning to teach me, but we were not ready. He was working on different, better ways. But of course, the fact we are here at all is the Crow's fault.

"Just let go of me," I say and I pull my arm away. But he's still there.

He opens his eyes, sees me. "Fuck," he says. "What the fuck is this?"

"What happened last time?"

"Someone pulled me in." He groans and doubles over.

"Who?" It's obvious I don't feel as bad as the Crow, and I feel a surge of joy. Blue Jay thought this would be easier for me. He was right.

"High Track," he says. "Up on the High Track."

"No."

"You asked."

"That can't be right."

"Shit, when I had the Time Locked box, someone pulled me in. Alright? With a fucking striped cane. And when I came back under Mac's instructions it was easier, but then I guess Mac was in control and not standing in front of the water tower about to be fucked over by Carine."

The speech takes a lot out of him and he spends the next little while recovering.

"Try the bloody phone," he suggests after a while.

I look down, but he pulls it away from me and pokes at the screen. He still has one hand around my wrist.

"No," I say. I don't know why, but it feels wrong to stop now, it feels as if the journey is not yet complete. I grab his arm, but it's too late; we've stopped shifting around. It's hard to know how I can tell, but it's obvious. And the Crow knows too.

He seals the phone onto his wrist and lies down on the grass. He's breathing hard and he keeps his arms crossed over his body, so I can't grab the phone back, but otherwise he's completely vulnerable.

"No need to thank me," he says.

I want to kick him. I want to jump on him until he is squashed and bloody.

Instead I walk away. We're in the same place, of course.

The water tower is still there. The farm looks wrong, but perhaps that's just because it's night and the only lights are the ones from the tower and, very faintly, from the High Track. All the garden beds are enclosed in plastic tunnels. I can see a house close by and the shed in the distance.

There are memories coming up that I don't want. I can feel them pushing at me, telling me they will be useful, reminding me there are actions I should take. I try and pull these memories up in such a way that I can look at them, but keep them away from me. But it is hard, so hard, and after not too long I push them back down. I can't have Olwin Duilis taking me over. I do know that the memories want me to walk towards the farm, knock on the door of the house, go inside the shed. Instead I turn and go back to the water tower. The opening at the bottom is shut and I doubt that I can shift it; but the ladder to the roof is still intact and I climb back up. I am halfway up before I realise I feel lighter and happier than I should. I feel free.

Crow

I FIGURED EVA would baulk at the farm and I was right, but I made sure to secure the best room first. Not that the water tower's quite up to scratch. The renovations are still there, but birds have got in, and some mice. And probably other animals, which I have no intention of looking for. No human's lived here for a while. The plumbing's not up to much either, but it's somewhere to stay. We both spent the rest of the night pretending to sleep: in my case, there wasn't that much pretence involved, to be perfectly honest.

I'm doing a recce on the roof, but it's hard to tell much from here. The most obvious difference is the polytunnels in the farm. Not that that's any sign of human involvement. If I know anything about Ed and Judith's ways, they'd both be up and about by now. The High Track's still there. Hard to see any difference from here. There's no sign of movement there either. I'd half hoped for the prophets, but even they seem to be taking a day off, assuming they feature in this reality at all. But the marketplace is up and running and the smell of foods is wafting over. I was out of readies before I came and this trip through realities hasn't made me any richer. But there's always ways and means, and I decide I'll avail myself of them in the near future.

I exit by the door in the base of the tower. It's a noisy bloody thing and difficult to shift, but I feel safer dropping onto the ground under the water tower. There's no big screen. Which only goes to show it really wasn't a well-thought-through idea. I mean, where's the wisdom in keeping the average citizen's brain alive and optimally functional, when the powers-that-be can't be bothered protecting something like the High Track from the likes of Guerra? As I get closer to the marketplace, I see some reasonably familiar stalls, though I recognise that I'm a little off-piste re the clothing trends. No-one's staring, though; I'm not that remarkable. People seem to be flashing their phones in exchange for food, and while I have a phone to flash, I very much doubt that it's backed up by anything so substantial as a bank account. Perhaps it is, seeing as it still seems to work and it wasn't originally acquired by me, but I'm not sure I want to put that to the test just now.

But then I see a familiar and very welcome sight: the Chemical Conjurers in all their glory. They haven't really got into their act yet. They're just floating things up into the air. Playing, really. Warming up.

"Kern Bromley," says Oscar. I can tell it's him because of the stars engraved on his face. "You shouldn't be here."

"Any chance of breakfast before you tell me why?"

Oscar begins to explain something about Time Lock and the necessary technology and the differences between Eva's body and mine, but before he can get too far into the dissertation, Felix appears bearing something that looks like pancakes. He also has a mug of coffee, for which I am extremely grateful. They're pretty well-synched, the Chemical Conjurers, but the appearance of food borders on precognition. Not that I care.

"I've a question," I say between mouthfuls of pancake.

"Ask away," says Oscar.

"Why is it that I'm fluttering around a fraction of a second in Time Lock, but now I've jumped, what, decades in time?" I actually had no idea about the time frame of this particular reality, but I was as sure as hell it wasn't a fraction of a second from the time and place I'd recently left.

"You *land*, Kern Bromley. That makes the difference," says Felix.

"How are the pancakes?" asks Oscar.

"Good," I say. Actually, they taste a bit odd, as if it's been made out of less-than-ideal ingredients, but they're hot and the syrup is sugary and I'm in no position to be fussy.

"Is there anything else you need?" asks Felix.

"No," I reply, which turns out to be an ill-advised answer, because Oscar has me in his hands and is lifting me up over his head. I am so surprised that I don't struggle, it'd be pointless anyway, given our relative strength.

"We are sorry," says Felix. But not so sorry as to stop what they're doing. For a second I think he's going to throw me and I imagine flying over the marketplace, a parabola of a human, moving in entirely the wrong way. But instead Oscar starts walking, moving through the marketplace, towards the High Track. Of course. Where else would I be going? You'd think such a sight would draw excited gasps as the very least, pointed fingers, even intervention by the authorities, but nobody seems to even notice.

We reach the stairs and Oscar puts me down. I'd half hoped he'd extend up and place me gently on the High Track, but it looks as if I'm expected to climb staircase number 3 by myself.

"I'm too heavy," says Oscar.

"Shame," I say. I walk to the first landing and stop. Oscar is still there at the bottom of the steps; while I suppose I could just stand here and sulk, there's no point trying to get down again.

"You used to help me," I say.

"We are sorry," says Felix, who has materialised, presumably as backup should I decide to do anything so foolish as attempt to slip away.

"We would help you again, if you asked," says Oscar.

I spread my hands, which I know the robots can interpret as *help me now*, but which they wilfully ignore.

"Are there prophets here?" I ask.

"Prophets?" asks Felix.

"Women who wander around singing wearing robes that change with the levels of pollution." It's not a particularly descriptive version of the prophets, but it'll have to do.

"No," says Oscar. "No prophets."

That's a damn shame. I wave them farewell as I begin my walk to the gallows. It's hard to stay mad at the Chemical Conjurers. I take my time, there's no point in hurrying, and so I can't help noticing there's some new artwork at the very top of the stairs. It's Eva/Olwin, of course, though this is a psychedelic version of her. It strikes me that I'd very much like to go to a world where this woman didn't feature so prominently, if at all.

There's no-one around to greet me, and so I head off in the opposite direction to admin. I'm only delaying the inevitable, but why the hell not. I last walked this part of the High Track with the Barleycorn King. Can't say that it's vastly different. I find a bench, take a seat. I'm looking out over gentrified Barlewin now, if it hasn't already found itself a new name, or defected to Wilton, the next suburb along. From up here, I can't really see much difference in realities. No gleaming towers, no apocalyptic holes in the ground. Shame, really.

On the armrest of the bench is another of those strange split-circles. This one has an ear in the middle. Which is appropriate really, because now that I'm settled and quiet I can hear the sound of singing drifting towards me. Just a lone singer, not a choir. And, if I'm not mistaken, it's a male voice and not a particularly gifted one.

The Barleycorn King strides into view. He's as old and unkempt as last time. Still has the cane, but the candy-striping is faded. I stay sitting. This is as good a spot as any. I'm not too near the edge, nor any staircases. He looks happy, which is new. His song is completely nonsensical. It's full of birds—crows and jays and the like—and some of it seems to be purely an approximation of birdsong. Which is off-putting to say the least. I'm listening because I have nothing else to do; I don't expect it to make any sense.

He sits on the bench beside me and finishes the song. Too close for comfort, but what choice do I have? His robes are still green and brown, still without the fresh look that regular washing might give them. His smell reminds of the farm: not unpleasant, but distinctive.

"What happened to the prophets?" I ask. Just to show him I'm in the know.

"They taught me to sing," he says. "I miss it here."

We sit in silence for a while, because, quite frankly, it's him that's brought me here.

"Have you met Eila?" he asks.

I can feel the phone on my wrist tingle. "No," I say because that seems the best answer.

"Then you must," says the Barleycorn King. "Let's wait here until she comes."

CHAPTER TWENTY-ONE

Green Jay

I KNOW THE Crow has left; there is no need to look for him. The water tower feels empty and peaceful without him. I miss Blue Jay, but the feeling of freedom has not left me. When I move, my body fails me. It craves the drugs Rose-Q gave me, it needs more doses from the box. But I can walk and I do not fall. I spend some time exploring the water tower, looking for a message from Blue Jay. It's unlikely—probably impossible—but I cannot help but hope.

The poor tower has suffered. Water has dripped through many things, and animals have found a home here. There is some food in cans, but not much. What I really need is sun. I could bask on top of the tower, but then a thought strikes me. There is nothing to stop me walking outside. Through the alleyways and back to my old home.

Of course, thanks to the Crow, I cannot know exactly where and when we are, I cannot be sure I am safe, but the greenhouse is pulling me and after all this time in captivity with Guerra, I cannot stop myself. I am down the ladder, standing under the water tower before I have truly thought.

I take a circular route under the High Track, staying away from the marketplace. I don't venture into the warehouses in the middle, just stick with the curve of the High Track above me. When it takes me close to the tenements I slip across the road and into the alleys. I should know the layout here, but somehow I am lost. I find dead ends where I thought there was another lane. But I am not yet fearful, because in each of these dead ends there is a picture.

A picture of me.

At first I thought it was a picture of a green goddess. Each portrait is a face covered with swirls and ornaments so that the only features that are clear are the mouth and the eyes. Even the hair is an extension of these curling patterns. The green goddess is always positioned at the end of the alley and underneath her are flowers and other gifts. Sometimes there are messages painted onto the wall. I stopped in front of one portrait to read them: blending, union, hope. And it was then that I realised that the eyes staring down at me were mine. And that the lips, if they were to speak, would know exactly who I was. I know they are mine, not Olwin Duilis', but how I know this I cannot say.

This brings me great joy, although I cannot claim to

understand it. And the joy carries me through to the right alley, towards the greenhouse. There is no-one by the doorway and it is not hard to open the bottom door and walk up the staircase. It seems deserted, but also clean. There is no urine on the stairs the way there often was when I lived here. No dark stains, no smells to rush past.

I come to the door of my greenhouse and I am almost too scared to open it. I don't want it to be as deserted as the rest of the building. I am worried the greenhouse belongs to a time past that has been and gone with nothing left. I close my eyes. I open the door.

Crow

WE SIT IN silence for so long that it's getting awkward. But then I see a figure coming up from the right. From this distance the person looks as if they're floating along. But as they get closer that illusion sorts itself out and I see that it's a woman, not that old, probably around my age. She's wearing something like the prophets' robes, but belted and not flowing. And there's no colour to speak of, just a plain off-white. This is as far as my sartorial expertise takes me. The woman herself is dark-skinned, and for a moment I worry that she's going to turn into yet another manifestation of the increasingly annoying Olwin Duilis, but that too proves to be an unnecessary concern. She's very much herself, this woman. Echoes of the minor prophet if anything, but I don't think it's her.

You'd think I'd be more certain on that score, but it turns out I'm not.

"My dear," says the Barleycorn King.

The woman bends to kiss him on the cheek, then straightens up again. She makes no move to sit down.

"This," he says, "is Eila."

"Kern Bromley," she says. Then she shakes my hand, which is also weird because her grasp bothers me. It's too flimsy, not quite solid. But it's also too brief to really be called a proper handshake. "You really shouldn't be here," she continues.

Why the hell not? is what I'd like to say. Instead I suffice with a low key, "Because…?"

"You're not made for all this, Kern," she replies.

"Too true," I reply. "And yet it seems to keep happening."

The Barleycorn King is staring away from us both, lost in contemplation of something else entirely.

"I've tried to help you," she continues.

"I don't think so."

"But I have. Did you not realise those messages on your phone were from me?"

"Same name, don't mean the same person."

Eila smiles again, and it's an infuriating smile, really. "Do you know any other Eilas?" she asks.

It's my turn to offer an infuriating smile into the mix and for a while it's a tussle of politeness, but truly, that gets boring after a while.

"Where are the Tenties, then?" I ask, because, from my point of view, she's the one that asked me to see that footage. And everyone else seems accounted for.

"We've tried," says Eila.

The Barleycorn King stirs. He looks straight at me and places a hand on my arm. His eyes are so wild that for a minute I think he's going to pick up his cane and escort me down the stairs again, but he calms, although the hand is still there and I'm not completely comfortable with it.

"If you didn't keep jumping around and changing things," he says.

He's blaming me? "I'm not changing anything," I say.

"But Brom, you are," insists Eila.

"You're the ones that got me into this in the first place," I tell them.

The Barleycorn King shifts in his seat, the better to freak me out. "We're not trying to blame you, Brom." *Oh, yeah?* "But no-one asked you to take that package. The very first day. It was unexpected. And it created patterns no-one was ready for."

So he's admitted he's Guerra. Or was Guerra, or a version of Guerra, but that's hardly a surprise.

"And Mac?" Not because I want to dob Mac in, but because Mac has a lot more, let's say, expertise in these matters. But I straight away feel shitty, because what kind of friend am I?

The Barleycorn King shakes his head. "I know I'm the one to blame," he says. This is not quite believable, but it has the effect of removing his hand from my arm, if only because Eila bends over to comfort him. I don't know why. As far as I can see, he *is* the one to blame. Him and Olwin Duilis and, I'm increasingly coming to suspect, Eila.

"Why'd you show me that footage, then?" I ask her.

"That isn't important, Brom," says Eila.

God, but she's a pain. I turn to the Barleycorn King. "Look," I say. "You're trying to tell me that you knew what you were doing back in the day when you were... "—a small deal criminal, is what I really mean, but can't bring myself to say it—"...younger. I mean you didn't seem to know much about this kind of thing, then."

"That's all too true, Kern. I fell into this. I thought I understood, but I knew nothing."

Once again Eila's with the comforting, but I'm having none of that. "*You* knew things, though," I say to her.

"Nobody truly understood," she says.

We are all quiet for a moment, reflecting on our various levels of non-understanding. Mine, I have to say, is definitely the winner. But I can't help myself. "So you mean to tell me that with all this mucking about, you went and lost the Tenties."

Eila looks at me as if considering whether to tell me what the Chemical Conjurers might refer to as a quarter-truth. But the Barleycorn King has had enough of that, it seems. "Not lost, Kern," he says. "Sent away. Got rid of."

"So they're okay? Just somewhere else." I'm the one looking for the half-truths now.

"They're adapting," says Eila. She's all excited now.

"They were put in Time Lock," admits the Barleycorn King. "And they became... stuck."

"Stuck?" I ask. "Just permanently zipping around, in between. You know that feels like shit, don't you? Like absolute shit. I mean, how long did they do this?"

They speak at once. "It's over now, Brom," says Eila.

"Too long," says the Barleycorn King.

"So where are they?" I ask.

And now it's all silence.

I TAKE MY time coming back down staircase number 4 and through the farm, and so I see there's some faded graffiti on the side of the tower which I think could be a bird. There's an eye, anyway, and something that looks like a wing. Which means we're further into the future than last time. Or they used crappier paint in this reality. Once you start thinking of possibilities, it leads you down too many paths and then... brain explosion.

I feel unaccountably sad about the Tenties. I'm not their greatest fan, that's the truth. But being the experienced inter-reality traveller that I am, I can't imagine that anyone, alien or otherwise, would enjoy an extended period Time Locked. I didn't ask the Barleycorn King for details, but it became pretty obvious that the Big Screen footage and the way everyone took that out on the Tenties was just the start of some not-very-well-thought-through actions. I mean, it sounds good 'n' all: this isn't working out, why don't we shift you along to a reality that will fully appreciate you? But it's hardly in the spirit of things, is it? An alien race goes to all the bother of showing up, adapting themselves to looks reasonably like you, and then you just say, thanks, but no thanks, why don't you try the next reality along? Especially if the next reality along is also doing the same thing. And, as it turns out, they didn't even do that. Just kept them jumping around, perpetually Time Locked. Even shittier.

I'd intended to just go back to the water tower, but as it happens hunger is overtaking and I decide to chance the farm. If I'm right, then probably Judith and Ed are too old to be here, or possibly old enough not to care. I can always show them Eva if it comes down to it, though it won't be my first move. I've not forgotten the footage where she was running away from the shed.

I take a peek inside the polytunnels as I walk, just to be sure that this still is a farm and therefore a likely place to get some food. It all seems normal as, despite the distinct lack of people. I walk up to the house and as I knock on the door, there's a feeling that this is very ill-advised. Just a feeling, though of course anyone with common sense would listen to it. But then who am I to listen to reason? Apparently, I've cocked everything up with my unexpected bloody behaviour. I may as well keep right on going.

CHAPTER TWENTY-TWO

Green Jay

THE GREENHOUSE IS as beautiful as I remember it. Even better, if I am honest, because someone has spent time bringing furniture up here and cleaning. Making things polished and shiny the way they never were while I lived here. There are shelves of books and a chair to read in. Even a bed. None of this was here for me. Though strangely, I wish there was no bed, that I could lie on the floor with Blue Jay.

I go and stand by the window. The view is not so different. The big screen is not there, but otherwise Barlewin seems as it always did. If I stand on my toes and stretch, I can see part of the High Track. It doesn't look remarkable either, though I notice something glinting in the light with lots of coloured ribbons twined around the rail and fluttering in the wind. But there is no-one there.

I'm exhausted now. I find the spot on the floor that Blue Jay and I used, and I lie down. There's a rug there now, so it's softer than before, more comfortable, although I feel less like a lizard than I want to. But I am overcome by a happiness all out of proportion to my circumstances. I drift quickly into half-sleep. I think about what it would be like if I really was the woman in the graffitied picture. Someone with swirls of colour on their skin. Someone whose hair rides up patterned and beautiful. I wonder if that is who I could become. A green goddess. Someone who could control their life.

There is a knock on the door and I realise that it is not the first time I have heard it. I let myself drift up, but before I can open the door, I hear it creak open softly and hear footsteps coming into the room. I should be more worried than I am, but I sit up, open my eyes, look to see who this could be. There are two people, both young: a man and a woman. They look as if they want to rush towards me, but they don't move.

"Oh, we are so sorry," says the woman.

"We'll go," says the man.

"Why did you knock?" I ask.

"We thought it was close. And we were right! But there's no need to stay now."

"Unless… you need anything?"

"What did you think was close?"

"The time. When you arrived."

I shake my head; they make no sense. "I used to live here," I say, "but it wasn't like this."

"Oh," says the man. "We know." Both of them have

moved forward now. They would rush in and hug me if they could, I think, but something holds them back, and for now I am glad of it.

"We knew that you would come," says the woman.

"Sit down and tell me," I ask. They find floor cushions and sit on them. The woman offers one to me and I take it.

"I'm Lona," she tells me.

"And Kolb," says the man.

"Eva," I say.

"Green Jay," they echo. I try to hide the tears on my cheeks. I can see them trying not to notice, though I think they are too shy to say anything. Instead, they tell my story. And even as they begin, I don't know if it can come true. I feel as if they are talking about someone who is not me. A life that cannot be mine. Parts of it are echoes of the Crow's strange fairytale. But that is their part. What makes me fear and hope and wonder are the parts that are mine.

Crow

I'M SITTING AT the dining table, which I remember well, drinking coffee, eating food, so all's good except that the two other people sitting with me are as different from Judith and Ed as you could possibly get. Come to think of it, the food is just sandwiches, and not exactly the high care, excellent-quality stuff that Judith always served, but then it fills me up and who am I to complain?

But the more important thing is the identity of the two men sitting here with me. They opened the door, greeted me, totally friendly, almost as if they'd been expecting me. There's something familiar about them, but there's also something I don't like. Can't put my finger on it. Perhaps it's the lingering weirdness of the Barleycorn King and the betrayal of the Chemical Conjurers, but I'm not sure about these two.

"How long've you lived here?" I ask.

"Not that long," says one of them, the older one, with a scar across his forehead. There's been no names given as yet.

"Stayed here once," I say. "Really nice people. Judith and Ed." Which is a bit lame as a conversational opener, but I'm claiming dibs if I possibly can.

The other man grins. His hair's getting to that length where it starts to get annoying and he keeps trying to get it out of his eyes. "Yeah, we met them," he says. We're all eating, which, of course, is a good thing, but on the other hand there's nothing like eating to evade a full answer.

There's silence. There's something about these two that's really off-putting, difficult to watch. But I make myself observe them. There's something here I need to know.

The younger one starts to make a noise that I can only describe as a suppressed giggle. "Shall we tell him?" he asks.

The older one's smiling too. He says, "You've not given us your name."

"Kern Bromley," I say. "Most everyone calls me Brom."

"Yeah, me too," says Scar and then they both drop the pretence and start laughing out loud. Which is disconcerting, to say the least.

And then, I get it. Not that it's much of a joke. They don't have to explain. And yes, I'm unbelievably slow. I am living the nightmare. I have met myself. *Two* bloody selves. "What the fuck," I say. Because no other comment will suffice.

"Yeah, Brom, you know it," says Hair. "Though actually, I'm probably less like you than you think."

"Whereas I …" Scar holds up his hands and gives me a half grin half grimace of apology.

"So you're telling me I've got to come back here and do this shit again?" I say.

"Maybe," says Hair.

"Maybe not," says Scar.

"It gets complicated," Hair continues.

"Better not to think about it," suggests Scar. A sentiment I can support.

We sit without talking for a while longer, finishing off our food. I'm trying to process the revelation and I'm trying to check them out. Scar is older than me, decades older, so I can forgive myself for not recognising him. And, in a sense, it's comforting to know that I'm going to survive at least that far. Hair is older too, but not by that much. Yes, he's got a different hairstyle, but there's something not quite right, something about the face that don't seem to belong to me.

"We don't look that much alike," I say to him.

Hair shrugs. "Whatever you say."

"Completely different upbringing," says Scar. Whatever that's meant to mean.

We both take a good long look at each other. And then, pretty much at the same time, we both decide to let it go. I mean, what are we going to do? Argue about who is the most authentic version?

"The thing is," says Scar. "You could be me, back in the dim dark past, but you're not the past him. On the other hand, we could be three entirely different people."

"Well, different realities," says Hair.

Scar shrugs. "I am you and you are me and we are none of us," he says. That's all very well for the old me to say, but it still don't make a lot of sense.

"Has anyone found the Tenties?" I ask.

They both look at me curiously, but don't reply.

"Because I'm thinking maybe I could go back, change things," I continue. A confession that surprises even me.

"Don't think you can do that," says Hair. He drains the bottom of his mug, then goes into the kitchen, looking for more coffee.

"Barleycorn King? That man knows shit," says Scar. "Why do you think he's become so crazy, trying to muck around with timelines and crap like that? Don't work."

"But he's Guerra, right?"

"Korbin, Barleycorn King, Fool on the Hill," says Scar.

"Fool on the High Track," calls out Hair from the kitchen.

It's hard not to laugh at your own bad jokes, and, quite frankly, none of us is making much of an effort to restrain ourselves.

"So you got any wisdom from the future?" I ask after we all settle down.

"What do you think?" asks Scar.

"I think you're about to say no, but there must be something," I say.

"Nothing you want to know," says Hair.

This is going nowhere.

"Disappointments, surprises, but there's no point trying to pre-experience it," says Scar.

"And, in any case," says Hair as he sits back at the table, "how do we know that, one, you're going to get the same future as we already got; and two, if we tell you to make different choices, it won't work out even worse?"

"Even worse," I repeat.

"Without as much felicity," says Scar.

"We're still here," says Hair. "That's the best we can offer."

"Thanks," I say.

"Our pleasure."

"More coffee?" asks Hair. Which seems to me the best thing he's had to say in a while.

Scar leans forward. And, for the first time, he looks serious. "Just don't get caught in the time nets," he says. His voice is quiet. And he gives a small shake of his head as soon as he finishes speaking.

"You get a sense after a while," says Hair. "Places not to go. A feeling for borders. A feeling not to go in and explore."

He's talking shit and we all know it, but we tacitly agree to allow him this bit of philosophical cant.

"There was this one place," he continues. "All I could see was birds. Big black things. Creepy."

"Yeah," says Scar. "But not as bad as the place where the graffiti came alive, embedded with some surveillance shit."

And they're off. Talking about all the Barlewins they've seen; all the weird and wonderful realities they've experienced. Which is interesting and all, but all I really want to do is get myself back to the Barlewin I know, complete with Tenties, complete even with Guerra if he insists. All I want is a bit of normality.

CHAPTER TWENTY-THREE

Green Jay

KOLB DOES MOST of the talking, but Lona is happy to interrupt and clarify things if I look confused. Or sometimes, I think, because she feels he has not explained well. Not everything they say makes sense, but I don't ask questions. I am content just to listen.

As I watch them, I realise they are not completely human. There is something about their skin which is like mine, though the tinge of green is very slight. They are, if I understand them properly, something like my descendants. Something like, but also something new. A new kind of plant people. Humants, the Crow said, though they don't use this word. And not truly male and female either, though Kolb is more male and Lona is more female. At least, it seems that way to me.

"Because of you," finishes Kolb. "Because of your

courage."

"But also because people felt so bad about the Trocarn. When they left. And there was a little of them in you and so something of them stayed behind. A legacy."

"What happened to the Trocarn?" I ask.

Kolb and Lona are quiet. "I forgot that you would not know," says Kolb.

"They... they were sent away. People felt..."

"There was a lot of anger," says Kolb. "People felt invaded, and they... They were an easy target."

"It was not their fault," says Lona.

"What do you mean, they were sent away?"

"They were Time Locked," says Lona. I can see her forcing herself to say it.

"Forever?" I ask. Time Locked does not mean sent away, it means banished.

"Oh, no," says Kolb. "They have found another place now."

"They found a way to adapt. People hoped they might."

"How do you know that?" I ask. "How do you know they have found a place?"

"They were monitored," says Kolb.

"So do you know where they are?"

"No," says Lona. "Not exactly another place; another *way*, another way to be."

"But it's better," says Kolb. "Better that they are safe."

"But you don't know that," I say. I am so loud that I shock them. I think of all the care T-Lily gave to me and the way Rose-Q released a screen to hide me from Guerra as I ran.

"They were too much," says Lona. "Too much for most people. Perhaps they are better off. Happier." She says this quietly, as if testing, but I can see it is her own belief. A strange belief for someone like her.

"And you?" I ask. "Are you too much? And me? What about me? Am I too much also? Should I prepare myself to be sent away?" I stand and walk away from them, because I don't want to see their puzzled faces that look at me with love, but would look at T-Lily with fear.

"You are honoured," says Lona.

I turn and close her off before she can say any more. "I would not be alive without them," I say. "In the beginning, in the early days, T-Lily would come here to this room and keep me whole. Keep me alive. And then, when I was with Guerra, it was Rose-Q who helped me escape. I have parts of them in me. That is the way that they work. But every human who was ever touched by them also has parts of the Trocarn inside them. It's impossible to send them away."

The two young ones are so quiet I feel ashamed. They cannot understand my anger.

"I never met the Trocarn," says Kolb.

I have forgotten. They are so young; they only know stories told by somebody else.

"Can they be found?" I ask.

Lona and Kolb move their hands, make small noises. They don't know what to say. I know I am asking too much of them, being unfair. But I cannot leave my friends in limbo. I need Blue Jay, and all I have is these two. All I have is the Crow.

* * *

Crow

HAIR'S TAKING ME down to the shed. Echoes of Ed here, but Hair's eager to show me something. I don't like to tell him I've already been inside the shed, discovered its multiple boxes and Ed's homemade protective gloves. In any case I've got nothing better to do, though I wouldn't mind following the example of Scar, who's stretched out on a couch having a kip.

"Does no-one live here?" I ask as we wander through the polytunnels.

"It's all automated," says Hair, though I get the feeling it's something he'd been told rather than any particular insight into the workings of the farm.

"What's the point of the shed, then?"

"Dunno," says Hair. "It's always here, though."

I don't much like the implications of that answer so I decide to delve no further. It's the kind of answer I'd give, though I'm still trying to weigh up the truth of Hair being an alternate me. A better-cared-for me, that's a possibility I guess. With a back history that involved more happy home time and less being out and about away from the fighting. But if they were the same parents, then less fighting means... What? An easier life, for all concerned. Mum not finding out about Dad's gambling ways? I give up. Too many possibilities and I'm not going to ask. Seems sorta like I should know, and also if I don't, then I probably shouldn't. And there's the possibility that I buggered my own life up, succumbed once too often to Guerra's offerings. Don't want to think that through at all.

Inside the shed's much as I remember it, though it has the air of being unused, vacant for a while. It's still as dark as, no modernisation of the lighting. In fact, no lighting at all, though the sun glinting through the cracks in the wall does its bit to help.

The shelf over by the wall has nothing on it at all: no boxes, not even remnants of boxes. I'm buggered if I know what it is Hair wanted to show me.

"It's cleared out," he says.

I shrug. "So?"

"So last time I saw it, there were at least four boxes here."

I'd shrug again, but I think my point's already been made.

"This stuff gives me the shits," he says. "But it's kind of like circles. Loops. Some things keep happening no matter what. Ed and Judith's daughter—that's Olwin Duilis, to you and me—goes mad scientist. Her double runs amuck and manages to stay alive with lots of help from various quarters. And Olwin, bless her, sends this bloody box, the contents of which will enable the double to live for longer, maybe become something new. Reasons for doing this are many and complicated. And Ed and Judith, being good people and loving parents, want to help but feel... let's say 'compromised.' 'Cause people keep turning up and boxes keep appearing and nothing seems to get sorted out. Especially as, understandably, the double wants to be herself, not a copy of somebody else. And of course you, or me, or one of us, gets tangled up in it somehow. And the poor bloody Tenties, but that's their own fault really."

"And Mac?" I ask.

Hair looks uncomfortable. "Mac's tangled up, yeah."

"But Mac knows what he's doing?"

"Yep," says Hair.

"So he'll get us out of this?"

"Maybe," says Hair. "The old one told you to stay out of the time nets, didn't he?"

"Yeah."

"'Cause there's nothing anybody can do if that happens."

"Where are Ed and Judith now?"

"Dunno," says Hair. "Maybe we're too far forward, this time around. Maybe it's all over and they've gone off and away."

"And they all lived happily ever after?"

"Yeah, maybe," says Hair. But neither of us believe that.

There's a knock on the door and Scar's standing there, looking bemused. "Thought you might want to see this," he says.

We walk out into the sunshine and I see straight away what he's talking about. There, by the water tower, under the faded bird graffiti, are three people: Eva and two others. They look a little like baby birds, although it's not clear if the water tower bird wants to feed them or eat them.

They're clearly waiting for us.

"They won't come closer," says Scar.

We walk towards the three. Eva's standing very still, and I wonder how she's holding up. She must be doing okay to have gone out and found herself these two, but it's possibly something she regrets.

"You've got retainers now," I say, when we're close enough for her to hear.

"As have you," she says.

"Eva, meet Brom," I say and the three of us bow. Understandably, that cracks us up a little, but she don't look amused.

"This can't be right," she says.

"Why not?" I ask.

"It should be impossible."

So should you, I think.

"You haven't introduced us," says Scar.

"Kolb," says one of them.

"Lona," says the other.

They both smile and bob their heads, but make no attempt to reach out a hand or come closer. They're pretty much peas in a pod. Same kind of clothes. A man and a woman, possibly, but I'm not totally sure.

"Humants," says Scar quietly. And then it all clicks. Eva's found some worshippers at her greenhouse. I liked mine better; these ones seem a bit too malleable.

"Will you come to the house?" asks Hair. "It's better than standing outside, and it's got to be better than the water tower." Eva gives me a look that manages to convey her displeasure that I've revealed our hidey hole.

But it's not *that* good a secret. "All of you," he says, obviously wanting to make sure Kolb and Lona know they're included.

"We only wanted to see Green Jay back safely," says Lona.

"You would be more comfortable in the house," suggests Hair.

Eva shakes her head. "What do you know about the Trocarn?" she asks my companions.

"They're gone," says Hair.

"There's nothing to be done," says Scar.

"It's your fault," says Eva.

"Why's that?" I say, because I can't help myself.

"How well are you?" Hair asks Eva.

And even I can see that she doesn't know how to answer that question. That perhaps she thinks she is not well at all.

"We will look after her," interjects Lona, and I can't see the two of them letting her run off on a doomed quest to save the Tenties.

"Yes, I'm sure you will," says Scar. "But she's not complete as yet, are you, Eva?"

"And whose fault is that?" she asks.

Yours, is what I want to say, but Scar keeps speaking before I have a chance. "You need to concentrate on getting yourself looked after," he reminds her.

"What do you think?" asks Eva. Everyone looks my way, and that's when I realise she's asking me.

"About the Tenties?"

I see Kolb and Lona visibly flinch, but no-one comments.

"I think," I continue, "Time Locking them was a shitty thing to do. But if they've found a way to get out of it, they're probably better off."

"And what if they haven't found a way?"

I spread my hands, because she's asking me to prove the unprovable. And anyway, if they are Time Locked, how the fuck would we find them?

"The lock was broken," Kolb insists.

"Have you ever seen them?" This time Eva's asking Scar and Hair.

Hair shakes his head. "No," says Scar, "but then, we're not likely to, are we?"

"What does that mean?" asks Eva.

"We're in your fucking reality," says Hair. If I can read anything into his tone—and God knows I ought to be able to—he's putting the blame squarely at Eva's feet.

Scar makes an attempt at peace. "So we won't find them, not while we're with you, but that don't mean they aren't there."

"Aren't you a little old to be still caught up in this?" asks Eva.

"You tell me," says Hair.

It's not so much the *old* comment that sinks in, but the fact that they're old and they're still here, farting around. Happy enough. But still.

"And why this world?" asks Lona. Which, after all, is the most pertinent question.

Scar shrugs. "Why not?"

Hair is silent, and I think about him showing me the empty shed. It's possible there's something else going on here. Who am I kidding? It's completely bloody obvious there's something going else going on, but I can't really be bothered figuring it out. What I want is a short cut home. And no-one here seems to have a way to help with that.

Eva takes a step forward. "Let me have the phone," she says.

"I don't want to be stuck here," I say.

"I just want to look for the Trocarn," she replies

"Then I'll come too," I say. And I can see that Eva had already figured I'd say that.

"Now," she says. And she gives me a look, that I might even interpret as *let's get away from these annoying sycophants and do something worthwhile for a change.*

I bring up the picture map on the phone and she grabs hold of my wrist and stabs at it as if she'd like to take a knife to someone. And straight away we're Time Locked together and the others fade away.

It's possible she looks happy. Deranged, but happy.

CHAPTER TWENTY-FOUR

Green Jay

I AM SURPRISED that the Crow was persuaded as easily as he was, though I suspect that the presence of his other selves was disconcerting enough to make him leave. He is of no help; his body can barely cope with the Time Lock. He has his eyes closed and is bent over slightly. So it is up to me to observe, to look at the realities we pass through for hints. It is like looking at a strange movie, with continuous frames of the same place, but where the camera captures slight differences every time. The difficulty will be to jump off when we have the chance.

I wonder if there is a better spot to be, a spot the Trocarn would be more likely to congregate. And I just don't know, but I think the marketplace will be better than here and so I start to walk, pulling the Crow with me. He mutters something—nothing polite, I don't suppose—but he moves and that is all that matters.

I like being the one who is strong, though even that won't last for much longer. Kolb and Lona have given me hope, but I could tell just by the way the other Crows looked at me that it will not be easy for me to survive. I suspect that there have been many times where I have died. And because of that, I must at least to try and find the Trocarn.

I have seen the Chemical Conjurers flicker up from time to time, and I am heading towards them. We will have to stop soon; the Crow will not be able to withstand this for long. But I make him walk the last few steps so that we're right in the middle of the marketplace. I keep one hand on his arm as I tap at the phone with the other and we're out of the Lock. The Crow doubles over and groans, no matter that we're surrounded by people. But no-one seems to be watching us. The Chemical Conjurers have, of course, noticed us; they beckon us over. I point them out to the Crow, but he shakes his head so I leave him. I am not going so far that he won't be able to find me, and I don't think he'll just up and leave.

They bend their bodies forward and then retract into themselves so that they are about my height. Their starred metal faces look closely at mine.

"How old are you?" asks one.

"Six weeks, perhaps eight. It was hard to tell when I was with Guerra."

The other lifts my arm and looks at the scar under my skin. "How many?"

"Only three," I say. "There wasn't time for more." The

Conjurer takes something and places it over the scar. I can feel its soothing coolness seep into me. For a second I wonder if they have also betrayed me, but there is no drug fog.

"Do you know anything about the Trocarn?" I ask. "Where they could be?" It seems rude to ask so soon, but the robots will not mind.

"We have been searching," says the other Conjurer. He is holding out his hand with its palm facing up. Right in the middle is one of Blue Jay's dragonflies. I put my palm out and it flies to me. I recognise the straight body, the delicate wings, the large eyes. It makes me miss Blue Jay; it makes me want to cry.

"Then you know where they are?"

"It would be safer not to follow," says the first Conjurer. But his voice seems far away and I see that they are lifting themselves back up to their normal height.

There is a loud *crack* and the dragonfly escapes from my hand and flies towards the Crow. I can hear people gasp and scream, but it is only the Chemical Conjurers and their tricks. There is something in the air, smoke, but I ignore it and focus only on the dragonfly. I run towards it, pushing through the people, not caring. And they are so scared they don't notice me, they don't make way for me as they usually might. The dragonfly has found the Crow. I am only a few steps away when I see its feet are on the phone. I have just enough time to grab onto his wrist before we are away.

*　　*　　*

Crow

THE BEST WAY of telling where I am is the graffiti. Depending on where Eva and the dragonfly drag me to, I take a look at the water tower. I take a look at the walls near the High Track. The less Eva/Olwin the better. I miss Ol' Stick Man, and I'd even settle for that mangy bird with the chicks, but you take what you can get. And what we can get in this reality is a picture of something that is undeniably Tentie. No sign of the actual beings around, even though the dragonfly appears to think it's done its job.

Personally I think I've accomplished sufficient Time Locked travel for one day and want to focus on getting something to eat. I'm hungry enough to risk waving my phone in the general direction of food and hoping it scans through. Failing that I'm hungry enough to try some other solutions, but I figure why not attempt a technological approach first?

The marketplace don't really seem to exist in this Barlewin, though there's a whole strip of shops lining the road. Bugger me if people don't ride around on souped-up bicycles. I've even seen a few cars. Well, bubbles on wheels, but it's a better car than I can lay claim to, so I can't be laughing too loud.

We approach a shop with the enticing name of *Amazing Grace Mini Mart*. I figure if they're true to their word, they'll forgive some transgression, technological or otherwise. Eva has refused to come with me, though I doubt she'll refuse to eat. Does she eat? I'm not completely up to date with the current state of her physiology.

The Amazing Grace Mini Mart is very bright inside, with aisles of packaged and canned food stuffs and cold stuff down the back. Same old. I grab a basket, casually pile some items into it and just as casually slip a few odds and ends into my pocket, just to be on the safe side. I grab a green-looking drink for Eva and a normal cola-type thing for me. Otherwise it's biscuits-and-cheese-type stuff. We've got no way of heating anything up. Though I do find a pre-prepared salad. It's old and wilted and probably still too healthy for my tastes, but I decide to make an effort, what with all this Time Locked travel shit.

I smile at the woman behind the counter. She's not seen a salad in a while, I'd guess, but she's a friendly sort with her hair piled up on top of her head. To counteract the heat, most probably.

"Hot today," I say.

"Hot every day," she says. "Rain'll cool things down. There's free slushies, if you want."

Now that takes me back. It's good to see some consistency over the realities. I wave the phone on my wrist in her general direction and it seems to work because she makes no comment and piles all of my goods in a not-quite-plastic bag. I decide to risk the slushie. "Can I take one for my friend?"

"Sure thing, hon," she says.

As everyone knows, it's hard to balance a bag of stuff and two slushies, but I manage. The heat of outside hits me hard after the cool gleam of the shop, but Eva's found a spot with a bit of grass. Just about the right distance away from the big screen, which has made a semi-miraculous re-appearance. Not that there's anything showing right now. Although there are other people out on the grass, and it's possible they're waiting for something to start. Which could be overly optimistic of them, considering the clouds building over in one corner of the sky.

I plonk myself down beside her. "Slushies!" I say, handing one to her.

She's less enthusiastic than I'd hoped; I don't suppose she has the same childhood memories as me. She presses the coolness of it against her face for a moment and then brings the cup down, looks at it and turns it slowly around.

"Or I got you this green drink. Look, I don't know what you want. Take your pick." I spread out my offerings on the grass. She's impossible to please.

"Brom, have you looked at the cups?" she asks.

Why would I do that? They're the same old slushie cups. Brightly coloured, probably not made out of quite the same earth-damaging plastic as they were in my childhood days, though it sure feels like it.

I take a good, long slurp as a reply of sorts, and then humour her by looking at the cup. There, on the side, and why the fuck didn't I notice it before, is a Tentie. A pretty unevolved Tentie, or at least very close to the way they looked when they first arrived: its tentacles are up and waving, its beak is out and proud, and the cup is designed in such a way that the Tentie's cloud is the colour of your slushie. It's quite disturbing, really, but that don't stop me from taking another slurp.

"At least we know they were here," I say. "Maybe still are."

"Have you seen anything like this before?" she asks. She's almost embarrassed. It's easy to forget that her experience of life only extends to a couple of months, and mostly fucked-up months at that.

"Haven't had a slushie since I was a kid," I say.

"So, last week, then," she says. It's almost a joke, and I'm slightly proud of her.

"Don't think there were any Tenties on the cups in our Barlewin," I say.

"It's not just Barlewin," she says. And she has a point there. It's not like anyone in Barlewin's making this kind of shit; it's not artisanal. It implies a whole-country involvement, probably a whole-planet involvement.

"We have to find them," she adds. I'm not sure whether she's talking to herself or to me.

I look around at the people gathered out here on the grass. It's just people, no Tenties, not even any slightly unpredictable robots. And no humants. At least not that I can see; but it's not like they advertise.

"We can't just wander around looking," I say.

"No," says Eva. "We need to go up to the High Track."

I take a particularly long, loud slurp. "Why?"

"Because that seems the obvious place," she says. She's not drinking her slushie, but she has started on her green drink. I've pretty much stuffed myself full of cheese and biscuits, but I could take more. The dragonfly's landed on top of the salad in a rather obvious let's-try-and-blend-in move.

"Do you want it?" I ask, nodding at her slushie. She hands it to me with an air of complete distraction. "If we're going to go, we need to go before it rains," I say, more to show willing than anything else. There's no way I think going up to the High Track is a sensible idea.

Eva finishes her drink and gathers up all her rubbish and puts it the Amazing Grace Mini Mart bag. It's getting dark fast, and quite frankly, we need to go somewhere that will keep us dry. And that's not the High Track. Most people around us are making a move, packing up their stuff, getting back to the safety of home.

"Come on," says Eva.

But almost as she speaks, there's a loud crack of thunder and huge drops of rain are falling. We run, both of us deciding that under the water tower is the safest bet.

But then someone pulls at my arm. "It's not safe."

The man's wearing a tentacle T-shirt and orange sunnies. I'd be inclined to ignore his advice, but the evidence is right in front of me: the water tower's a mess. It's still standing, but one side looks as if someone unexpectedly set off a reasonably devastating homemade bomb. The roof is very obviously sinking in. The only option now seems to be the underneath of the High Track, far too close to Eva's obsession for my liking, but still, beggars and all that. We change direction mid-stride.

Our new friend sticks with us. We're under the High Track's protection, but we're all fucking wet and I can see him giving Eva the eye. I don't exactly blame him, but I don't exactly care for it either; especially as she's not looking so good. Time Locked travel is one thing, but running in the rain appears to be another. She leans against one of the posts and closes her eyes. The dragonfly's in her hair and the man sees it and stretches out his hand to touch it. So, of course, I knock the hand away and then it's on for young and old.

CHAPTER TWENTY-FIVE

Green Jay

THE NAME OF the man wearing the Tentacle T-shirt is Reen. Which makes the Crow laugh, even though he probably shouldn't, because he's sitting on the ground gasping for breath. Which is entirely his fault. It's all been explained, everyone has apologised, but I can see the Crow would do it all again given even the smallest of chances. Right now he seems mostly upset that his drink is ruined, though how he could have expected it to last through the rain I don't know.

I ask Reen about his T-shirt, partly to make up for the Crow's behaviour but mostly to see if there's anything we can learn about the Trocarn. Reen is sitting down too, not breathing quite as hard as the Crow. "Oh," he says, "I'm a supporter, you know. Do what I can."

"A supporter of what?" asks the Crow, which is a

question I would also like to ask, although I would have taken a different approach.

"You know, of the Trocarn. We miss them around here, would like to get them back."

"And that's a sentiment shared by the majority of people?" asks the Crow.

"You know, you look familiar." Reen is talking to me, ignoring the Crow, which is usually wise. "But you're not from around here, are you?"

"No," I say. And that is as true as it can be. Of course, it is possible that there is someone *like* me here. Having met the other versions of the Crow, I know it is possible. But the fact that the dragonfly led us here makes me think that I have never existed in this world. We've not seen any green goddess graffiti, though we've not really been here long enough to explore properly.

"You'll have to do better than that," says the Crow. He's teasing Reen, of course, but I realise he's partly spoken to break the silence.

"I'm sorry," I say. "I'm a little tired." I wish that T-Lily was here, even Rose-Q, but these are not thoughts I should hold on to.

"You look like you need a place to stay," says Reen.

"No, we're fine, just didn't expect it to rain," says the Crow before I have a chance to speak. He is right, of course. We cannot go with this man.

"Won't last for much longer," says Reen. I hope he is right, though the rain truly shows no sign of letting up. It's impossible to see out to the marketplace, because of the water sheeting down from the edges of the High Track.

"Take us to see them," I say. The words are out of my mouth before I can stop them.

Reen and the Crow both stare at me.

"Take us to see the Trocarn," I ask.

"No," says the Crow, but Reen agrees at the same moment and the Crow has no choice but to follow.

Crow

AS IT TURNS out, all of Reen's talk was so much shit. We're doing nothing we couldn't have done ourselves and, quite frankly, exactly what we were just about to do: that is, climbing staircase number 3. The only difference is that we now have his dubious company. Given the similarities to his other-reality namesake I feel like I should be running in the other direction. Reen, Carine... a friendlier approach does not mean we really had a choice.

Nevertheless, we're trudging up the metal rungs, sending drops of water flying and of course, me being the final party, I'm getting my jeans wet all over again. Eva appears to be handling the stairs just fine; I'm not completely convinced her fainting spells aren't largely attention-seeking. Or this one seems to have been, anyway. The clouds have gone, but by now it's evening so it's still dark. The High Track's lit up in a softly glowing fairy-light kind of way that don't do much for visibility on the stairs.

"Mind the puddle," says Reen at the top of the staircase. Eva politely steps around, but I stomp right into it to splash him. Which is just plain childish, but there you have it.

Then, unexpectedly, we turn to the right, away from admin—or where admin would be if we were in our true and rightful place—and walk towards the place I'd had the talk with the Barleycorn King and Eila. Of course, there's no sign of them. In fact, there's no sign of anyone, though admittedly it's only just stopped raining.

"Happy now?" I say to Eva.

"Look around, Brom, it's beautiful," she says.

She's right, of course, though I'm in no mood. We walk in silence through the High Track. They've got some of that tickly grass here. Which reminds me again of the Barleycorn King. I don't know why I'm so anxious to see him.

We reach a part of the High Track I've never been. At this rate I'll have made the complete circuit, albeit in different realities. That's disappointingly touristy of me. I'm half expecting a convenient bench, but Reen stops, as far as I can see, in the middle of nowhere. He grabs Eva's hand and she lets him hold it.

"It takes a while," he says. "You need to let you eyes adjust, watch until you see it."

There's not much light in this part of the High Track, so for a while we're standing in the near-dark looking at, well, nothing. The rest of the city stretches out. Lights have come on, but there's still enough daylight to make out shapes. The sky's that deep blue colour that makes me a wistful fool. A fool who could almost believe this could turn out alright.

"Oh," gasps Eva, and I'm glad to see she's taken her hand out of Reen's grasp.

And then I see it too.

It's a shimmer in the air, nothing more. It looks like a dome at first, and then inside there are shapes. Some moving around, some still. Shapes of what, I can't say. Some creature, some obviously living creature, but the name of such a creature does not immediately come to mind. Not even the Tenties look like this.

"This is the Trocarn," says Reen.

"What have they become?" asks Eva.

"They've adapted."

"So they're still Time Locked here?" I ask. Just to clarify, because that's sure not the message Eva's friends Kolb and Lona were spinning.

Reen remains silent.

"That's all of them?" I ask, 'cause I'd like to get some information out of him.

"No," says Reen. "Of course not, just the Trocarn from this area. But we believe they are able to fuse their bodies as well as adapt them. So the exact number of individual Trocarn may be different."

"That's true," says Eva. "That's how they travelled here."

I can't tell if she's okay with this or not. Right now she seems to be marvelling. But I'd thought the whole point was to get them out of this mess, not observe them in it.

"Are they happy?" she asks.

"We believe so," says Reen.

"How the fuck can you know that?" I say.

"Observation," says Reen. "Although of course we would like them back."

"And what would *they* like?"

"We can't know that," says Reen.

"Exactly," I say.

"Is it possible to release them?" asks Eva. "Whoever set this up must know how to stop it."

Reen sets forth on a spiel about agreements and decisions and difficulties which I cease to listen to after about three seconds.

It's darker now and you'd think the Tenties would be harder to see, but they're not. Maybe I'm just getting used to the whole thing, but they seem to be *glowing*. Eva takes a few steps towards them, but Reen pulls her back, which is educational to say the least.

"Be careful," he says. "You don't want to be caught."

"So you could just walk in?" I say. "Ask them how they're doing yourself?"

"In theory," says Reen. "Although the timing would have to be perfect."

I can see that Eva would like to run and jump, but Reen's keeping a steady grip on her arm. She's not resisting, which is possibly a good thing, but I'm not sure that I like the way this is panning out.

"And of course, says Reen, "you'd be stuck too. And without the protection the Trocarn have. It would be excruciating for a human. Too long and you'd die."

It's possible the fact that Eva is not entirely human has eluded him. At least she has the sense to keep quiet about it. And it seems that Reen, tentacle T-shirt or no, is getting bored.

"Do you need somewhere to stay?" he asks again. "I mean, you're new to Barlewin."

"No," I say, "we're good." Unfortunately at the same time as I'm brushing him off, Eva is saying yes, that would be wonderful.

"I know a decent place," says Reen.

And before I can protest, he and Eva are walking away from the poor Time Locked Tenties and further up into the better-lit sections of the High Track. I watch them for a moment, then bow to the inevitable and say a mental goodbye to the beings in the dome. At least, I figure, we know where they are.

It's possible Reen is leading us up the garden path in more ways than one, but probably not. It don't seem his style. And to be fair, Eva probably does need to rest. I can see what looks like a staircase up ahead: the elusive staircase number 1. My thoughts turn to food. Perhaps this place Reen knows has something better than biscuits and cheese; they were good and all, but they only really amounted to a pre-dinner snack. The night has cooled to the point where I could even contemplate hot food. And a bath. Clean clothes would be nice. Or at least dry ones. I'm deep in my fantasy of warm and dry when a body rushes past me. Eva. The surprise stops my brain for a moment.

"No," says Reen, but we both know that's a futile gesture. And we both know where she's headed and what she's about to do.

"Now's your chance to find out just how happy they are," I tell him.

He looks at me as if I'm mad and I half expect him to grab me and stop me following her. But it seems he don't really care what choices I make. And then we're both off running. Reen, presumably, to stop Eva. Me too, I think. I'm running like a mad man; I can feel my various aches and pains announcing themselves with every step.

Reen is ahead of me. He's close to Eva. He reaches out a hand, touches her, but she moves away from him. But it's a sideways move, not into the Tenties' dome, so I guess he's stopped her after all. Reen bends over a little to catch his breath, but he's still got an eye on Eva. She don't move. She's looking at me. I'm still running, but I'm truly buggered, so I slow and walk the last few steps, largely concentrating on not sounding like some kind of steam-powered elephant in its dying moments.

"Coming?" she asks. Which, after all, is the question I knew she was waiting to ask.

And we step into the dome together.

CHAPTER TWENTY-SIX

Green Jay

As SOON AS we step through the dome, we are surrounded by the Trocarn. They are very different in this form, but I do not mind if they envelope me. They are like the memories of the Trocarn I knew: T-Lily, Rose-Q and the ones who tended to me in the early days, ones whose name I have forgotten, or did not think to ask. I can see the Crow beside me. Poor Brom, it was brave of him to follow. He will not want the Trocarn to touch him, but he must allow it if he is to survive. I think he knows that. But he does not appear to be enjoying himself. His face amuses me.

No-one has spoken yet. Their bodies are not made for speech any more. They are fluid and flowing, more like vines than anything else. Although they are not just plants, they are animal as well. I feel emotions as they embrace me, emotions I suppose they wish to transfer to me to convey their state of mind. It would be easy to drift here, locked into a chemical oblivion. I see that the Crow has closed his eyes, and it occurs to me that we may never leave. I close my eyes and let myself drift for a while. It is good to feel so refreshed. Untangled. Whole. It is good to stop running.

But I force myself awake before I float away completely. I cannot succumb. I feel my hair and the dragonfly is still there. I wonder if the Chemical Conjurers are monitoring it, if they know what we have done. It may be that our only hope is that they pull us out of here. Or that Blue Jay finds us. Blue Jay seems a long way away now. Too far, too distant.

I have a question. If the Trocarn can travel through space, surely they can get out of Time Lock? I wonder how long it has taken them to achieve this form, why they have chosen to adapt rather than escape. Why they have chosen to surrender. There is no way to ask. Or perhaps there is and I do not know it. If I allow it, I am sure they will make me more like them. I could ask my questions, mesh with them, learn their answers and their reasons. I would be so far from Olwin Duilis that she would be no threat to me anymore. But I would also lose myself.

There are moments when the world outside lights up. Perhaps it is the time nets searching for us, perhaps just different lighting. But the world outside is blurry, hardly there. We are inside a strange, alien cave. The pull of the Trocarn is too strong, and I sink into it once again. I am so glad to have found them and I hope they can feel it in my skin.

* * *

Crow

SHIT, BUT THIS is good. I was weirded out at first, too slow to stop the tendrils finding me. Too half-hearted when I tried to tear them off. Because the thing is, once you're settled in, you're doing fine. There's no nausea, no sense of tangling with the universe and losing. It's all just fine. Which is dangerous shit, and I should know, but that don't stop me from melting in. The real me would not want the Tenties wrapped around me. I mean, I never let them touch me even when they looked vaguely human. But it's too late now. They've got me. Not even sure how long we've been here.

Not that I should be complaining. Whatever stupid impulse made me jump into the dome with Eva, I regretted almost before I was completely in. You'd think I would know enough about this Time Locked shit to not voluntarily put myself through this. It's just that that Reen bloke was so annoying. And after all, this is what we came for. Save the Tenties and all. Though it appears very much as if they didn't particularly need saving, thank you very much.

Eva's a little way away. I can still see her, but I can't touch her. She seems to be drifting too, and I can't say as I blame her. She's used to the Tenties, after all. She pretty much needs whatever it is they're pumping into us. It's a shame not to be able to talk to them. Scrap that: it's a pleasure not to be able to talk. And though I'm well aware it would be wrong to drift along like this for too long, it's nothing if not pleasant.

I feel a scratch on my wrist. The dragonfly has detached itself from Eva's hair and flown over. A reminder to wake up, I'm guessing. It puts two dainty feet on my phone, wakes that up too. Not quite sure who it wants me to contact, or what it wants me to say. Perhaps it's trying to tell me to get out of there. I'm going to be very pissed off if it activates a shift back out of Time Lock, leaving me on the cold outside and Eva in here with the Tenties. I brush it away, and it humours me slightly by sitting on the back of my hand. Thing is, I don't want to hurt it. It's as if it was alive, which of course it's not. Just a tiny machine sent to both save and annoy.

The outside world is indistinct, to say the least. Every now and then, there's something bright. Too bright, I'm thinking, but whatever it is, and it's probably the time nets, it don't seem to be able to get inside the dome. So it's safe and snug here, and impossibly floaty, except that the bloody dragonfly is scratching at my hand again, preventing me from drifting off. Just what I need, an insect sponsor, but it's right. I can't stay too long in Tentie land. Though they're not really Tenties any more, more like vines. Friendly triffids. I'm not completely sure where one vine stops and another begins. Maybe they're all joined.

The thought that I'm up here on the High Track, passing, albeit briefly, though the land of the Barleycorn King and the prophets and whoever else likes to hang around up here, makes me smile. I wonder if anyone walks through us by mistake. Though of course that's impossible, seeing as we're not really here. The mind-boggly shit starts again. Best to abandon that train of thought.

I think about a way to get over to Eva. By the look of her, she's sure as hell not coming to me. It's not that far, just far enough that I can't stretch out and give her a kick. I try unwinding myself from the tendrils, but that's about as effective as telling the dragonfly to piss off. And so I lurch myself into the middle of them all, as if I was wading through a particularly nasty river. It's slow going—incredibly slow going, considering she's not that far away—but finally I'm close enough to be able to touch her.

I stop. I let her be. She's happy.

But unless we want to live out our lives in here, we're going to have to go. And I'm damned if I'm going looking for Eva all over again just because she exited Tentie land at a different time to me. That, and Mac would never forgive me. I hope to hell he's tucked away safely with Guerra, if such a thing can be contemplated, and not trying out his own schemes to find us. Because, as mean as Guerra can be, Mac is probably better off just staying put. Acting as a kind of hostage. I can't see Guerra doing too much damage. Though who am I kidding? Guerra's more than capable of getting someone else to kick the shit out of you. He usually has the sense to only do it when he thinks it'll do some long-term good, but that's about all the restraint he's got. It's the notion of the Barleycorn King that's got me all sentimental. And I don't know why. He's the one that threw me down the stairs.

The thought occurs to check my phone, and perhaps

that's what the dragonfly was trying to tell me all along. Because there's a message. No name. Which could mean anything. Could even mean Eila. I tap on the screen to open it. It's Mac: *Olwin here. Eva safe?* There's more, but a tendril curls around my wrist. Either the Tenties are trying to read my message or they're just being particularly friendly.

The Tenties are more than just a tangle of vines now. Shapes appear. Almost human shapes sometimes. I give them time because they're probably trying to communicate, but I wish they'd hurry up. It takes a while before they coalesce into something that resembles human. In fact I'm reminded of Kolb and Lona, though that could be the green tinge more than anything else.

I seem to have been released from the tendrils. And, at least for the moment, I feel just fine. I deliberately don't want to think about what they've pumped into me. Eva is released too, although she looks less than completely alert. To be honest, she looks as if she is dreaming.

"You have brought us Green Jay," the shapes say, the both of them together. Which is disconcerting, but then not so long ago I was hoping they would speak.

"We were worried," I say. Which is about as lame a reply as you can get. How to articulate the fact that the Tenties' predicament is quite possibly all my fault and that while I probably can't do anything about it I feel the need to try? That, and let's be honest, I'm a victim of my own poor impulse control.

"This is the best place for her," they say.

"I think she'd like to return," I tell them. Because for

all this Sleeping-Beauty thing they've got going on, the princess was, after all, waiting for the kiss.

"She won't survive," they say.

"You sure about that?" I ask. Because, unlike the Tenties, I've had the privilege of seeing her museum greenhouse and her acolytes and, let's face it, a mountain of graffiti that looks just like her.

"Olwin Duilis wants her returned."

"Yes, I know, Guerra too, but the fact is, *she* wants to go back. Eva. Green Jay, or whatever you call her."

"It is not going to work," they say. "Not for her."

"You can't keep her here forever," I say. "I mean it's impressive and all that you're living in permanent Time Lock, but don't you want to get out?"

"We were not wanted."

It's way beyond my abilities to articulate the capacity of the human race to get rid of the very things they should have kept. Let alone the tendency for the milder humans to let the fuckers get away with a wide variety of crap. "That's not true," I say. "There's people out there with pictures of you on T-shirts, drinking out of cups with tentacles. They want you back. You'd be like rock stars if you came back." Which, once again, is supremely lame. Do Tenties even know what rock stars are? But I never asked to be a diplomat. Though perhaps, to be fair, I cast myself in the role when I jumped into the dome.

There's a great silence, which I, as usual, feel the need to fill up. "Perhaps one of you could come with us. Just one. See what it's like. Take the lay of the land. Scout it out." There's a tendril around my wrist and I know it means *shut up*, so I do. And we wait. It's very peaceful. Very floaty.

Very fucking boring.

CHAPTER TWENTY-SEVEN

Green Jay

I KNOW THAT what I'm seeing is a dream. I know, but it seems so very real. Kolb and Lona—only it is not them—are taking me, showing me different places. It is always Barlewin. I can never escape Barlewin. They show me my greenhouse, they show me the High Track. They take me on a walk through the marketplace. We watch the big screen. And always there are people like me. People like them. That is, not people, not completely; part person, part plant, part Trocarn. Because, and I did not realise this before, Kolb and Lona have more of the Trocarn in them than I first thought. And I understand, though I remember it is a dream, that this is true outside of this dome.

We walk through the crowds and we are unremarkable. There is no flinching away if we touch someone by mistake, no making room so there is no chance of contact. It is wonderful, but it makes me want to cry. They are showing me this to comfort me. Comfort me for what? What has happened that is filling me with sadness?

The person I long for is Blue Jay. I try to tell them, in this dream. But he is never there, wherever we go.

And at last they take me to the farm. I do not want to go, but I know I must. And there is part of me that wants to look, the way you want to look at something decaying and old. You want to face it in all its awfulness.

We walk under the water tower. The opening at the bottom is closed and the ladder looks crumbly and unsafe. I want to climb in, look around for Blue Jay, but we keep walking. We are in the gardens now. There are no plastic covers the way there were last time. Instead the plants grow green and free. There are people in the house; I see them through the windows, but they do not come out to us and we do not knock at their door. Instead we continue to the shed.

I do not want to go. I pull at Lona's arm. I plead with Kolb.

"You must," they say.

"But I've already looked," I tell them. And it is true, though I can't remember when or why.

"Do you remember?"

No, of course not. But I cannot say that. My feet keep walking even though the rest of me wants to turn, wants to run. My head is full of fizzing and I want to stop, but I know that I must. I must.

We are at the door. Lona opens it and Kolb goes

in. Lona smiles. She knows I am scared; she is gentle, understanding. But terrible. She holds the door open for me. She insists.

I walk in. It is not so awful. Just a shed. Dim and dark, hard to see clearly, but there is nothing here to terrify. It smells of the earth and of must. A few of Olwin Duilis' memories bubble up, but I let them free, they cannot trouble me here, in the dream. I see tools and containers. Everything is neat and orderly. And Kolb. He is at the end of the shed. Not far, but so far away. By the bench.

There is something on the bench. A body. Mine. Of course. I am so calm. So calm as I walk. I see my hair, fuzzy, unkempt, falling out in patches. My eyes are closed but my mouth is open. There is no red on my lips. My skin is a greying green. There are places where it has fallen away, where it is bruised and wrong. I see the faint marks of the cut that Blue Jay made in my skin, on the underside of my left arm. It has healed. It was made a long time ago. Too long.

I do not run. I look and look and look and make myself understand. I cannot survive. However long I manage to live, it will come to this. There is no Blue Jay.

"There is us," says Lona.

And I don't know if that's enough.

Crow

THE DRAGONFLY BUZZES at my wrist. I've been trying to look outside, mostly 'cause I'm completely bored with what's happening inside. Kolb, Lona and I have come to a stalemate. In that they're not speaking, and my diplomatic prowess, crap under the best of circumstances, is all used up. I notice there are tears on Eva's cheeks. So the Tentie drug heaven possibly has a downside. Which is good to know.

"You need to let her wake up," I say. "You need to at least let her decide for herself."

"There is something we need to show her," they say.

So now they're claiming to be inside her mind, which, impressive as this Time Locked dome is, is a bit of a stretch.

"It won't be long, Brom." This comes, not from Kolb and Lona, who I notice are gradually beginning to lose their shape, but from another voice off to the side. It's disconcertingly familiar, though I can't quite place it.

"T-Lily," she says.

"Of course. Hi." And I recognise her now.

T-Lily performs that Tentie smile which is so disconcerting, with the beak and all.

"You're coming with?" I ask.

"Yes, Brom."

"Good," I say. Which is true. This is, after all, what I asked for.

"And Eva?"

"It is up to her." Which I hope means T-Lily is a little more flexible than Kolb and Lona, but is not exactly a 'yes.'

There's a flash of light outside, the brightest I've ever seen, eye-hurting bright. "Will this hold?" I ask T-Lily.

But I see she's already joined herself to Eva and me. There's a scrap of tendril around my wrist like a bracelet. I want to flick it away, but T-lily's holding my other arm. The tendril seems particularly persistent. I'd really like to get rid of it, but I don't have time. T-Lily's walking us swiftly through the dome. She'd be running if Eva wasn't so out of it.

The tendrils and other assorted shapes fall away from us, until we're right on the edge of the dome. The outside world is still no clearer, but I can see a shimmer in the air like heat haze. T-Lily stops, and gathers Eva even more tightly to her. She's still hanging on to my arm, but it seems pretty obvious who's going to get the bulk of attention if any difficulties arise.

"Ready, Brom?" she asks.

"Yeah—" I begin, but T-Lily's obviously taken it as a given because we're already stepping through the dome into the outside world. This time it hurts. It can't take more than a fraction of a second, but it feels as if I'm being torn in two. Slowly. The outside world is bright, like artificial lights.

I hear T-Lily say something, but I don't know what it is. I can see she's released a cloud of murky green, a colour I've never seen before.

We're right on the edge of the High Track, almost up against the railing, and I see that there are metal locks on the edge here, too. For all the good they did. There's a flash of something and I feel T-Lily pull at me. She's trying to get us away and into the dark, but the lights have found us and they're not letting us go. This is worse than coming out of the dome. Needles of pain shoot through my whole body, as if the light had found my nervous system and had decided to examine the limits of its resistance. I want to ask T-Lily if this is it, if we're caught, but she shakes her head. And despite it all I still find the movement of her tentacles slightly creepy.

We can walk. I'm not sure that this is anything more than the movement of dying fish in the net, but we're walking anyway. T-Lily's dragged us to the railing, and she has to let me go to climb up and over. I help her with Eva. T-Lily stands on the outside ledge between the railing and the very edge of the High Track. It's just big enough. She's holding Eva in her arms now. She turns, to tell me something, or to see if I'm going to follow, but then the light gets stronger and I feel a booming. *Feel* rather than *hear*, as if my body and my feet know it. My internal organs.

T-Lily jumps. I scramble over the railing, I rest my feet on the ledge, still with one hand on the rails. There's no point looking down. There's nowhere else to go. So I jump too.

I'M REASONABLY SURE I blacked out for a while, and, to be frank, that was a better state than the one I'm in now. The High Track's only a few stories high and, if anything, I should probably have smashed into the ground long ago. Instead, my spine is on fire, there are barbs of pain up and down my arms and leg, and the tendril on my wrist is digging into my skin. There's no doubt that a time net is trying to pull me up; what I'd like to know is what's trying to pull me down. Oh, yes. Gravity. I look at the tendril. Either the Tenties have turned nasty or it's trying to do something helpful to my body. God knows what. If it's a choice between death and being turned into a Tentie, I'm not sure which I'd choose.

Who am I kidding? I'd choose survival any time. But God I hope it don't have to come to that. I dig at the tendril to see if I can persuade it not to dig into me. It winds its way around the tip of my finger. It's still attached to my wrist, and I can see the skin is red and raw. Shit. I think about all the Tentie-lovers way back when they first showed up. The way their skin became scaly and itchy. The way we all laughed at them. And now it's me.

A blast of pain lances through me. I hear a scream and I know it's me, but my brain's processing it as someone else. Someone who should have known better and now has no fucking idea what to do. The pain subsides a little, just in time for the tendril to go back to its work of infiltrating my skin. I dig at it, furious. It won't save me, but it's the only thing I can do. Though it's got itself under the phone now, hiding. I'd forgotten about the phone. I imagine myself making an emergency call to Mac, or even that crazy Eila. *Help*, I'd say. *I'm stuck in a time net being dragged apart in at least two directions; what do you suggest I do?*

I peel away the edge of the phone. I figure I'll take it off, flick it out, put it in my pocket and address the question of the tendril. The phone comes off in a rush, and even that hurts now: I feel something like electricity in my fingers, trying to dig through, take a hold of the thing. So I let it go. Which is a remarkably stupid thing to do, given that it's my sole contact with anybody in this reality or the next. But I'm glad. Because I can feel the electric net that used to be my spine and nervous system leave my body to chase the phone. Goodbye, I say. Which, again, is ill-advised seeing as I'm trying to pretend not to be here. But I seem to have become slightly addled. Who cares? I'm finally completing the rest of the journey down from the High Track. Addled or no, I'm about to hit the ground.

CHAPTER TWENTY-EIGHT

Green Jay

WHEN I WAKE up, the first thing I see is a large blue jay looking down at me. Not the real Blue Jay, but a bird and even then only a picture. It makes me both happy and sad at the same time. He is looking after me, but he is not here. I don't even know where *here* is any more. I don't know where I am. I try and sit up, but it hurts too much to move. I can feel cold, hard concrete underneath me. I seem to be on a landing at the top of a short flight of stairs.

"Where are you?" I ask the blue jay.

"Here," says T-Lily, and of course I do not tell her that the question was not directed at her. She is sitting behind me, or at least that is where her voice is coming from. I try to twist up and around to see her, but she puts a hand on my shoulder to stop me. "We have lost him," she says.

The Crow can take care of himself, I think. But I say nothing.

"He helped save you," says T-Lily.

"Do you think he is dead?" I ask. I don't want him dead. He followed me into the dome, after all. He is Blue Jay's friend.

"It is impossible to know. He is more likely caught by the nets."

"Then he is back with Guerra."

"Perhaps." T-Lily's voice is soft. She smells different from usual, though she has only just come back to this form. I don't imagine I smell that pleasant either, though I am too tired to care.

"Where are we?" I ask.

"Somewhere we can be found," she replies. "Rest now. We are safe."

We are completely out in the open, and I wonder that T-Lily has allowed this. But I trust her. She has released a cloud of blue-green mist. Turquoise. It swirls around us and then down the stairs. She is resting her arm on the back of my neck and my shoulder and I can feel her releasing chemicals into my body. I let myself drown in them for a while. I bring my hand up to hers to tell her thank you, and I see that there is still a tendril on my wrist. It has fastened itself to my skin so that is has almost become part of me. I don't mind. They have done so much for me, the Trocarn, I am glad to have a little part of them.

I think of myself lying on the bench in the shed. Lying in the dark with no-one around. I would much rather die here with T-Lily. Out in the sun with the picture of a blue jay looking down over me. The little dragonfly is still here. I can feel it buzz around my head. I close my eyes and let the drugs wash over me.

Crow

RIGHT NOW I'M lying on a bed and the world around me looks all gleam and high-tech. Not that I've examined much of it. Just an 'open my eyes, take a quick peek, close them again' type of thing. I have no idea where I am. I have memories of someone injecting me with what looked like a big-arse needle. Right into my leg. A leg I can't move right now, incidentally.

The fall wasn't that far, as it turned out. Or maybe it was and I just fell fast. Don't know. I made an attempt at that curl-up-and-roll shit. All very stunt professional, until I caught my leg on some sharp metal thing sticking up unexpectedly which naturally ripped it to shreds. And then it just fucking hurt. I don't know how long it took, but eventually there was fuss and what not. I seem to remember drones. The kind of ones that used to bring the Chemical Conjurers' parcels. Could be I was just imagining that.

There's nobody here in this room with me. It's big enough. Other beds, nobody in them. The door is this strange black thing that looks like two pieces of rubber. I've seen it open a few times: it slides to the side and the two pieces roll up and around. It's weird shit, but it's fun to watch. Unfortunately there's not much door action. No-one's much interested in the state of my health, it seems.

Which is not to say I've not been cared for. There's a drip in my wrist, handily inserted under the Tenties' tendril, which seems to have irretrievably attached itself to my wrist. I'm feeling fine, though it's the kind of fine that you know will stop just as soon as the drugs wear off. And I've not really tried moving, except to note that my left leg is quite determined to just stay put, thank you very much.

There's a shitload of bandages around it, so it's hard to know what the damage is. The memory of the metal spike resurfaces and I try not to dwell.

I close my eyes, but then I hear the door doing its thing. It's a swishing sound, very distinctive. I'm expecting the usual robot thing to emerge. So far I have not seen a living person in this building, not that I've been paying much attention. But it's not a robot. It's a completely human being of the male persuasion. And I recognise the face: Mac.

I've never been so glad to see anyone in my whole life.

I pull myself up as far as I'm able; which, to be honest, is not that far. Mac walks over and gives me a swift hug, which hurts like hell. Then he sits down on the black chair conveniently placed beside the bed. We grin at each other like idiots for a while.

"How'd you find me?" I ask.

Mac spreads his hands. "Long story."

"I've got the time."

"Tracked the phone, used the drones when that fell through." So I was right about the drones. "I'm glad you didn't get caught in the time nets, Brom. I tried to stop it. Tried and failed. Sorry."

"Wouldn't have thought you'd have much of a say about what was going on."

"I promised to bring them Eva." He says it with a grin, so I know it's a trick, all part of a cunning plan, but there's something about his voice I'm not sure of.

"Have you found her too?"

Mac looks down at his hands for a moment. "Not yet." Much as I'm glad to see Mac and all, there's something about this that makes me glad that Eva and I got separated. Which makes no sense. I mean, I should be handing her back to him, all thank-God-the-lovers-reunited. I trust Mac completely, even with my life. So why this feeling?

"How'd you do it?" I ask. "How'd you slip through to different places?"

"I worked on something with that glove you showed me. And the Chemical Conjurers helped. They send their drones around all the time."

"But you're the real you?" I ask. And because Mac gives me the look I'd give myself if I'd been him, I say, "I mean, I've met versions of me. Older. One super old. But, they're... not me. So it's possible you're not really Mac."

"It's me, Brom. There's not as many of us out there as you'd like to think."

"Yeah, but there's some." And then an unwelcome thought. "How many Guerras are there, Mac? All with time nets?"

"I don't know, Brom. I seriously doubt that you and Eva are the main concern of all the versions of Guerra that exist."

I think about telling Mac about the Barleycorn King, with his artificial companion. Seemed like an alternate version of Guerra to me, albeit one that had gone a little mad. "What's with the time nets, anyway?"

"There has to be some way of retrieving Time Locked parcels that have gone astray," says Mac. "That's all they are. They weren't really designed to look for people." He looks kinda tired, Mac does. But then I don't imagine I'm at my best either. "Brom. I'm sorry. I really am. This has all got complicated and messy and, look, I don't know if I can make it up to you. But I'm asking you to go back."

"I'm not going anywhere for a while," I tell him. Which is stalling, 'tis true, but also a matter of fact.

Mac sits forward and runs his thumb along the surface of the chair. It's a black rubber thing that kind of matches the door. But what I really notice is the blue dot on his thumb. There's a whole past to Mac I don't know anything about, never wanted to know anything about. I wonder if it's catching up with him. But, after not too much reflection, I realise I don't care. I trust him. He went to all the trouble of finding me, after all. And he's a friend, for better or for worse. (And it can't get much worse than this, can it?)

"What do you need me to do?" I ask.

"She's there," he says. "I mean Olwin Duilis. The person, you know…" I understand he don't want to say she's the *original* person, Eva's creator, so I nod. "She's not who you think she is, Brom. But Eva doesn't want to see her. I understand... But if you went back instead? Maybe that would be enough."

"I doubt she's going to be satisfied with me instead of Eva."

"But you could explain. Tell her about Eva, and the way she's been living, and..."

"There's a shitload of things I could tell her, Mac. I don't think she'd be interested in any of them."

"Maybe not," says Mac. He's back to tracing something onto the chair again. But it's a crap plan and he's got to know it.

"What about Guerra? Maybe he can talk her around?" Which is also a crap plan, but possibly a more likely one.

"Guerra's got nothing to offer her," says Mac.

I want to tell him about the Tenties and Guerra's role in their exile, but now don't seem the time. With the older Guerra, you could put a spin on it, make him feel guilty. I doubt the current Guerra's got quite to that stage yet.

"What does she want? This Olwin Duilis. I mean, apart from wanting to see Eva? What's it all about?"

"She grew up in Barlewin," says Mac. "I don't know, it's all mixed up, all sentimental. It was never meant to happen like this." He pulls himself upright, looks at me straight for the first time. "She wants to see what she'd be like if she got to live a normal life," he says.

"Eva's living a normal life?"

"More so than Olwin," says Mac.

"Then we show her that," I say. I grin, and Mac's fool enough to grin back at my non-plan. And then someone else comes through the door; this time, as expected, a being of the artificial variety. The kind of metal-and-plastic construct that seems so much easier to deal with than biological doubles and creatures that can mimic different looks and insert their tendrils into your arm. The robot comes over and does all its monitoring and checking. It also does something with my pain medication that makes me sink back into the sheets. I wave feebly at Mac. Enough's enough for now.

CHAPTER TWENTY-NINE

Green Jay

THERE'S SOMEONE SITTING on the landing beside me. At first I think it is T-Lily, but the feeling is different. Someone warmer, hairier. It is a dream, I am sure. A dream that Blue Jay is with me. Only because of the picture on the wall and because I am letting myself drift. I am dying; why not imagine the life I dreamt I could have? It is the only way it can come true.

But then he speaks and I know that it is not a dream. I hurt too much for it to be a dream. He swims in and out of focus. His hair is too long and he looks grey and worn, but it is him. Blue Jay. Perhaps he has come too late, but he is here.

The dragonfly is buzzing around his wrist. He brings out something small—a piece of plastic, it looks like, but I'm sure it's more than that—and it settles. Feeding. Communicating.

"Where is T-Lily?" I ask.

"She's gone," says Mac. At first I thought he meant she wasn't there, that she'd gone to look for food or shelter, but he looks over and I see her body collapsed onto the landing. She is still sitting with her back to the wall, but her head is bowed and her tentacles are dark and flaccid. Something is oozing out from her side.

"We jumped," I say. "We had to."

"The time nets, I know," says Blue Jay.

"Will they hurt the other Trocarn?"

"I don't know. I don't think so. Not…"

"Not now we are gone."

"I found Brom. He's okay. His leg is pretty bad. But he landed in a good place, I mean a high-tech kind of place, and they should be able to help."

It is not right that the Crow should live and that T-Lily should die. I move over to her. It's not far and I don't even have to stand; I just pull myself up to sitting and shuffle along until I can feel her. The connection that is always there when one of the Trocarn touches you is gone. There is no exchange. There is nothing. I have made it worse for her, not better.

"We can't leave her here," I tell Blue Jay. Though neither of us has anywhere to go, any place to take her.

"I can't let you be caught again," he says. He's still sitting on the landing, as if he's collapsed. For a moment, I feel as if I want to push him off. I don't understand why. But then he looks at me, and the feeling goes.

"We could take her to the greenhouse," I suggest.

"Okay," says Blue Jay, but I can see he thinks it's wrong.

That he would have to carry her up the flights of stairs. And then, what would we do with her? I do not even know how the Trocarn treat their dead; what is considered right.

"Or to the High Track, back to her own people." I make myself say it.

"No, not there."

"We can't leave her here."

"Can you stand?" Blue Jay holds out his hands, and I pull myself up. Once I am standing, it's not as bad as I thought. I hold on to the railings while Blue Jay lifts T-Lily. I want to cover her, but there is nothing. Blue Jay holds her in his arms and starts down the stairs. T-Lily could be asleep. Asleep in his arms. He walks slowly and I follow them, and there is a part of me that wishes I was asleep too.

Crow

I'M BACK BY the water tower and luckily I had some help to get this far. I'm as right as I'm ever going to be, which is to say my leg is completely fucked. And if it wasn't for the fact it's full of God-knows-how-much ultra high tech, it would be a write-off. They told me that at the hospital quite a few hundred times. I'm not sure who they thought I was, and it's not like I was giving them a rundown of my own complicated history—I don't even know if I could anymore—but they seemed to know very well I wasn't from there and then. So to speak. And didn't seem much troubled by it.

In any case, I've got a clean bill of health, despite some prolonged fussing over the tendril embedded in my wrist. They offered to get it out and I surprised myself by refusing. So far no harm done, I reckon. And if they can fill part of me full of shit, then so can the Tenties. Talk about loyalty.

Anyway, once I'd expressed an interest in the water tower and they divined that taking me there was a way to get rid of me, I got some help. I could have managed on my own. I mean, I can *walk,* although I've been advised not to run for a while; things are still settling in. And I can't say it's the most dependable walking I've ever done. So a friendly robot helper was provided. It looks like a stick insect standing upright, and it has all the personality of one. No offence to stick insects.

The robots here are nothing like the Chemical Conjurers, more's the pity. There's no personality, no chance for a chit-chat and a laugh. On the other hand, you know exactly where you stand; they're a mine of information, and extremely helpful. Can't see this one helping me out with any necessary escapes, but you never know. I'm not even exactly sure if this one's coming with—I mean, back home, and elsewhere. That's the one bit of extremely good-to-know information I haven't been able to extract.

The hospital turned out to be not all that far from what should have been the marketplace, and so it wasn't long before I was back in familiar territory. Same old, same old. The High Track was as obvious and intrusive as ever, and my thoughts naturally, if reluctantly, turned to Guerra and the task at hand.

I'm not looking forward to it. I've got a new perspective on Guerra now. There's the man he becomes, the crazy tortured Barleycorn King, feeling more than a little guilty about the Tenties if nothing else, but more immediately there's the man who sent the time nets out for me and Eva. And bloody unpleasant things they turned out to be. But that's the Guerra I know, and I know ways to get around that one.

At least, I hope I do.

But first I have to meet up with Mac and Eva. Rendezvous at the water tower. Which, despite all the high techiness of this particular reality, is still very much there. There's not much chance for graffiti, the whole thing is covered in screens. Thin, bendy screens that sometimes show all sorts of different things and sometimes band together for the one big, slightly overwhelming image. Beats the big screen back home, have to say that.

We stand under the water tower for a while, but bugger that, I give up and sit with my back against one of the support posts. It's not the one with the ladder, but I can see the entrance to Mac's lair. Don't look like it's been opened in a while. The farm's pretty much nonexistent, unless this world somehow get its sustenance from grass and wildflowers. It's pretty. There's no shed, which comes as something of a relief, but the house is there. I watch it closely, just to see if there's any sign of life. It's somewhere to sleep if I have to. I don't fancy climbing up into the water tower, even with the help of my robot friend.

I close my eyes for a moment. I wouldn't have thought

I slept, but after a while there's a clucking noise from the robot. It's half-human, half-dog as far as I can tell. I mean, it can speak and it's usually intelligible, but it also makes these weird sounds. Kind of annoying, slightly endearing. I suppose I'll get used to it.

Not that there's anything happening when I do open my eyes. Everything is much of a muchness. There's a bit of a breeze rustling through the grasses, a bit of heat haze, but that's hardly enough to provoke clucking in a robot. Or maybe it is. I had a dog once that used to bark his head off at insects and completely ignore the birds stealing his food. That was a while ago, that dog. The thought makes me homesick.

I close my eyes again and make a mental note to mess with that clucking somehow. For now, I just ignore it. And so I'm surprised when the robot gives me a kick in the shins. Not my bad leg and, to be fair, not that hard, but it does surprise.

"Look," it says, pointing to the outside world in what I can only describe as an exasperated manner.

There are two people walking towards us. One of them's carrying a third person, who looks, from this distance, to be either gravely injured or dead. You'd think I'd be more concerned about prospective visitors. Or at least up on my feet. But there's something about the drugs I'm fairly sure are still pumping through my system that makes me chilled. And these people don't appear that much of a threat. One of them's encumbered and the other one appears to be struggling; she, and I'm fairly sure it's a she, lags behind. The first one waits, she catches up, they keep walking. Obviously heading over here, but taking a bloody long time about it.

The robot takes a few steps forward. It's changed its configuration so that it is actually more like a dog. Down on all fours. Not sure why: it could stand up under the water tower. I can, and it's not much taller than me. It's at the edge of the water tower, hovering between shade and sun, and then it decides and runs out to greet them. At first I thought it was some kind of an attack, but no, it wants to help. All that first-aid programming kicking in. It stretches out its body so that the injured person can be laid on its back. Which would not be a comfortable ride, but then they're probably in no state to care. The injured figure is delivered to the robot, the woman leans on the first figure, and they all keep walking.

I'm standing too now, at the edge of the water tower shade. And recognition kicks in: it is, of course, Mac and Eva. Who else was I expecting? I can't tell who the robot's got. A Tentie would be my first guess, but I'm reserving judgement. I lift my hand in greeting and get a half-hearted response from Mac. Who looks, with all due respect, like crap. Eva's not much better, but that's par for the course.

CHAPTER THIRTY

Green Jay

WE WALK FROM the landing where Blue Jay found me, across to the High Track staircase. It is not that far: T-Lily, so hurt, so brave, had brought me to the closest hidden place she could find. But when we get to the staircase, there are no stairs. Or, better to say, the stairs are damaged and unusable.

"There'll be others," says Blue Jay, though I can see he is already tiring. I forget that he, too, has been through so much. I have not yet asked him how he managed to get away from Guerra, what harm was done to him, and I feel ashamed.

In the Barlewin I was born into, there are buildings under the High Track. Most of them used to be warehouses and they probably still are. Guerra uses some of them, I am sure. People live there, not many—because, I think, it is hard not to feel that you are under Guerra's watchful eye. It is not a place I have ever been. Me, or even Olwin Duilis. It is not somewhere you would *want* to go.

This Barlewin is not so different. Perhaps because it's beginning to get dark, so that there are shadows and mysteries. I do not want to walk between the buildings here. The tenements where my greenhouse is are also shadowy, but at least you know there are people living there and it is possible they will be friendly, and that they will allow you also to live beside them untroubled. But in this place anyone you meet is here for a purpose, and that purpose is unlikely to be friendly.

There's a lot of neglect. Broken windows, doors swinging open. Grass growing up where there should be pavings. I imagine a lot of the plants are ones whose seeds have floated down from the High Track; but here they have changed from beautiful to sinister. I stumble a few times, but I know I must not. I must walk as if I have no fear, as if everything is fine, as if we are in a safe, well-lit area.

Blue Jay is moving straight across the middle. It would be quicker to try and reach one of the other staircases, but I know what he is thinking: at least in this direction we are heading to the water tower and the marketplace, to places that may offer protection.

There are sounds. Bumps, scrapes, stifled laughter. They've been there for a while. It means nothing, I tell myself. I try to walk faster. I know it is not fast enough.

And then there are five people standing right in front of us. They moved so fast I can't even tell where they came from. And there is nowhere to go. No side streets, no open doors. Although what we might find behind a door could be even worse. I see flickers of light that could be knives. I draw close to Blue Jay.

"Give us the Tentie," says one of them. He's skinny. His clothes are too big for him. He reminds me of the Crow. But even the Crow would not behave like this.

"She's injured," says Blue Jay. "We're taking her to get help."

"There's no help here, mate."

Blue Jay looks at me quickly and then down at his arms. I know what he's thinking. We may have no choice but to Time Lock, and for that we need his tech. He can't move his arms. He needs them both to hold T-Lily. I find the dragonfly in my hair and then link my arm through his as if I am scared, but I've moved it as close to the technology wrapped around Blue Jay's forearm as I can. I hope the dragonfly understands. I can reach the top of the device; I need the dragonfly to get to the underside. The skinny guy is watching me, but I don't think he suspects. Why would he? This does not seem to be the kind of place where Time Locked travel would be common. Blue Jay is still talking. Making things up about hospitals and being lost and if they could just let us through we'd be out and away so soon.

One of the others—not the skinny guy—laughs. "It's dead," she says. The five of them crowd closer. Some of them are poking at T-Lily. One of them's trying to pull her away from Blue Jay. Another has his knife out, and is flicking at Blue Jay's arm. "Give it up," says another. "Give it up." His voice is getting louder.

The skinny guy steps back, spits on the ground deliberately so that I can see. I don't dare look down at the device. And I cannot be at all sure where we are going even if the dragonfly knows what to do. The skinny guy steps towards me. There's a grin on his face that I know and understand. I close my eyes and will the dragonfly on. Anywhere we go is better than here.

Crow

THEY MAKE IT to the water tower, and pretty much collapse onto the ground. At least Eva and Mac do; there is a Tentie on the robot's back and I think probably T-Lily, but she's too far gone to know for sure. Tentie features were never my strong point. The robot gives me a look and then lowers itself right down low so that it can slide the injured Tentie off its back, releasing something flat underneath it so that it's not lying on the ground. I help, because I'm not such a heartless bastard as all that. Then the robot starts fussing with Eva so I go to Mac. Not that I can offer any medical skills, but I have some water. He sits up and leans back against one of the water tower support posts. I sit down too because standing, for some reason, hurts like hell.

"You looked better last time I saw you," I say.

"That's T-Lily," says Mac. "She's—she didn't make it."

And somehow that makes everything worse. All this running around with the time nets and Eva's quest for personhood and Guerra's madness in whatever form

I encountered him, never seemed much more than a fucked-up version of normal life. But we were meant to save the Tenties. Eva and me. Get them out of Time Lock and back to disturbing us in real life.

"We thought we'd take her to the High Track, but we didn't quite make it that far." Mac tries for the self-deprecating grin, fails. He's got his head as much wrapped around T-Lily's death as I have, which is to say not at all. And then I realise that Mac has to have carried T-Lily through Time Lock to get here.

"Trouble?" I ask.

Mac nods. He holds up a piece of flimsy tech which looks pretty much ruined then closes his eyes and I disturb him no more. The robot pushes me out of the way so it can fuss with him.

"How's Eva?" Mac asks.

"She is stable for now," says the robot. "She requires extra care. I could take her to hospital?"

"No," says Mac.

"Can you do anything for T-Lily?" I ask.

"The Trocarn?"

"Yes."

"She is gone," says the robot. "Unnecessary, given her restorative powers."

I look at Mac and he's looking up at the bottom of the water tower. We both know what that means. T-Lily could have saved herself. She saved Eva instead. Mac flinches. The robot is suturing a cut on his arm. "You would benefit from a hospital visit too," it remarks.

"No," repeats Mac. "Is anyone else around?" he asks me.

"Don't know," I say. "Haven't seen anyone. Can you scan?" This last addressed to the robot.

"Not accurately. I am designed for personal care and monitoring, nothing more."

"Doing a great job," says Mac.

"Thank you," says the robot.

"Do you have a name?" he asks.

"I have been called Tal."

"Tal it is then," says Mac.

A half hour later, Mac's recovered enough to take a look inside the water tower. (Tal believes there isn't anyone inside, but he gives no guarantees.) It's completely empty, no sign of the half-done renovations, no sign that Mac ever lived there.

But that's not the worrying thing.

On the inside of the tower, painted right at the eye line for someone standing on the top rung of the ladder, are three birds. One is green, one is blue and the other is black. They are all wearing gas masks, and they are standing on barbed wire. Not that I climb up to see; Mac takes a picture on his phone to show us. And even I get this. It's a warning.

We all of us look at T-Lily.

"What do you know about the Trocarn?" Eva asks Tal. "What is the right thing to do with her?"

"Let me take her to the hospital," Tal says. He's reverted to his stick insect form, although he is not as tall as I remember him. Perhaps that is only because he isn't walking beside me.

"Can you access anything beyond your first aid script?" asks Mac.

Tal shakes himself a little. "The Trocarn have had many forms," he says after a moment's contemplation. "Death is unusual because of their self-healing capabilities."

"We should take her back to the vines," says Eva.

"If they still exist," I say.

"Eva's right," says Mac. "She has to go back to the Trocarn."

"Which means the High Track," I say.

"The High Track is weird here," says Mac.

"The High Track?" asks Tal.

Mac points in the general direction of the High Track. "Big circular thing, floating above the roads. Ramps coming down."

"The bicycle ring," says Tal. Which explains the swooshing noise that has been bugging me for a while.

"Right," says Mac

"Then we take her there," says Eva.

"At least there's no stairs," says Mac.

"Was it ever a garden?" I ask.

"No," says Tal. "Always for bicycles." He turns to look at me. "You cannot go through Time Lock, not with your leg." Which is news, and not welcome news, not that I had any intention of taking T-Lily back to the vines. "I assume that is your plan? To take the Trocarn back to her people in another reality?"

"Somebody has to go," says Eva. And she looks at me as if to say, *well, it should be you.* I return the look, but I doubt she interprets it correctly.

"We'll all go," says Mac. "At least as far as the place where the Trocarn should be." He helps slide T-Lily onto

Tal's back. The plan is to walk up to what I think of as staircase number 1, which in this world is a smaller ramp designed for people. It's a bit of a trek, but otherwise we'll have to deal with cyclists. So off we go.

It's a forlorn procession: Eva leaning on Mac, unnecessarily as far as I can tell; me hobbling along; and Tal carrying T-Lily.

As we walk, I give some thought to Tal's no-Time-Lock-travel prohibition. It's an edict I could have done with some time back. But there's no way I'm going to stay here, not indefinitely. Though now is not really the time to be asking Tal for details.

Eva seems oddly reluctant to walk under the High Track. I know what she means; not the most pleasant part of town. But right here and now it's just gardens and pathways. There's one building that I think I might recognise, but nothing else. In any case, Mac consoles her and we trundle through to the ramp. Which, as advertised, swirls around at a gentle slope until it reaches the High Track, just about at the point where the Tenties' dome was located. My leg does not appreciate the climb and I find a place to sit down as soon as we reach the top. Eva will fuss over T-Lily; I'm happy to leave all that to her.

There's one of those split-circle decorations on the bench. This one with a nose in the middle, which, I have to say, looks a little odd. It's all plastic and new, and I'm thinking probably a copy of something older. Barleycorn King era, if such a thing ever existed. Or, given that this was never the High Track, perhaps it's some kind of cross-reality bleed. That really don't bear thinking about. I watch the others try and figure out whether or not the Tenties are actually here. Well, not so much *here* as accessible from here. I lift my face to the sun and wonder what the Barleycorn King would have to say.

CHAPTER THIRTY-ONE

Green Jay

TAL HAS INSISTED that the Crow not come with us. He does not seem to mind, though he did get up and say goodbye to T-Lily. He touched her arm lightly. He has a tendril embedded in his wrist too; he is not as separate from them as he once imagined he was.

Surprisingly, Tal helps us step into the dome. He does something so that the shimmer of the dome is clear, so that it is almost possible to see the Trocarn inside, and then we step in, Blue Jay, T-Lily and me. Blue Jay is holding her as he did before. Tal wanted to stay with the Crow.

I expected that we would be surrounded by tendrils as soon as we were in the dome, but instead the vines draw back and there is a space around us. Blue Jay is coping better than the Crow, but he cannot stay here long, even with the help of the Trocarn, even with the technology he has developed to make travelling through Time Lock easier. He holds T-Lily out to them but nothing happens. There is a great, green silence. I think perhaps it is shock.

"We did not know what to do," I say. I am trying not to cry. I am so ashamed. Perhaps it would have been better not to return. At last, Kolb and Lona come to us. Lona takes T-Lily from Blue Jay's arms and disappears back into the vines. It is hard to tell what is happening to her. It is almost as if they are blocking the process from view. Kolb places his hand around Blue Jay's wrist and I see the relief it brings.

"Thank you for bringing her home," says Kolb. He looks down and away as if he cannot bear to meet our eyes.

"We... I... I am so sorry." It bursts out of me and it is not enough.

"T-Lily chose," says Kolb. "She was exceptional."

"Can you heal her?" I ask.

"We will send her home, back to the stars." Kolb looks up at me. "But she is forever gone."

I start to sob. I am thinking of the Trocarn's journey to such a strange and cruel place; but I am also thinking of the other Eva, the one lying on the bench in the shed. And I wonder how many of those have also been sent to the stars.

Crow

I'M SITTING ON my bench, minding my own business, when things start to happen. Bicycle traffic has been slow but steady. There's a continuous *whoosh* in the air without it being overwhelming. Or maybe I'm just getting used to it. But now people are turning up, people without bicycles but with equipment. I'm not sure what kind of equipment, but there's a lot of it. Speakers, I think, which probably means music. No-one asks me to leave and I'm not inclined to. I'm not particularly in the way, though someone's used the rest of my bench as a place to store a few bits and bobs of a decidedly electronic nature.

It's getting dark, and there's one or two people already with things that look to me like miner's lamps on their heads.

"Any ideas?" I ask Tal. Frankly, I'd hoped he'd be more forthcoming, but he's been silent for a while—in fact, since the others disappeared into the dome with T-Lily.

"Music," he says. "You should turn around."

As it turns out the back of the bench lifts up and over so that the prospective sitter can face any which way. I manage to do so without dislodging anyone's stashed equipment, then take the opportunity to stretch. Only for a moment, because I want to reclaim my seat before someone else takes it.

People have brought food, which makes me hungry. And I can see people with drinks, alcoholic drinks, which there's no way Tal would allow, but which are still very tempting. Back in the day, Guerra would have loved this, prime market for his wares. Not that he'd have let them hold a concert up on the High Track.

Tal reads my mind, which in this case is not particularly difficult, and manages to acquire some chips with enough salt and grease to keep me happy. And some sort of non-alcoholic juice with a straw, which makes me feel like a kid.

It's properly dark by now. There have been sound checks and tests of various sorts. There's a hum, like a distant buzz of a very large hive, which builds until it's almost unbearable and then scatters. And then I see why Tal told me to turn around. There are light projections on the leftover buildings in the middle of the High Track. And, somehow, in mid-air between the trees. Sometimes showing people I assume are the performers, sometimes pictures chosen for cultural reasons outside my ken. Sometimes just patterns. The patterns are the best.

There are flags waving, both here up high and down in the gardens below us. It's fucking wonderful. People come and take their equipment and then finally somebody comes and sits down on the bench with me. Which is only fair. I turn for a quick peek. It's dark and there's weird light patterns everywhere, but it looks a lot like the minor prophet to me.

"Catelin?" I ask.

"Oh, hi, Brom," she says. "Thought I'd find you here."

And so what started off as a nice surprise quickly turns to creepy. I look at her closely, or as closely as I can given the circumstances. She don't seem that much older. Not that I have any idea of time frames here. But, shit, I thought I was in a different reality altogether.

"I can't say the same about you," I say. Which is not very gracious, but I'm a bit put out.

"Fantastic concerts," she says. "Can't be missed."

"Yeah, but—"

And then she stops me with a touch of her hand. "Oh, but you're the young Brom. Sorry, thought you were... You're not looking so good."

"Buggered up my leg," I say. "Still recovering." I look around for Tal to introduce him, but he's nowhere to be seen.

"Ah," says Catelin. Though there's something about her that's wrong. Then a stray beam of light wends its way over our bench and she flickers badly. So much for Time Locked love, then.

"You're not Catelin," I say.

"Never said I was. But we've met, Brom. Remember? It's Eila."

"Guerra sent you." It's all making sense now. Any minute, these beams of light will turn out to be time nets and that will be that.

Eila laughs. "What makes you say that?"

"Isn't that your thing? You're Guerra's companion. Or the Barleycorn King's. Or whatever name you want to give him." I'm talking a wee bit too much, but it's mostly to combat the amused look on Eila's face.

"And you think Guerra sent me to find you."

"Yes," I say. "Probably. He's been kind of actively looking." I look down at my leg in what I hope is a meaningful way.

"True," says Eila. "But that's not why I'm here."

"Then why?"

"Just came for the music," says Eila.

We're silent for a while, both having come to the end of

half truths. She startles me by touching my wrist. "Lost your phone?"

"And you want me to believe you're really not trying to track me down?"

"No, Brom. No. I think you've probably jumped to a few wrong conclusions. I haven't had anything to do with Guerra for a long time."

And then Tal shows up with Mac and Eva in tow. There's introductions; some, I think, unnecessary given the expression on Eila's face, but I'm beyond caring what conclusions she thinks I've jumped to and presume she doesn't know anybody.

"We should go, Brom," says Mac. And he's right and I can see that he's exhausted and Eva's not looking much better. And that Tal is hovering. But I don't want to go, even with Eila sitting here. The music's just that good.

More than that: it's strange enough, it's weird enough, it's big enough to be a wake for T-Lily. That's not something the others are going to believe, so I don't even try to explain.

"One more song?" I ask.

"Sure," says Mac. And I can see that he's deliberately got in quick before Eva can protest or Tal make one of his medical pronouncements. Quite where we're going to after this, I don't know. I suppose Mac does.

I ignore them all and listen to the music. Let myself be swept away. I don't even care about the light projections or the flags waving or the whole carnival atmosphere. I just want to disappear into the sound.

CHAPTER THIRTY-TWO

Green Jay

WE ARE BACK in my greenhouse. The Crow is here, of course, and Tal but also Eila. I remember Eila from my time with Guerra and I don't trust her. Especially not in this form, pretending to be human, but really an illusion. A trick. But she came with us when we left, just followed along with us as if she was invited. Even the Crow seemed surprised by that.

I would have liked to stay up on the High Track, but Blue Jay was right to leave. He needs to sleep. Tal is with him now, and that makes me worry. He is more badly affected by the dome than I realised. He has his eyes closed and has stretched out on the floor. The Crow has found a spot too. I suppose that I should also sleep—I can feel the pull of sleep on my body—but my mind is awake. I keep thinking of T-Lily and the sad greeting of the Trocarn. And I do not want to sleep with Eila here.

The greenhouse makes me sad. Having seen it made so beautiful with Kolb and Lona, I was not expecting this shell. Some of the windows are broken and there are leaves and dust and drifts of rubbish on the floor. No furniture. We are lucky it is empty, I suppose. Lucky that it is still here at all. But it makes me feel that I have been forgotten.

The sounds of the concert drift through. And there are sparks of light. I sit with my back to the wall. Tal is doing the same now, having satisfied himself that Blue Jay and the Crow are fine. He has not checked on me.

I close my eyes for a moment to see if sleep will come. But my thoughts are tangled and won't let me go.

"Eva?"

Eila has come to sit beside me. Too close. I keep my eyes closed, and will her away.

"I know you're not asleep," she says. "And I need to talk to you."

"Why? What can you tell me?"

"You can't let them keep doing this," she says. "They need to return to their own reality."

"And me?"

"You know what will happen to you, I think."

"I will join T-Lily in the stars," I say. "I don't mind." It is a lie, of course it is, but it is one that must be said.

"Not always," says Eila. "Not for all of you."

"I am only me," I tell her. Because there is no point in thinking otherwise.

"And perhaps you will be the one."

I shake my head and look away. There is no point thinking like this. There is no point having this conversation. Already I can feel my body weakening, now that I am away from T-Lily. Blue Jay has forgotten about me, and what I need to keep living. But I cannot blame him, he has hardly survived himself.

"I have seen your children," she says softly.

"So have I," I tell her. I am thinking of Kolb and Lona, because who else could they be?

"Part-human, part-plant, part-Trocarn?"

"Yes," I say and I am glad to know more than she does.

"They are honoured, you know. They are cursed and divine."

Kolb and Lona would not agree with that description, but I say nothing. "So people still fear them?"

"Of course," says Eila. We're both silent for a moment. She touches the raised ring of tendril around my wrist. It is covered by my own skin now. Eila's touch is feather-light, a whisper.

"We need to copy you," she says.

"I know," I say. Because I've known it all along.

And because I want to pretend that this can be my own choice, my own doing, I follow her down the stairs and through the almost familiar streets. I had thought we might return to the place of my birth, the public 3D printer box, but of course this is a different reality. Eila takes me to another building, somewhere close by. This one is open, like a warehouse, but full of machinery and life. There are people everywhere, and robots like Tal. And, at one end of the building, an area that seems almost like a hospital, filled with beds. People are lying down, and robots are fussing. But there's no blood, no screams, no distress. We are met by a larger version of Tal, who takes us to one of the beds. Nobody talks. Perhaps this has all been prearranged. I lie down; the robot fixes something like a curved plastic roof over me. There is a mist. It makes me think of T-Lily and of Rose-Q and I feel myself falling into a green darkness.

Crow

THIS WORLD'S NOT-REALLY-A-HIGH Track is all a bit sad in the morning. Lots of tattered flags and leftover picnic scraps. Not as much as I might have expected, though that's probably explained by what looks like a robot cleaner crew off in the distance. A few mad keen cyclists are already on the track.

Tal is here with me. He's not happy. He says my leg's not healed, it won't do well on the journey. In fact, he wants to come with, and I've been saying 'no,' but it looks like he's coming anyway. I'll admit there's a part of me that wouldn't mind showing up at Guerra's with my handy robot companion, and quite possibly that's the wiser part.

Of course Mac's here to help with technical stuff, though it's a very silent Mac. My feeling is he'd like Tal to stay and look after Eva. Could be something else.

Eila's buggered off, back from whence she came, I guess. Which is a shame, really, because I'd hoped to have her onside too. In fact, there was a time I'd imagined she'd do all the talking, persuade Guerra of the rights and wrongs of the situation and leave me to stand in the background, smile charmingly and have Guerra pay as much attention to me as he normally does, which is to say none. Not that I'm so optimistic as to think I'll be rocking back into my old job.

And Eva. Well, there's the Eva that's coming with me and the Eva that's staying here. It's not that difficult to tell them apart. For a start, one's got a raised tentacle around her wrist and, to the keenly observant, a faint scar from the implants under her left arm. To the not-so-keenly observant, one looks fresh and new and the other looks like she's been to hell and back—which, for all intents and purposes, she has. But Guerra's not likely to know that. Anyway, a bird in the hand and all that.

I can't help but think it's a bit hypocritical. Saving one Eva, sacrificing another. Which might help explain Mac's silence. And the other Eva's, the real Eva's, absence.

There was a time it wouldn't have mattered to me: she's a double, she never was meant to last. But it's become clear that Eva is more than a double. Which, of course, opens the door for the possibility that doubles are more than doubles. Don't look at me, I'm just caught up in all this.

Mac and Eva have assured me that this one, this sacrificial Eva, will be okay. That Guerra won't hurt her, that Olwin Duilis, of all people, will look after her. Olwin Duilis, the one person Eva's been running from this whole time, if I understand anything at all. Mac was the one who mentioned Olwin Duilis, not Eva, and the name didn't come easily out of his mouth. The real Eva didn't say anything at all.

So maybe they've built a copy. A shell, not meant to exist for more than a few hours, and under no illusions that there might be other possibilities. Someone that knows its place.

But there's something else going on here. It was all fait accompli when I woke up this morning. There's something not being said.

Don't get me wrong. I like the idea of fooling Guerra. I like the idea of getting him off my back, of stopping the bloody time nets. I even like the idea of handing him a fake package, so to speak, of tricking him. I just don't buy the argument that the package doesn't matter anymore. There's a part of me that thinks, *well, go back, fool Guerra, make sure this double/copy is okay,* but that part is kidding itself. Especially given all the success I've had so far, which is none at all.

Still, I'm going along with it. Because, quite frankly, I've had enough. We ran around trying to save the Tenties, and all we managed was to kill one of them.

So here I am, back where it all began, up on the High Track, as close to the spot that we guess Guerra's admin should be, without being actually inside the building. I'm not expecting a warm reception, but I doubt that attempting to sneak up on him will be profitable in any way. And neither will a debate with security. I mean, the whole point is to show him Eva.

So here she is, the sacrificial Eva. I take her hand,

because, why not? "It's okay, Brom," she says. Already, I like her better than the real one. I see the dragonfly in her hair. So Mac can keep track of her, I guess. The plan had been to use Mac's tech, but now Tal's providing transport. I'm kind of glad about that; no disrespect to Mac, but stuff he uses looks wildly improvised and unsafe. Not to mention damaged by his previous expeditions. Tal and Mac have been in some kind of deep tech consult for the past while. Which makes me think my protestations that I'd be okay by myself were doomed from the start.

Tal approaches us, stretches up to his full stick-insect height and then splits himself almost in two, so that he surrounds us. We're inside a freaky robot cage, which gives me the giggles. I hold up my hand to Mac. I should have said goodbye. I should have said something, because already I can feel that familiar Time Locked nausea. Dampened this time, although perhaps I'm just a jaded traveller. The world flickers in and out, and then, before the urge to throw up makes itself fully known, we're back. Back on the High Track proper, in my reality. Where I fucking well should be.

And if I throw myself down and kiss the ground, well, who could blame me?

CHAPTER THIRTY-THREE

Crow

TAL HAS THROWN himself around my leg like a brace. Which, I have to say, is a cunning plan. He's injected something into me, too, which I'm grateful for, because the leg did not appreciate the journey. As warned, as predicted. But hell, I'm home.

Mac and Tal did well. We're just outside the doors of Guerra's admin. How I would love to have him come out and see us. But, no, our arrival is pretty much without fanfare.

I turn to the fake Eva. "We could go," I say. "Say that we tried, but no-one was home."

She smiles, squeezes my hand. "No, Brom. Let's go in." I wonder if they've somehow programmed her. And yes, I definitely do like her better.

We go into the building. The foyer is deserted, but not

for long. Carine shows up, gives me a look and a nod. "Brom," is all she says. And, belatedly, more security. They're following Carine's lead, for which I'm grateful.

I spread my hands. "No box. Time Lock stuffed it. But Eva's back. And she'd like to speak with Guerra."

Carine gives me a look which I interpret as *you sure about this?* Luckily I don't have to answer because, hell, I'm not sure at all. "Stay here," she says at last. She gives a nod to the remaining security, which they interpret as *stay here too*, and then disappears into internal Guerra realms.

I expect him to materialise, but no, Carine's back and we're following her inside. Naturally, as I have never been this far in before, I'm having a bit of a stickybeak. The Eva with me, for whom this is also new, is showing a surprising lack of interest. Which works in our favour.

Guerra is sitting in a room that looks something like a gentleman's library. Any minute you'd expect cigars and brandy. I'm not holding my breath. He's sitting in a luxury black chair and so is someone else; someone who makes fake Eva gasp. Someone who I can't help but stare at. There's no prizes for guessing this must be Olwin Duilis. And if I thought the real Eva was the worse for wear, Olwin Duilis is well beyond that. Even sitting down, you can't help but notice the strain and illness. Oh, yes, and a metal tracery around her arms.

Guerra smiles the smile of someone who knows they're about to provide you with unwelcome, but possibly liberating, news. "Take a seat," he says. There are two, slightly lesser quality, but still perfectly serviceable black chairs just in front of us.

We sit—what choice do we have? Fake Eva chooses the seat opposite Guerra, as far from Olwin Duilis as she can get. Which is, admittedly, not that far. In turn, Olwin Duilis has eyes only for fake Eva.

Guerra makes some introductions. He knows they're unnecessary, he's been ironically polite, or at least that's the way I read it. The only surprise, he calls fake Eva 'Aleris,' which is a name to be getting on with, at least. It makes me suspicious at first, but it turns out to be the name Olwin Duilis has given her in absentia, and that Guerra, businessman that he is, has adopted without question. Fine with me. Keeps things in order.

And then there's an awkward pause after which Olwin Duilis tears her eyes away from Aleris and looks at me.

"You've hurt your leg," she says. Her voice is faint and more nasal than Eva's, but—and perhaps I'm kidding myself—friendly. Before I can answer, she stretches out a hand and lifts up the edge of her long skirt. Her legs are both laced with metal, from the ankle and up as far as I can see. She grins and it occurs to me that Olwin Duilis is not old. I'd always imagined her as middle-aged, at the very least, but she's not.

But she's tired, and obviously damaged in some irreparable way.

"Impressive," I say.

She smiles again, lets her skirt drop back down to the floor. As she sits back I notice a flash of metal at the top of her spine.

"But you've brought Aleris back to us," says Guerra,

obviously eager to get back to the business at hand. "You took your time, Kern."

I spread my hands. "The technology has its flaws."

Guerra gives me a look which is less than encouraging, but is interrupted.

"How is MacIver? Was he hurt too?"

It takes me a beat to realise Olwin Duilis is asking after Mac. "Mac's fine. I did this to myself." Getting away from the time nets, I remind myself, but there's no way I'm bringing that up.

But, of course, Olwin Duilis is not really talking to me. She is looking at Aleris. And there's something about the tilt of Olwin's head, that makes me think: she knows. She knows this is not the real Eva. She knows Mac has run off with the real double and left her with this. And if I was to travel even further into fantasy land, I'd say she's okay with that. But what do I know? The dragonfly spins out of its hiding place in Aleris' hair and flies across to Olwin. It lands on her open palm and I see a metal filament grow out of Olwin's exoskeleton and attach itself to the insect.

"Don't mind us," says Olwin. But of course the three remaining people have nothing at all to talk about. We let the dragonfly and Olwin commune in silence.

"How are you feeling?" Olwin asks Aleris at last. Though I get the impression it's to break the silence; Aleris is obviously doing just fine. "I am sorry that we do not have the help of the Trocarn," she continues, and Guerra has the grace to look unsettled. Though I wouldn't go so far as to say he was approaching the guilt levels of

the Barleycorn King. If that's to come, I don't see any
evidence of it.

"About that—" I begin. Which is unwise but probably
the only chance I'm going to get.

"This is not the time, Kern," says Guerra. He gives me a
look which makes the early deployment of exit strategies
a high priority, if not the *only* priority.

"I would like to lie down, please," says Aleris. Which
surprises us all, particularly as she don't seem physically
distressed in any way.

"I am sorry," says Olwin. "It must be a shock." But
she makes no move to help her. Guerra stands, holds out
his hand, which Aleris takes. He leads her away. And,
even though it's exactly this that I've agreed to, it's deeply
creepy.

"He's not going to hurt her," says Olwin.

He hurt the first one, I think. Pumped her full of drugs
and chased her down the stairs when she tried to escape.
But I'm not quite ready to lift that cat right out of the
bag. "I hope not," is the best I can offer.

"I never expected a double to have a mind of her own,"
says Olwin.

I almost snort, thinking of Eva, the most mind-of-her-
own, self-obsessed being I have ever encountered. "What
did you think?" I ask.

"I thought I was being clever," says Olwin.

I shift about as if to say, *well, so do we all,* but that's not
really what I was asking. There's no real need, though;
she seems in a confessional mood.

"I'd heard that the Trocarn who lived here were in

charge of the 3D printers. I thought they might help her if asked. And they did. I persuaded Guerra to keep an eye on her. I sent him the package. I knew that if she managed to survive the first few weeks, it would help keep her alive." Olwin looks down at her hands. "I was naive. I didn't quite realise who he was or what he does."

I leave that unlikely assertion for another time. "How did you ask the Tenties to help?"

"It was MacIver's idea," she says. She looks straight at me and smiles. *MacIver,* I'm thinking, and I must have looked blank. "He's the one who realised what the Trocarn had to offer. And he was right, of course. I wish I'd known them like he did."

"Mac," I say. Like an idiot. "It was Mac's idea."

"I thought you knew." Olwin's head is tilted to the side, trying to assess my stupidity. It's deeper and wider than she knows.

"So you and Mac cooked up this idea of keeping a double alive because…" And I can't bring myself to say what now seems obvious: because he wanted a better version of Olwin. The thought makes me feel sick.

Olwin looks away. "No," she says. "It was only me that thought that. MacIver left."

"So all this time…"

"All this time it's been me, Brom."

"But that's why you sent her here. Because Mac was here." It wasn't even a question.

"Yes." She's looking at me now, straight and fierce. An *I don't really give a fuck what you think* kind of look.

Which may be completely true, given the events of the past few weeks and the company she's kept.

"What will you do now?"

"With Aleris?"

"Yeah, with Aleris." But I'm thinking, *And with Mac, with the Tenties*. With the whole fucked-up mess.

"Help her stay alive. Give her a life."

"With Guerra's help."

"At first, yes. Not for long."

I stand up. Because I've had enough. And it seems a good time to get out.

"Show me where she lived," she asks.

"She's not you," I say. "She doesn't have a life you can look into and take."

Olwin stands now. I hear the soft whir of the metal cage helping her to stand. Once she's upright, she looks fine, but it reveals just how fragile her body is. "Please, Kern."

"No," I say. "No. I've done enough."

"I could help with the Trocarn."

"And how the fuck would you do that? Make some copies of them and plant them around so that we all feel better about ourselves? You and Mac? They're aliens, they're fucking aliens. There's no way you can help them."

"I can get them out of Time Lock."

"Yeah, right."

"I think you'll find she can and she will, and in the meantime it might be best if you did everything Olwin asks." Guerra is back.

"They're not the same," I say. Because I can't help myself. "They may not even want to come back."

"You've seen them?" asks Olwin.

"Yes."

"Then show me that."

I shrug. Because I don't have a choice. And because at least I won't have to climb all those stairs up to Eva's greenhouse.

CHAPTER THIRTY-FOUR

Green Jay

BLUE JAY AND I are lying naked on the floor of the greenhouse again. It fills me with calm, even with joy, although it is a sad joy that is matched by the broken windows and the dirty floor. His fingers are twined through mine, but he has come no closer to me than that. If I ask him to take me to hospital, he will. A thousand Tals will comfort me, a thousand doctors examine me. They might even be able to keep me alive for a while longer. But I would like to fade away here. Now that I have brought the new Eva into existence, I have done all that I need to. I would like to pretend that Blue Jay and I can fly away together for a while longer. But I can't. I ask the question I know I shouldn't.

"Will you find her?"

Blue Jay turns to look at me. I can see the tears on his

cheeks. He is tired too; dirty and tired and worn. "No," he says, but I cannot believe him. "Let me tell you about her."

I know he wants to talk about Olwin Duilis. I know and I cannot stop him, because he needs to tell me. Things I probably already know, if I allowed myself to look. Things I cannot allow myself to know, because then I will be lost. I will be another her.

"Yes," I say. "But let me say goodbye first."

I stretch over to kiss him. My lips find his and our tongues meet. He strokes the bare skin of my back and down to my buttocks. We twine ourselves together so that he is me and I am him. My brown-green skin mingles with his cream and pink and the blue twined into him. It is almost the same as floating in the Trocarn tendrils. We have never done this before, Blue Jay and I. I cannot say why. But now is the right time. Now, before I go.

We lie, dusty and sticky and half asleep. Blue Jay begins the story of Olwin Duilis. At first the story is slow, but then the words come out faster and faster until they pour out of them and they could never be stopped. He tells how he first met her. How her body was broken, but her mind was extraordinary, the smartest person he had even known. Smarter than him? I wonder, but he waves the blue dot on his thumb around as if to show me, his brain has help. He does not explain this, but I understand.

He tells of the way in which they became friends and I can see that even then, they had fallen in love, though they did not know it. I know they would have lain naked too, somewhere. Olwin barely able to move. Blue Jay with his fingers entwined through hers. He tells me how they invented a way for her to move around. A metal skeleton, but on the outside so that it was a kind of cage. I thought she'd run away, he tells me.

And then, the part that I did not want to hear. The night that Olwin Duilis made a double of herself. A double, but changed, so that she would be healthy and strong and able to move without the cage. A double for Blue Jay. Except, of course, she called him Mac, called him MacIver. But, of course, the double only lasted a few days. And Blue Jay had been entranced and repulsed and had fled to Barlewin.

"Why Barlewin?" I ask. Because I don't want to ask how many doubles he saw die before he ran.

"I wanted to see the Chemical Conjurers," he said. I think back to the day the Chemical Conjurers helped me hide. "Did you know I was coming?" I ask.

"No," he says. "But somehow they did, and once I met you, I knew, and I knew straight away that you were not Olwin, that you were you and that you were running from her, just like me, but that you were enough like her that I couldn't help but..."

His fingers are still in mine, but his face is turned away.

"I'm sorry," he says. "I'm sorry."

I take my fingers away from his and he turns further from me, but I stretch out my hand and turn his face towards me. "I can't let myself be her."

"I know." I can't tell if he means it's good or bad. But it does not matter. I can only be who I am. And then I feel the parts of Olwin Duilis that Blue Jay has talked about rise up. They can't help but be part of me now. I hold on to myself for as long as I am able.

Crow

GUERRA HAS LEFT Olwin Duilis to my tender care. (There are enough of his people around for him to be secure and certain: Carine, for one, made me tell her exactly where we were going.) All things considered, it's not a bad outcome. But it's not one that has me feeling comfortable. We're walking the High Track and Olwin hasn't said anything at all. I'm fine with that. At least I was; the silence is weighing in now, making me want to speak. All that I can hear is the whisper of Olwin's cage, the thing that's keeping her upright, helping her walk. Keeping her alive, for all I know. It's creeping me out.

I stop at the spot where it's easy to see Eva's greenhouse. This much I can show her. Though I figure she already knows. There's a bench, but neither of us use it. And there's no broken symbol with an eye or any other body part. Instead I tell her about the locks. The way those other-reality people put locks on the railings to protest the Time Locked Tenties.

"What's it like, travelling Time Locked?" asks Olwin Duilis.

"Bloody awful."

"But isn't it worth it, to see other places and other people?"

"Not really. I mean it's just more of the same. Saw a mad Guerra. That was… interesting."

So she makes me tell her about the Barleycorn King and the prophets with their pollution-sensing garments and the way he drew me to safety with his striped cane.

"You sure that's Guerra?"

"Who else could it be?"

Olwin Duilis smiled. "Doesn't seem much like the Guerra I know."

"He threw me down the stairs."

Olwin laughs. "Okay, that's a bit more like Guerra."

"Theory is, he's been tortured by what he did to the Tenties." Even as I say it, it seems wrong, but I'm sticking with the theory.

"Still not convinced."

I'm being drawn in. I can see why Mac liked her. She's smart, but easy to talk to. And she's beautiful, too, in a drawn and terrible way. But you don't see that after a while.

"So you and Mac…?"

"MacIver and I are friends, but nothing else. I'm not even sure if we're friends now."

Yeah, me too, I think. I can't get my head around Mac's life. I guess he hasn't exactly lied. But he hasn't exactly been forthcoming either. Seems like a betrayal to me.

She looks out at the greenhouse so I can't see her face. "Will he come back, do you think?

I can see the dragonfly sitting in her hair. "Why don't you do it?" I ask. "Travel between the realities, see the sights?"

"Track him down?"

"No. Just do it for yourself?"

"Look at me, Kern. I wouldn't survive."

"Not even with all that tech shit you've got going on?"

"Not even with the tech shit."

"The Tenties might help." I stick my wrist out so she can see the raised ring around my wrist. "There's a part of them in me. It helps, I think."

"Maybe."

"And Aleris"—I nearly say 'Eva,' but I remember in time—"she can travel. Don't seem to bother her."

"I know, I made her that way. Some plant matter. Helps a lot. Quite strange, really."

"Humants."

Olwin laughs and looks at me and I see that this, at least, has pushed her out of her melancholy. "What?"

"Part-people, part-plant. Probably part-Tentie. I met some. They hang around the greenhouse worshipping you."

"Not me," says Olwin.

"Well, not exactly."

"She's a different person. You know that, Brom. Don't try to cheer me up by pretending she isn't." She turns around, her back to the greenhouse. "The Trocarn?" she reminds me.

We walk further up the High Track, to the place the Tenties should be. Approximately, that is, seeing as how the High Track is all much of a muchness. But we're past staircase number 1 and this spot looks as good as any.

"Here," I say, feeling slightly stupid. "In theory, anyway."

"Was there any indication?"

"A shimmer. If you look close." If it's here at all, I think. I mean, maybe the Tenties have given up and gone home. Maybe the dome never cycles into this world. I haven't asked where the Tentie dome is, in this reality. Not on the High Track, that's for sure. And that seems like a considerable flaw in my guided tour.

"Where are they here?" I ask.

"Oh, I'm not sure. Not up on the High Track. Close by, I think." But she's distracted by something. I see the dragonfly searching for the dome, buzzing around loudly, searching, but never settling. I remember the way Tal lit up the dome for us, realise I could get him to do that now if I was willing to show Olwin who and what he was. Which I'm not, not just yet. Maybe not ever.

"It's not here," she says. "Or if it is, I can't find it."

I'm tempted to bring out Tal, but no. We're too close to the spot where I watched Eva and T-Lily jump off the edge to get away from the time nets. We're too close to the spot I did the same thing.

"Can you manage stairs?" I ask. Because if I know Guerra, I know just where the Tenties are.

"Can you?" she asks, and she grins.

The fact is, stairs are probably not the best option for either of us, but we manage. Slowly, awkwardly and with a fair bit of swearing on Olwin's part. We sit for a while on the bottom step. At least, I sit; Olwin leans against one of the posts supporting the High Track. There's another of those big hands there, painted to make it look like it's holding the whole thing up.

"Okay, Kern, now what?"

"For a start, call me Brom."

"Okay, Brom, now what?"

"Warehouse. Figure they're in one of Guerra's warehouses down here."

"More walking?"

"Not that much." Not if I choose the right warehouse. I have a mental sort through the options. Something with space, but something he don't use all that often. Something he wouldn't have to clear out. And something reasonably out of the way. Not that anyone much comes down here. There are a couple of choices, one likely option: the warehouse with the old Black Kraken sign on the outside. That's the kind of thing that would appeal to Guerra's sense of humour. "I could go on ahead, come back to you?" I suggest.

"Don't think so, Brom."

Yeah, I'm on a leash, and don't I know it. "Okay, then, ready?"

The two of us propel ourselves forward like the mechanical men we've become. It might even be funny to the outside observer. It isn't to me.

"How does it work, then?" I ask. "Tenties in one reality hovering around on the High Track, Tenties in another reality, hovering around down here."

"You don't cycle through all the realities, Brom. Just some of them." And then, as if it's been playing on her mind, "Did you never meet yourself? Just think of all those versions of you. I doubt if any of you are in exactly the same place."

I already regret asking, but I persist for something to say. "Yeah, but we're not flicking back and forth in Time Lock."

"Even if you were, why would it matter? There's still the same number of you."

"And if we were Time Locked in the same place?"

"You'd explode."

It takes me a moment to realise she's joking.

"I don't know, Brom. It seems unlikely."

We're near the warehouse. I can see the Black Kraken sign. Much faded, though you can still make out the unfortunates grasped in the tentacles. And as I hoped, there are none of Guerra's people around. No need, really: it's not as if the Tenties are high risk. Which doesn't mean there aren't security cameras and the like. But what the hell, I'm here with Olwin Duilis, which seems to amount to a get out of jail free card, at least for the time being.

I manage to get a side door open without too much of a fuss. It was locked, but not so as to pose much of a barrier. Olwin says nothing, just releases the dragonfly inside. It's quite dark, but I don't look around for lights because—and maybe this is my imagination—I reckon I can see the shimmer of the Tentie dome.

"Yes," says Olwin. The dragonfly's still buzzing around the dome, further out in the warehouse, so I don't know how she can be so sure. But then I realise that the dome's changed. I look down at my leg and Tal's pretending that he's just an exoskeleton, but I strongly suspect he's helped things along. He must be bored as hell down there. Assuming he's capable of feeling such a thing.

We walk forward, close enough so the Tenties are quite visible. It's like looking into an alien greenhouse–which, I suppose, it is.

Olwin takes a step forward and before I can even think, *No, not again,* she's grabbed my arm and pulled me into the dome.

CHAPTER THIRTY-FIVE

Green Jay

BLUE JAY HAS taken me to the hospital. I did not want to go; I wanted to fade away before Olwin became too strong. But that hasn't happened. Not yet, at least. She is there and it is hard to tell the borders of her and me, if there are any. But I am not lost. Not completely. From time to time I touch the tendril around my wrist and remind myself that Olwin Duilis does not have this. That already I have memories that can never belong to her.

Blue Jay sleeps on a chair beside my bed. I am glad of him, so glad, but it is easier to think of myself without him. Without knowing that it was Olwin Duilis he loved first. And he will draw her out of me more than he already has. I must leave him, as soon as I am well enough. I don't think I can stay.

I lie still so I don't wake him up. He has a pole beside

him; a white pole, quite tall, the kind of thing a tightrope walker might use to balance. That is Olwin Duilis' thought. I know that. It doesn't seem so bad anymore.

I watch him and despite myself I want him to come to the bed and kiss me again. Unravel me. He opens his eyes, stretches and then comes and sits beside me. He is too scared to touch me. "How are you feeling?" he asks.

I smile and hold his hand, but only because I can't answer that. I am a mixture, now, of so many things. Of Olwin Duilis in the beginning, but not truly because of my green skin and other things borrowed from plants. I have offerings from the Trocarn, and now I am also partly held together with the microtechnologies of these future people. I am surprisingly whole.

"Don't leave me," he says.

"You should go back to her."

Blue Jay shakes his head.

"You must."

"I said goodbye to her before you ever came," he says.

And that is true. Perhaps even enough. I pull him towards me and we lie in the hospital bed holding each other. I cannot go.

Crow

OLWIN'S COVERED BY tendrils, but I've just got the odd one wound around my arms. I'm feeling fine, considering, and by the looks of Olwin she's okay too. I've seen all this before, of course, so the novelty's pretty much worn off.

I'm hoping someone materialises out of the vines pretty soon. It'd be easy to lose yourself in here, but the thought of using an alien species as a type of immersive drug den seems wrong, even to me.

There's a shape emerging from the tendrils; quite fast, at least as Tenties go. It's not Kolb or Lona, but it does remind me of the first humant I met, Fay. An androgynous figure, very green. Perhaps this is the new Tentie look.

The figure moves towards me and embraces me, early Tentie style. I don't object. How can I? I'm in their dome, after all. But then the whole thing becomes awkward. It's hard to think of a way to convey that I'm only here because someone pulled me in, without sounding rude.

"I'm sorry that you're still here." It's the best I can come up with at short notice.

The Tentie holds its head to the side, a very human gesture, but not all that comforting. "We don't need saving."

"You're telling me you like it here?"

"As much as anywhere. And you visit."

Was that a joke? "I do my best." The dragonfly has transferred itself to my leg, to Tal actually; he's obviously decided that he's going to hold me together come what may. And I see that Olwin has stirred. The tendrils release her enough so that she can move closer to us. The Tentie embraces her as well. It's a long, uncomfortable hug, and probably more about DNA exchange than friendship, but you never know.

"Thank you," says Olwin.

The Tentie bows. "Quickly," it says. The tendrils draw

back from Olwin. She takes a step towards the edge of the dome and Tal does something to my leg so that I move too, and we're out. Back in the warehouse, the dome just behind us. Olwin's grimacing, but she's still upright. Though I don't suppose she has much choice about that. I look at her wrist, but there's no tendril there to match mine or Eva's.

I give her a moment, walk back to the door. There's no-one in sight, but I'm fairly sure that Guerra knows where we are and that someone will be round fairly shortly.

I hear the sound of her exoskeleton, feel her hand on my shoulder.

"They're extraordinary," she says.

"Yep," I say. "But they shouldn't really be there." Despite what I was told. I guess the Tenties can choose their own Time Locked life if they want it that much. Olwin doesn't contradict me, so I decide to push. "So can you do it, get them out?"

"Can I convince enough people? No. Can I turn off the machines? Sure. They'll be in here somewhere."

That takes a moment to process. "They'll just put them back."

"Maybe, maybe not." She's grinning now. Still looks dreadful—pale, sweaty, almost grey—but also happy. "Technology breaks down all the time. At least this way …"

My mind comes up with a whole lot more excuses, but that's all they really are. "I'll take a look around," I tell her. And before Olwin can say no, I begin my search. As much as she'd probably like to keep me within sight, she's in no state to follow me around. I'm frankly surprised that I'm in a fit state to move, but that's me, seasoned interreality traveller.

But not a seasoned technology expert. I turn and call back to her, "What am I looking for?"

The answer I get is the dragonfly. If I'd thought about it for a second longer, I would have thought of Tal. On the other hand, perhaps it's better that I still have some secrets. It's not that big a warehouse, and it's pretty much the one open room, but there's a mezzanine walkway type thing at one end and that's where I start. More bloody stairs. The dragonfly loses patience and zips ahead. It buzzes impatiently around one section, barely waits for me to get there. Yep. There's panels, buttons. Not much in the way of instructions, but I figure, what the hey, I'll just turn everything I can see to zero. It occurs, possibly too late, that I could be doing the Tenties more harm than good. So I look up, see a sight I had in no way expected: Olwin Duilis surrounded by Hooks.

It figures. The Hooks hate the Tenties with an unreasonable obsession, and they haven't had the opportunity to focus their hate on anything or anyone else yet. None of them are wearing the T-shirts with red writing, I guess even they had figured out that if the Tenties can't see red in real life, they're not going to see it when Time Locked. But a few of them still have fish hooks in their hair, which has got to be one of the more inconvenient forms of protest. The dome is non-existent, at least from up here. I hope to hell I haven't just released the Tenties into a group of moronic haters. But there's no sign of the Tenties at all. It's possible the Hooks are Guerra's half-arsed security system. If that's true, I hope he's alerted them to Olwin's special status.

"Go," I say to the dragonfly, because there's no way I can make it down to Olwin Duilis with any kind of speed. Not that the dragonfly can do much to protect her. For possibly the first time in my life, I actually hope Guerra's looking. Surely he's not going to let Olwin Duilis come to harm.

My mind skips ahead to a brief vision of tendrils pulling the Hooks into the dome and disposing of them, but that's not Tentie style. Co-operation rather than revenge. Of course, they also co-operated with Guerra, which don't show the best judgment. Eva, for one, might have something to say about the moral compass of some of the Tenties, but still, I don't think they'd outright kill the Hooks. Which is a pity.

They've surrounded Olwin. I should go down and help her, although that's a course of action I know I'll regret. There's a tickle on my hand and there's the dragonfly, which is proving as courageous as I am. But I see a light blinking annoyingly on the panel. One last button. If the dragonfly thinks it's okay, it must be, yes? So I press the button which flashes once, red.

It's the prelude to a whole shitstorm of happenings:

One, there's a loud crinkling sound as the dome first appears and then disintegrates.

That reveals the Tenties who are, understandably, in a state of considerable disarray. Some are back to old Tentie state, some are in the new green Humant form, some are still tendrils. I'm surprised they're this prepared, but I guess they figured I was about to go and do something stupid. They know me disturbingly well.

Some of the Hooks take one look and run. Some of them start laughing and jumping up and down in complete disbelief. Some of them seem to be readying themselves to fight the Tenties. They've got knives out, that kind of thing. There's no action, though. I guess they've never seen so many Tenties all in one place at one time.

At least the attention's not on Olwin. She looks up at me, gives me a thumbs-up and shakes her head. I'm interpreting that as, *Don't come down.* I start to move anyway. Why, I don't know. And then—and this is the least expected thing of all—the Chemical Conjurers make an entrance. Felix and Oscar. They pull themselves up to full height once they're through the door. Most of the Hooks take the hint and run. A few of them are helped on their way with a robot hand. Once they're gone, Olwin gets the full attention of Felix, and Oscar comes up to talk to me as I make my slow way back to the centre of the room.

"Well done, Brom," he says. I'm hoping he means the release of the Tenties and not my complete inaction in the face of danger.

"Thanks," I say, which he can interpret however he likes. "Will they be okay?" Probably a question I should have asked earlier, but better late than never.

"Will they adapt to this reality after having been caught in Time Lock for several months?"

"Yes." Although I'm thinking, *Several months?* Several

weeks, maybe, not several months. Though in the future, several years. Shit, I hate this stuff.

"I believe they will be fine," says Oscar. We both take a look at the Tenties. Just a whole crowd of tentacled beings, some tending towards the unashamedly green humant, some tending towards the original Tentie form. There's very few tendrils left.

But there's some of that orange cloud of happiness hovering over them, which is a good thing, because although some of them seem to have found clothes, others appear to have forgotten the need.

"They're remarkable," comments Oscar.

"That's what Olwin said."

"She is also remarkable."

"You've known about this all along: Olwin, Mac, the whole thing. You just watched me make a fool of myself."

"No," says Oscar. "Not a fool. Except for one thing. Olwin will know that Aleris is not the real double, Brom."

Maybe, maybe not, but I'm not about to get into this discussion. Luckily we're close enough to the others that a reply isn't strictly needed. I throw myself into the meet and greet, put up with a lot of Tentie hugging; but the fact remains, releasing the Tenties is nowhere near as satisfying as I thought it would be.

CHAPTER THIRTY-SIX

Green Jay

BLUE JAY AND I are returning home, back to the greenhouse, my hospital stay over. It is evening, almost dark, but still a touch of blue in the sky. We are walking through the alleyways of the tenements when I feel someone pull at me. A fleeting grab to the arm, then release. I should be scared: it was not always safe here, and perhaps that is still true in the place we are now. I turn, I can't see who it is, but then I see the lights a little way off. I know those lights. I call to Blue Jay, stop him, and he sees it too. The Crow has failed us again. The time nets should have stopped. Even if my double has not survived, if the Crow did his job, they should think it is me that has died. My arm is grabbed again, more strongly this time, though I still cannot see who is pulling.

"Eva," whispers a voice I recognise. I take Blue Jay's

hand and we move quickly into the darkness. There is not much space, a few steps then a wall. But the arm pulls at us again and we move to the side, and then up a few steps so that we are standing with our backs to a door. I am caught in a hug. I don't understand why it is so dark, why I cannot see clearly, but I know that this is Rose-Q. The feel of her, the smell. The memories of being caught with Guerra come back. And she is somehow here, somehow released. I hug her back, but it makes me miss T-Lily and, unfairly, I wish that it was her rather than Rose-Q. Maybe this is just another form of time net, one of Guerra's people come to get me.

She stands close to me. I take Blue Jay's hand and we all three of us stand in the dark, waiting for the time nets to pass. None of us speak. I am sure the time nets cannot hear us, but we have become like trapped animals, too frightened and unsure to speak.

When the lights fade, Blue Jay pulls me back into the alley, away from Rose-Q. She follows, of course. "Thank you," I say, because we would have been trapped without her. We move as quickly as we can towards the greenhouse. Not running, not quite, though I wish we could.

Crow

THE CHEMICAL CONJURERS say goodbye to us at the water tower. Olwin seems to have recovered. In fact, she's recovered enough that she's now insisting that we visit the farm. Who am I to complain? Most of the Tenties have gone their own way—back, I suppose, to whatever lives they previously led and whatever homes they previously inhabited. We have a retinue though, a few stragglers. I don't recognise any of them. One in humant form, the others as the Tenties we've come to know and love. I don't mind that they're here, but I don't want to talk to them either. I think about telling them about the water tower, showing them it's a place they can stay if they need it, but that reminds me too much of Mac, so we walk past Ol' Stick Man without a word.

There's no sign of anyone working in the garden, but the door opens as soon as we knock and Judith is crying and laughing and ushering us in and hugging anyone in sight, including Tenties. It's obviously Judith—a younger version, but the same earth mother vibe. I wasn't sure how they'd react to me, but I suppose, for them, this is our first meeting. And that's quite possibly a good thing.

We're fed, of course. Tenties too, and if Ed looks less than completely comfortable with the idea, he says nothing. He looks almost exactly the same as last time I saw him. There are, of course, remonstrations that Olwin took so long to come to see them.

"You could have come up to see me, Mum."

"No," says Ed. And I can see, straight away, that we've moved to a delicate area of family disagreement. I can't say I blame them. Even as a former employee myself, I don't know that I'd want my daughter making deals with Guerra. But they move past that. Probably because of the Tenties, maybe even because of me. And then it's family reminiscence and catch up and I feel completely out of place.

"How long will you stay?" asks Judith.

"In Barlewin?" Olwin asks. "I don't know."

"One night?" asks Judith. "In your old room. And of course, your friend is welcome. And the Trocarn, if they would like to stay."

The Tenties release a cloud of orange happiness, apologise in the confusion, profess their exhaustion, and then follow Judith up the stairs and to a spare room.

Ed looks directly at me. "You got them out of that Time Lock?"

"Yes," I admit. Because I have to show some courage.

"Good job. Strange beasties, the Trocarn, but the Time Lock was cruel."

Which pretty much sums up my own feelings, so we sit in silence, drinking tea. Ed takes his leave, off to address the afternoon's farm work. I get the feeling he's considering asking me for help. But luckily he's only just met me—as far as he's concerned—and my leg is obviously buggered up.

"I've been here before," I tell Olwin. More making conversation than anything else. "Your mum gave me a phone from the future."

"She did?" Olwin's question seems more polite than I'd expected.

"Yeah. I lost it though." Accidentally on purpose. "And the dragonfly visited."

Olwin is distinctly disinterested in my adventures in time and space. "And Aleris, did she come here too?"

This, I could answer truthfully, even supposing by Aleris she meant Eva. "No, she was a little… freaked out by the farm."

"She didn't want to remember me."

Olwin is right, but only partly right. I think of the footage up on the big screen, of Eva running from the shed. "How many times have you done this?" I ask.

"Done what, Brom?"

I don't really need to answer that question.

Olwin looks down. "Only the once," she says.

"You sure about that?"

"Don't forget you've been in different realities. Seen lots of mes, lots of ways this might have played out. Don't confuse them with what has happened here."

"So you wouldn't try it again?"

Olwin stares into the dregs of her tea. "No, Brom. I won't try it again." She swirls the cup around as if she was a fortune-teller looking for portents. "I want to see her," she says.

Of course I know who she means, but I can't admit to it. "You have seen her."

It's possible Olwin might be crying, but if she keeps looking down at her mug I can ignore that. "What was it like?"

"You're asking the wrong person," I begin. But then I realise I'm just being cruel. And that maybe one of the reasons we're here is so that she can ask me questions out of Guerra's hearing.

So I tell her as much as I can. About Eva in the greenhouse, how she was captured by Guerra, about all the ways she was kept alive, including Mac's surgery. I tell her about the three of us holing up in the water tower, because, fuck, I'm still mad at Mac, and what do I care if that knowledge comes back to bite him? I tell her a little bit about the alternate realities, though that's hard to do without sounding like you're off your tree. And last of all I tell her about the scenes on the big screen, the ones that got the Tenties Time Locked.

"Was she always so scared?" asks Olwin.

"No," I say and I think that's true. "She was"—and it takes me a moment to find the polite word for *annoying and self-righteous*—"determined."

Olwin snorts a little bit at that. And it's difficult to ignore the tears and snot and the rest of it. I get up, find her a tissue. Well, not so much find, as have Judith hand me a box when I'm in the kitchen.

I sit down again and Tal untangles himself from my leg and pulls himself into stick insect form. This, unsurprisingly, catches her attention. He hasn't drawn himself up to full height, but he's still taller than either Olwin or me.

Olwin looks up, grins. "Very cool," she says. "And hi."

"Hello," says Tal. He shakes Olwin's hand in a formal gesture that might have made me laugh in a time before I was used to the ways of robots.

I stretch out my leg and rub my hands along the muscle. It feels unsupported and weak, but somewhat more human.

"You can't do that anymore," he tells me. "Mess about with Time Lock."

"You said that before. Nothing happened."

"A lot happened. I did what I could. But you've prevented proper healing and your leg will not survive another outing."

"Oh, Brom, I'm sorry," says Olwin.

"Don't be," says Tal. "He would have done it anyway." Which, I will admit, is a reasonable insight into my personality. "But"—and this is addressed to me—"you absolutely can't do it again."

"Could you protect me," Olwin asks him, "if *I* wanted to do it again?"

Tal makes a noise which I interpret as a robot sigh. "Time Lock wasn't designed for travel to alternate realities. It's crude, it's frankly unsafe even for the short periods messengers use it. I don't recommend it."

"An unintentional side feature," says Olwin.

"Yes," says Tal, convinced that she's onside.

"Yeah, but you're from the future," I say. "Maybe things have improved a bit."

"It may surprise you to learn that the focus of most research is not on travel to alternate realities."

"But the Trocarn," Olwin says. "They adapted."

"Because their bodies are malleable and because they learnt from your offspring."

"Are you sure that the offspring aren't just the Tenties with a new, improved look?" I ask.

"No," says Tal. "If I understand the Trocarn correctly, it's a homage. In the same way they copy your form."

"They helped Brom," says Olwin. She picks up my wrist and shows Tal the raised patch of flesh. It's a desperate bid and she knows it, seeing as Tal has already banned me from Time Lock.

Tal is as unmoved as only a robot can be.

"Looks like we're both stuck here," I tell her. Trying to cheer her up.

"No," says Olwin. It's a quiet no, but it's also a statement of belief. Just at this moment, I can't blame her; I'd probably want an out too if I was stuck in that exoskeleton. But, speaking purely selfishly, I'm more than happy to have what amounts to doctor's orders to stay in the one place.

Judith comes in and if she's surprised that there's a new guest standing in her dining room, it doesn't appear to worry her. "Perhaps," she suggests, "you could all do with a rest." Olwin shakes her head, but stands up and walks up the stairs, presumably to her own room.

"I'm sorry you've had to see all this," says Judith. Which is extraordinarily polite, given we were the ones who brought the trouble to her door and not the other way around. But perhaps this is not the first time she's experienced strange, emotional events connected with her daughter. And even if it is, it probably won't be the last. "Can I get you anything else?" she asks. "Another cup of tea?"

I let her fuss, because yes, I would like another cup of tea, but also because she seems to need it. So much strange needs a little ordinary.

While I'm waiting, I leave Tal at the table and go for a wander into the adjoining room. There are faded, comfortable chairs, books and a television. It's almost exactly as I saw it before. It's strange to observe a life where almost everything stays the same, but perhaps that's Ed and Judith's injection of sanity, given their daughter and her propensity for the bizarre.

But there is one difference: a picture of Olwin up on the wall, a framed photograph. It's the same shot as the one I saw on the phone Judith gave me, as the one superimposed over the map. It's head-and-shoulders, no hint of the exoskeleton, even though now, in real life, that neck shows definite touches of metal. Even so, it can't have been taken long ago. Olwin don't look any younger in the photo.

It makes me wonder what will happen to make her ever-loyal parents take it off the wall.

CHAPTER THIRTY-SEVEN

Green Jay

I FEEL SAFE in the greenhouse, even dusty and abandoned as it is. The hallway has graffiti I never noticed the first time. And the very front wall of the building is painted, so that the front door is part of a woman's yawning mouth and one of the windows is an eye. Blue Jay and I only plan to stay here for a while, he wants to work on the pole, something he has developed to move quickly and easily through Time Lock to other realities. He will still need more protection than I do, of course. Partly because of that, I hope that we don't need it, but the time nets are still searching. I wonder if there is anywhere else I could make my home. It is strange to look up and see the bicycles whooshing past. A High Track without plants. A High Track without Guerra.

Rose-Q is not quite the same as I remember her.

Perhaps it is only that I am not drugged, but I suspect that she has not had time to fully form. She told us of the way the Crow released the Trocarn. Too fast, and almost without warning. Just like him. And the scattering of Trocarn released over different realities. She thinks it was unintentional; she does not blame him. But I do. He never does anything without causing more harm and confusion.

It is a strange thought that there are still Trocarn caught in the dome on the High Track. Unless a different Crow from a different reality released them too. That should be my job, when I am well and whole. I will ask Rose-Q to help. She will understand how to do it properly. Although she does not appear to have been hurt by her time in the dome. She does not describe what it was like to take such a different form. It is almost as if those memories have faded away. I find that sad. As though they have lost a part of themselves, even if it was a part we forced them to create in order to survive.

I tell Rose-Q about Aleris. I know I'm using Rose-Q as a confessor. I am worse than her. She did as Guerra asked her to and drugged me, but she also kept me alive. And in the end she did not abandon me. She helped me escape. I have made another and left her entirely to the care of Guerra and Olwin Duilis. I understand now why Blue Jay trusted Olwin to care for her, but that does not make it right. There is enough Olwin Duilis in me to know it was very wrong.

*   *   *

Crow

IT'S SOMEWHERE AROUND two or three a.m. There's no clock, and of course whatever phones I once owned are long gone, but the night has that feel of the early hours. I'm lying in the room that Judith found for me. Because of course, Olwin was persuaded to stay the night, which means, so was I. Judith apologised several times for the room's small size. I don't tell her it's one of the best places I've had to sleep for quite a long while.

My brain, as usual, has taken a long time to catch up. It seems to me this is the perfect opportunity to get the hell out of here, away from Barlewin altogether. I'm feeling virtuous because of the Tenties. And, quite frankly, I don't really want to experience more of the drama that is Olwin Duilis. I'm not without my sympathies for her, but I can see why Mac wanted to get away. Not that I've forgiven him.

I take a piss and have a quick wash. There's really nothing I can bring with me—I've had a quick check through the drawers. They live simple lives, Judith and Ed: food from the farm, money in the bank. Not much stuff around. It's probably a good thing. I wouldn't have felt all that bad if I had snaffled something, but it's nice to leave quick and clean once in a while.

I close the door to my room. I want them to think I'm having a sleep in for as long as possible. There's voices coming from Olwin's room. Soft, but I think she's having a heart-to-heart with Tal. Which is a shame, he would have come in useful.

I move past them and down the stairs. It's dark, but I remember the house well enough from my first time here, so I'm out the front door without any fuss. I stand for a moment, taking in the lights of the High Track and planning my move out through the farm, past the shed and into the great unknown.

Well, that's an exaggeration. It's not like I've never been out of Barlewin at all. Just not within recent memory.

There's someone standing in between Ed's rows of beans or whatever it is he's got growing there. Someone who looks a little like a ghost, though I'm not going to be fooled twice. It's not a prophet, minor or otherwise, but Eila. Of course it is. She's checking up on me, Aleris, the whole plan. I was stupid to think otherwise.

She stands still, waiting for me, and I've half a mind to go back inside, but instead I walk towards her.

"Hello, Brom," she says. As if we'd planned all along to meet in the middle of the farm at two a.m. by the light of the High Track.

I don't say hello back. It's childish; can't help it. "The time nets are still out," she says.

"So he's not convinced."

"It's not Guerra we need to convince."

And with that it all falls into place. It's Olwin Duilis I should be worried about. It has been all along. "She'll never be convinced," I say. "She… she'd turn herself into Eva if she could."

"She probably thinks she already did."

I shrug. "She's the one with the time nets."

"And Eva's the one with Mac."

"Yeah, don't remind me."

"Eva's not safe yet."

"What do you care? I mean, I've never understood this. You can't be speaking for Guerra, because he don't give a shit as long as he's getting paid, which I'm guessing he is. So who are you speaking for?"

"Maybe I'm speaking for myself."

"How is it that you're in all these places? Following me around, up with the Barleycorn King, and then at the concert, and tapping into my phone and showing—"

Eila puts her hand out to stop me and I'm kind of glad she interrupts because I'm getting more worked up than I really want to. "Have you ever done anything you regret, Brom?" she asks.

Yeah, about a thousand things, but nothing that I'm going to admit to at this moment. "Maybe."

"And did you ever want to fix it?"

"I've been told by authoritative source"—i.e. myself—"that's a waste of time."

"Maybe," Eila smiles in a truly irritating manner.

"Goodnight," I say and I turn to walk back towards the house, because what other choice is there? I'm still stuck in the middle of this crap, and somehow I need to convince Olwin to let me out; that's the only way I'm really going to be able to wander off. But I can't help but ask one more question. "Who are you?"

"Ask Felix and Oscar, they'll tell you."

Which is a half-arsed answer if ever I heard one, but it's the middle of the night and all things considered, I'd rather be back in a bed. I lift my hand in farewell then trudge back through the farm. The door squeaks a little as I open it—thank God it didn't lock—and I sneak back up to my room. Disappointed, but I'm getting used to that. Or that's what I tell myself. The lights are out in all the rooms; Tal and Olwin seem to have finished their heart to heart. No-one will be any the wiser.

Tal, of course, is in my room ready with the questions.

"Don't start," I tell him as I climb into bed. I've taken off my shoes, but that's all. A wave of tiredness has hit me and sleep seems very appealing. I don't want to give Tal any conversational openings.

Actually he seems more worried about my leg, but I show him that it's working just fine by kicking at him. And then I'm asleep.

The next thing I know there's light streaming in the window, and people are expecting me to get up and going, back to the High Track. I take my time, why the hell not, but then it's all goodbyes. I give Judith a hug, which surprises her, but I'm actually glad to see her again. Ed too, but he's not a hugging man.

Of course I angle for a detour through the marketplace, hoping for a heart-to-heart with the Chemical Conjurers, but nothing doing. Olwin wants back to Guerra, so back to Guerra we go. The short way, up staircase number 4 and then to the left.

Both of us make a better fist of the stairs, though neither of us is what you'd call elegant. Carine is waiting at the top, along with a couple of other buddies. Guerra's obviously glad to see us back where we belong. No sign of any Tenties, which is probably a good thing; I'd hate to think I'd released them into Guerra's tender care.

We walk in the direction of admin, Olwin happily ignoring our guards. It's awkward, to say the least. We've just passed staircase number 3 when we see Aleris lying out on a deck chair, taking in the sun with one of Guerra's people standing guard close by. I don't recognise the guard. Tal, I think, would like to go see how she's faring. As would Olwin: she stops, and so do we all.

She takes a seat beside Aleris. They're the kind of push-back chairs placed side by side but oriented so that the head of one is beside the foot of the other. Olwin don't lie down. She just sits sideways and leans over a bit so that she can look at Aleris eye to eye. The rest of us stand around, waiting, our lowly place in the scheme of things underlined by our lack of movement.

So I've plenty of time to look around and admire the High Track. And that's when I see Mac and Eva, standing close to the outside railing. They're behind some kind of sculpture and, of course, there's plenty of that fluffy grass between them and us, but still, they're completely out in the open. It will only take a moment of distraction on the part of a guard and they'll be spotted. And shit, there's someone with them. A Tentie. They've probably brought her back for Aleris, more fool them.

Olwin straightens up, her heart-to-heart with Aleris obviously over. We'll be off in a minute, leaving Eva and Mac to whatever foolish plan they have in mind. I look over towards admin, hear a crack, see Olwin fall back onto the chair. She's been pushed over by one of the guards, who is running towards Mac and Eva. Tal disentangles himself from my leg and shoots over to Olwin; she's got enough tech of her own, but he can't help himself. Aleris is sitting up, when she'd be better off lying down. Carine gives me a look, which I interpret as, *This better not be anything to do with you, Brom.* And for once, it's not, though Carine is probably betting the other way.

Then all four guards are running into a murky yellow green mist the Tentie's released. One of them pushes at me as he goes past, so I stick out a leg to help him on his way. He stumbles, but then he's up and off. That's as much help as I can give, I'm afraid. Olwin, Aleris and Tal are moving towards admin, which is a fine plan, but not one I'm particularly interested in. Instead I walk to the side, across to the stairs and then down.

CHAPTER THIRTY-EIGHT

Green Jay

As soon as I see the Crow I know our plan will go awry. He is the only one who notices us; the others are paying attention to Aleris or looking around bored. Rose-Q is trembling and letting off a little mist, but it drifts away without being noticeable. Blue Jay is calm, so calm and still. I see the Crow look away and I try to see what he is looking at. And perhaps it is because I turn my head, or perhaps it is just bad luck, but one of the guards sees us and comes running.

Blue Jay lifts the pole, ready to draw us into Time Lock and away, but, of course, the guards think it is a weapon and then all four of them are running, yelling, guns drawn. Rose-Q is so afraid that she surrounds us with mist. It keeps us safe, stops them from firing, but Rose-Q is agitated. She keeps moving up and down the edge of the High Track so that Blue Jay cannot create the field. And then it is too late. Hands grab at us through the mist; someone has my arm and is pulling me back towards the middle of the High Track. Rose-Q screams, a strange noise that I have never heard before. I hear the guard hit her; I hear something like a sob. I pull away from my guard, trying to get to Rose-Q, but the guard is stronger than me and I am forced to keep walking.

And then we are out of the mist, standing in front of Guerra's building. Olwin Duilis is there, with Aleris and Tal. Tal has pulled himself into some type of shield, but Olwin Duilis steps around it and out into the open. She holds out her hands and the guards soften their grip, but do not let us go. She looks at Blue Jay, looks for so long, in complete silence. Me, she will not look at, but I suppose I do not especially matter to her. I am one of many.

And then Blue Jay steps to the side and the guard lets him go. He moves the pole up and across and I pull myself away from my guard and step inside the dome he is making. Olwin Duilis watches us all the while, watches us disappear. We have left Rose-Q, but they will not harm her, they will ask her to help Aleris. And of course, we can come back for her at another time, although it will be more difficult now.

Once again, we have failed.

Crow

I'M WALKING THROUGH the marketplace. Easily, not drawing attention. Though it's good to recognise the market stalls, nod to the owners. It makes me feel at home. I head towards the Chemical Conjurers, who are towering over the rest, doing something with streamers. There are small things like flying jellyfish about their shoulders and head. The jellyfish push themselves up on unseen air currents and then drift off around the marketplace. They remind me of Tenties, though I couldn't tell you why. Maybe it's just the jellyfish/sea creature association.

If I had any sense I'd drift away with them. But though I've got myself out of whatever's happening up on the High Track, I seriously doubt that this is the last I'm going to see of Olwin Duilis; and the only people I can think of that might actually help with that are Felix and Oscar.

Okay, not technically people. In some ways, better.

Their trick this morning seems to be knocking down empty takeaway coffee cups by standing way back and pointing something like a cardboard box at them. It's a good trick; it looks like there's a bit of magic in the cardboard box. Of course, it's just air. I've seen them do it before with smoke, which takes away the mystery but adds a bit of atmosphere. So the theme today seems to be light and airy, which may or may not work in my favour.

I choose a spot where they can't help but see me, settle down to watch. For a while, it's as if I'm not there at all. But that can't last.

"Didn't think you'd run away," says Felix. He sends a jellyfish flyer my way.

"Wouldn't call this exactly 'away,'" I tell him.

Oscar makes one last pass at the coffee cups and manages to get them to spin up and around before they inevitably fall to the ground. Felix sends the rest of the jellyfish flyers up high into the air, so they float away over the market and disappear. Some appear to be heading to the High Track.

"Sick of dragonflies?" I ask.

They take a seat beside me, one huge robot on either side. It's almost like I've come home. At least they don't seem to be about to pick me up and take me back to the High Track. But they do seem ready to comment on my moral choices, robot to human.

"I thought you were a better friend," says Oscar.

"I thought I had better friends." That's a little unfair, but only a little. I haven't forgotten the time they lifted me up and took me to the High Track. I'm still extraordinarily pissed off with Mac, but then if your best friends turn out to be a pair of robots, what does that say about you?

"Explain it to me," I say. "Tell me what's going on."

"You're asking us how to help Olwin Duilis?"

"I'm asking you how to get Olwin Duilis off my back." Which probably amounts to the same thing, but I want my position clear. Admittedly not leaving her up on the High Track in the middle of a fight would have been a good step, but it's a bit late for that now.

"You can't do anything about Olwin's problems, Brom."

They're probably right, but it don't help to hear it.

"Then tell me how to get away so that she don't harass me anymore."

"There's no need," says Oscar. "She will find a different way."

"A less biological solution," says Felix.

And that's about as much information on Olwin Duilis I'm going to get out of them. And at least they're not insisting I go back to the High Track.

"You have damaged your leg," says Oscar.

The leg in question is stretched out in front of me, because it aches when I bend it. "Yeah," I tell him, "no more Time Lock for me." I look up at the stars on their faces. "Is this what you've been doing all along? Trying to get into these alternate realities, find out what's going on?"

"That, of course, is a contradiction," says Felix

"By their very nature," says Oscar, "they are alternate." Both of them are highly pleased with themselves.

"And if we sent you to see an alternate version of yourself, that does not mean you have seen your future."

"A possibility, at best."

"So Guerra don't become the Barleycorn King?"

Both of them start laughing, a deep metallic rumbling that is incredibly disturbing and may actually be damaging some of my remaining internal organs. And maybe because of that, I miss something important, because all of a sudden there's Mac standing in front of me. He's wearing fingerless gloves and holding onto some kind of long plastic pole as if he was a destitute ninja. Presumably it's yet another alternate reality device. Less dodgy than the last one, I hope, though it pretty much looks cobbled together from pieces of the previous incarnation.

"MacIver," say the Chemical Conjurers. Mac hands Oscar the pole and they toss it from one to the other and wave it alarmingly through the air.

"We would need something larger," says Felix.

"But still," says Oscar, "impressive."

"It's easier to work with," says Mac, "but it's not entirely stable."

"No," says Felix in a who-the-fuck-cares, this-is-quite-cool kind of way.

I stand up, because this seems a good a time to go as any.

"I'm sorry, Brom," says Mac. "For everything."

The blue tracings have worked themselves further down his arm. Right now he looks to me just as alien as the Tenties, and certainly as strange as Eva. They deserve each other. I shrug, which is about all I can manage.

"I have to get back to her," he says.

"Of course you do."

"I... I didn't think that Olwin would become so obsessed."

"Why not, Mac? You knew she'd made a double of herself. I mean you helped keep the double alive. You can't really criticise anyone for being obsessed. And now you get to dance through all this Time Lock shit and I'm left here with bloody Guerra and Olwin Duilis. Who is, frankly, a *less* obsessed version of herself than Eva. And I can't just wave some ridiculous pole and get away. Well, fuck you. Just—fuck you."

Mac offers me the pole. "You can take it now and go."

I stretch my leg out in front of me. "Can't. Medical advice."

"Since when do you take advice?"

"Since I can feel my leg disintegrating underneath me."

Since I've realised it could be *me* who turns into a crazed man up on the High Track with only an AI for company. But I'm hardly likely to admit that.

Mac spreads his hands. "Then what do we do?"

There's really only one thing that can be done and Mac knows it. "How about you have a heart-to-heart with Olwin Duilis?"

Mac looks deeply uncomfortable but he agrees.

"Okay, then," I say and somehow things with Mac don't seem so bad. I like having him around; I'm used to him, after all. And I guess his love life is his own business as long as I don't get dragged into it. And since we've come with up a tentative dealing-with-Olwin-Duilis plan, we decide to get something to eat and coffee first. Because you can't go into battle on an empty stomach.

CHAPTER THIRTY-NINE

Green Jay

BLUE JAY HAS left me on the High Track, up in the section overlooking my greenhouse. I am safe here, at least for now. He wanted to leave me back in the world that has become our home, but I refused. I need to see that Aleris is safe and cared for. No, more than that. I need to see if Aleris can choose her own life. And then Blue Jay and I will be free.

I find the spot where I can see the greenhouse most clearly. It is strange to be looking in from the outside. I feel so foolish thinking about my younger self, thinking that I was unobserved and free in that space, when all the time Guerra was able to look straight in at me and report back to Olwin Duilis. I was never free at all.

I wonder if Aleris will feel about me the same way as I feel about Olwin Duilis. That here is a person who claims to be part of you, but whom you want nothing more than to push away, to bury them so far that they cannot influence you at all. She seemed so passive, so young, so malleable. It makes me sad to think I was once like that.

I think of all the things Eila told me. About the other Evas, about the humants. Aleris cannot be sacrificed too. I think about my time in Guerra's care. I know where they will have her. I know the room, and the books that are in there. I imagine Rose-Q bending over her, filling her with drugs because Guerra and Olwin Duilis have asked her to. Rose-Q may have no choice, not up here under Guerra's nose.

And I know I must not wait for Blue Jay. If I am careful, I can sneak in, find her, at least tell her what she needs to know. I cannot wait here for Blue Jay to do all the work.

Crow

WE MAKE IT all the way to the top of staircase number 3 before anyone stops us. Even then they don't do much; I guess we're heading in pretty much the direction they want us to. It's almost like old times: me, Mac and Carine wandering the High Track, Carine pissed with us for some minor misdemeanour. Yeah, it's not really like that at all, but I'm pretending for the next few steps that we've got things all under control. Because, really, we have no plan, other than Mac talking to Olwin Duilis. Carine's taken his ninja pole away from him but, as usual, Mac seems okay with that.

Olwin Duilis comes out to meet us, and it's a strange little moment. The dragonfly detaches itself from her hair and flies over to Mac, who holds it in the palm of his hand. He says nothing, and it's almost as if the dragonfly is telling him all he needs to know. But bioenhancements or no, Mac's got no way of directly communicating with the small machine, or none that I know of.

"Where is she?" asks Olwin.

"Couldn't you just let us be?" asks Mac. "Turn off the time nets, live your life?"

Nothing like getting straight to the point.

"This *is* my life," says Olwin. "All of this. You know that, MacIver. All of it is a way for me to live my life."

"Except that it didn't work that way, Olwin. You didn't create a better version of yourself. You created someone else."

Olwin says nothing. There's a look on her face which seems part-fury, part-sorrow. I'm not sure I can tell which way she's going to tip. There's movement by the admin door and I'm stupid enough to let my eyes focus there.

Because it's Eva. Of course it's Eva, trying to sneak in and rescue Aleris, I have no doubt. Because both she and Olwin are just the same, in that they can't leave well enough alone. They're both obsessed. With themselves, above anything else. And now, with their doubles.

I look at Olwin and Mac and there's no sign that either of them are any the wiser. On the other hand, there's no sign that this talking is going anywhere either. The dragonfly has settled back in Olwin's hair, but I'm not sure that means anything much. Carine, naturally, is focused on us. I doubt that she's seen Eva. In fact, she seems almost bored; she's swinging the ninja pole back and forward. You can hear it swish through the air.

Mac turns to her. "Don't. It's not safe."

Carine turns the pole in a complete circle just to piss him off. Mac makes a grab for the pole, but it's too late; Carine's gone, presumably into Time Lock.

"That's got to hurt," I say.

And then Carine re-appears, except now she's extremely pissed off, but, luckily for us, also extremely nauseated. Mac tries to take the pole. Carine holds on to it, even while doubled over and retching. A consummate multitasker.

"That's clever," says Olwin.

"That's really, really stupid," says Carine.

They're both right, actually. Carine shifts the pole from one hand to the other and I can see the burn the pole left. No wonder Mac wears gloves. Rose-Q appears at the doorway. She looks over at Mac. Mac shakes his head slightly, which, naturally, is enough to make Olwin look around. Rose-Q's one step out of the doorway, two figures behind her. Figures with dark green skin and a cloud of black curls. They're holding hands. Rose-Q turns her head, tells them something and then steps backward so that she's blocking the door.

"Let me talk to her," says Olwin.

Rose-Q don't move. But Eva does.

She walks forward and Rose-Q lets her past. She don't come far, just a few steps out of the doorway, but there's no pretending this is someone random, an alternate reality glitch. She's more like Olwin than Aleris is. More worn, more obviously troubled. Though she's obviously found strength somewhere. That whole damsel-in-distress thing is over. There's no sense that she's about to collapse at any moment. Maybe it's because she's finally standing up for herself.

Olwin is very still. So is Mac. Carine positions herself so that she can grab Eva, but she don't do anything to stop her. What's to stop? Eva's just standing there.

They've never met, Olwin Duilis and Eva. That's an odd thought. I look at Mac, and he's got no idea what to do. Although it's obvious he'd like to grab that ninja pole from Carine and get Eva out of here. Shit, that's what I want to do, and I'm not in love with her.

Eva holds out her hand. Olwin laughs, a bitter, sad sound, almost a sob, almost a cry of derision. But then she takes the hand, grips it fiercely.

"I'm Eva." Her voice is unsteady, but it's clearly her own. They may look the same, but their voices are different.

"Eva," says Olwin, and a sound escapes her, more the sound of a wounded animal than anything else. She stretches out her other hand towards Carine, never taking her eyes off Eva. Carine hands her the ninja pole in an act of mind reading I hadn't thought was within her capabilities. Eva's still holding Olwin's hand, but she seems a deal less sure of the arrangement. Presumably she's not keen on heading into alternate realities with Olwin Duilis. Who could blame her? But it's Olwin who lets go of Eva's hand. She grips the ninja pole and twirls it around, up and over her head. Mac takes a step forward, hand outstretched, but he hesitates, and in that hesitation the pole comes down, completes the circle, and Olwin Duilis disappears.

Eva looks at Mac. I'm not sure I'd want to be the recipient of that look, and then she leaves too, turning back inside admin.

And then everyone reacts. Carine grabs Mac. Which is altogether too late, but I guess she feels the need to do something, maybe because Guerra has materialised from wherever he's been hiding. Rose-Q runs back inside, and almost immediately runs back outside. A stream of yellow cloud follows her. Eva and Aleris are nowhere to be seen. If Tal's still inside, he might help them. Although he's more medical–emergency-help than fighting machine.

And then there's a *crack*. The kind of sound that makes you think the air has been torn in two. Followed by the jangle of falling concrete. The ground we're standing on moves around, settles. I fall onto my knees, and I'm blaming my dodgy leg for that. Carine falls too, and Mac uses the moment to wrench himself out of her grip.

"Fuck," says Guerra. His voice is controlled enough that I spare a moment to admire his calm. But then I see what all the fuss is about. Right where staircase number 3 used to be is a whopping great hole. Luckily for us, this section of the High Track is resting on top of one of the support poles, but the other side isn't faring so well. Bits of the platform seem to be weighing their options, deciding they have none, and then dropping down into the gap.

When most of the debris has found its rightful place,

a head appears. A large robot head with engraved stars. Oscar. At least I think it is.

"Sorry about that," he says.

And the sight is so extraordinary, so completely *wrong*, that Mac and I start laughing.

For a moment, that's all there is. The sounds of the night, the echoes of settling rubble, and the two of us laughing our heads off.

But nothing good lasts for long. "Get the fuck out!" yells Guerra. "Just—get the fuck out, and take that bloody Olwin Duilis with you, and all her bloody little doubles, and—fuck! *Fuck*." He's sitting down, covered in dust. Carine comes over, tries to give him a hand up, but he swipes her away.

We don't need any more encouragement. It's hard to walk because my leg's even more buggered and also we're still laughing quite hard. But we make it over to Oscar, who grabs us and brings us back down to earth with relative gentleness. In fact, he transports us all the way over to the grass by the water tower, a place where we can survey the damage at our leisure.

We watch some under-dwellers emerging. Apparently unscathed, but frankly there's no loss if that isn't the case.

"Don't tell me, you made a larger pole," says Mac.

"Yes. It needs some work." Oscar makes a noise that could be amusement, could be a robot snort. The thought that this may all have been a complete accident don't completely sit true, but I'm willing to go along with it if Mac is.

"What about Eva?" I ask, surprising even myself.

"I'll get her," says Oscar. And somehow that's funny too and Mac and I lie on the ground laughing until we're fit to puke.

CHAPTER FORTY

Green Jay

I'M WITH ALERIS in my old room when I hear the world split in two. I see that I am shaking, but I feel as if I am watching myself from the outside. Aleris is sitting on the bed, completely still, as dust falls down on us both. I don't know if we are safe inside, but I cannot think of another place to go.

"That was her," says Aleris. "The first one."

"Yes." I can't think of anything else to tell her.

But then, I think of everything: T-Lily, the way the Trocarn came through space. The way Rose-Q saved me in the end. I even tell her about the other Evas, the ones who died. The ones who lay in the shed and were sent to the stars. I hope that she will not join them. But I tell her about the future, about Kolb and Lona.

It takes so long that neither of us notice that the world

has stopped shaking.

"I will stay," says Aleris.

"No," I say, because it seems so wrong. "Olwin has gone. You'll have no protection."

"She has me," says Rose-Q. I'd forgotten she was there. She looks singed. Her tentacles are flat to her head, and it makes her seem defeated and lost. But that isn't so.

"But Guerra…"

"Guerra won't hurt me," says Aleris. "But I don't mean to stay *here*, I mean stay in this world."

"You could live in the greenhouse," I suggest.

"I would like to visit," says Aleris. And I realise that I must leave her to find her own life.

I take her hand, because I don't know what else to say. I would wish her a long life, but I'm not sure this can be. Even now I can see the signs of deterioration, a wilting of the skin. But she leans back into Rose-Q and I know that she will be as cared for as she can be.

Tal is still in the corner. I had assumed he had lost function, but he moves now, stretching up into his tall form. "Your chariot awaits," he says. He is as obscure as the Crow sometimes.

"Do you mean you, Tal?" I ask.

"No, I am not the chariot. I believe you call them the Chemical Conjurers. One of them is here for you."

I kiss Aleris on her forehead, and she smiles at me. I follow Tal out of the room, through the corridors of Guerra's building and into the sunshine. I can see the great hole in the High Track. But there is one of the Chemical Conjurers, standing taller than I have ever seen him, so that his head is sticking up through the hole. There is no-one else in sight.

We walk towards him, Tal and me. Any minute I expect to slide away, the High Track collapsing further, but the ground is solid and I reach my chariot without damage.

"I will take care of her," says Tal.

And now I know that Aleris will be safe. Not only because Tal will keep her as well as he can, but because she and Rose-Q can escape if needs be. But Tal already understands that, I think. He has already thought this through. "Shall I tell Brom?" I ask.

"Thank you," he says. I would hug him if I could. I remember the way he carried T-Lily, the way he cared for Blue Jay. I extend my hand and he takes it and shakes it gently. And then, without warning I am borne up in the air by larger robot hands, lifted up and out of the High Track and deposited on the grass by the water tower.

The Crow and Blue Jay are there, lying on the ground, and as soon as they see me they start laughing. Normally I would be cross with the Crow, but I don't care. It makes me feel like laughing too.

Crow

NOW THAT EVA'S here, the fun's pretty much over. She and Mac are more cautious around each other than I'd expected. At least there's no lovey-dovey to contend with.

"What will you do now that Olwin's stolen your ninja pole?" I ask.

Mac shrugs. "Make another one?"

I nod my head at the wrecked High Track. "After that."

"Maybe some extra safety features," says Mac. I can already see him itching to get back into the water tower, start work on modifications.

"The time nets are still looking," says Eva. "Olwin Duilis never turned them off."

"Yeah but now they'll be after her," I say.

And that thought makes me sadder than I expected, though not completely. Serves her right and all that. "Will she survive, do you think?" On the one hand I'm probably asking the wrong people; on the other hand, who the fuck else would know?

"Yes," says Eva.

"No," says Mac.

They look at each other and smile. Of course they do. There's nothing like complications and contradictions to make them long for each other. My money's on Olwin Duilis. She's a tough lady in a metal cage and not one to jump to her own death. Plus she's got the dragonfly, which, admittedly, is more of a good luck charm, but it knows a thing or two about travelling between realities.

"But what will you do, Brom?" asks Eva.

"Free the Tenties," I say. I can see Eva's downright surprised, but it seems fair enough. It gives me a goal. It won't be as easy as the other time, especially as they'll figure out I'm coming pretty soon. And I dare say most places have better security than Guerra. Yes, theoretically the Tenties could free themselves; but hell, they're not going to, are they? Maybe they injected something altruistic into me via the tendril, maybe I figure I owe them.

That said, I'm confining myself to this reality, and this reality only.

"Tal's going to stay with Aleris," says Eva.

"Fair enough." Though I can't say I'm not disappointed.

"Maybe Felix and Oscar will help out," says Mac. And that's a thought. Me travelling the world with my two giant robot companions. That's a thought I like a lot.

Eva and Mac retreat into the water tower, but I lie on the grass for a little while longer. I don't expect to see much of them. I don't really expect them to stay in this reality either, time nets or no. I wonder what Guerra will do now. Whether he'll stay up on the High Track, or give it back to the government now it's wrecked. Could go either way.

But then hunger takes over, as it usually does, and I'm back in the marketplace, looking for food. Not that I've got any dosh. I have a brief yearning for my lost future phone and its tap-and-go credit, but I figure I can persuade somebody out of something. That's my gift, after all.

Somebody's pumping some music into the air. Nothing as good as the concert up on the bicycle High Track, but it's happiness-making. Maybe it's a celebration of Guerra's downfall. Who knows? I can see a few brave souls with ladders and climbing gear heading up and over the High Track's railings. I wish them luck.

I watch as Felix pours what looks like a glass of water onto a tray. Instead of just making a mess, as you'd expect, he's sculpting what appear to be ice towers. "Sodium

Acetate," he tells me. Not that I particularly care. Oscar, meanwhile, is tossing jelly snakes into a large test tube and watching them dance around in the violet flames. They've both collapsed their bodies so that they're not quite so robokiller, destroyers of large structures, but given their role in the High Track collapse, they seem remarkably unphased. Well, they're always unphased; they're robots, after all. And they've an audience who don't particularly seem to care that the Chemical Conjurers, aka Felix and Oscar, were recently seen demolishing part of the city.

I sit on the kerb and watch them for a while. A kebab seems to have found its way into my hand, and I munch on it and watch the show. The Chemical Conjurers keep up an educational patter, but I let most of it wash over me. There's rainbow fire which is somehow associated with metal salts and then later a crowd favourite— elephant toothpaste—which is foamy and messy and fun and hotter than you'd expect. I watch them and I think about ways I might persuade them to come with me on my Tentie rescue jaunt.

Maybe they'll come with, maybe they won't. I'll have to wait and see.

ACKNOWLEDGEMENTS

HEARTFELT THANKS TO David Moore for his judicious editing. Michael Foster gave me some unexpected encouragement along the way. But, most especially, thanks are due to my family. Amina was brave enough to read an early draft. And while Albert and Rehana probably had no idea what I was writing, they believed in it anyway. I am grateful for you all.

ABOUT THE AUTHOR

DJ Daniels is an Australian author and musician. She writes when she manages to get her husband and two daughters out of the house and during lulls in the ongoing dog-lizard war. (Lizards are well ahead.) Her first novel, *What the Dead Said*, was followed by a raft of short stories which have appeared in publications such as *Aurealis*, *Andromeda Spaceways Magazine*, and *So It Goes*. She was a judge for the 2012 Aurealis Awards and is one of the Sydney Story Factory's Ambassadors of Ink.

FIND US ONLINE!

www.rebellionpublishing.com

/rebellionpub   /rebellionpublishing   /rebellionpub

SIGN UP TO OUR NEWSLETTER!

rebellionpublishing.com/sign-up

YOUR REVIEWS MATTER!

Enjoy this book? Got something to say?

Leave a review on Amazon, GoodReads or with your favourite bookseller and let the world know!